TO SAVE HER SOUL, SHE'LL HAVE TO PUT HER FAITH IN THE DEVIL.

When Death Blooms

G.E. MASTERS

Content and Trigger Warnings

Some content may be disturbing and/or triggering to some readers. Please read responsibly.

This book includes:

-Sexual assault

-Mental health issues, specifically PTSD, anxiety, and depression

-Suicidal ideation

-Torture

-Verbal and emotional child abuse (discussed)

-Blood

-Character death

-Infertility for a secondary character (mentioned)

-Sexually explicit scenes

-Consensual non-consent

-Primal play

-Anal play

-Bondage

-Choking/gagging

-Praise and degradation

-Squirting

-Shadow play

-Use of sex toys

If you have experienced sexual violence and need someone to speak to, the National Sexual Assault Hotline is free, confidential, and available 24/7. Call them at 800-656-4673.

If you are struggling with your mental health, the 988 Lifeline is here. Whether you're facing mental health struggles, emotional distress, alcohol or drug use concerns, or just need someone to talk to, their caring counselors are here for you. You are not alone.

For those who see themselves in V and V—the storm will always pass.

Prologue

Venus

The battleground is littered with bodies. Broken, mutilated, dead bodies.

Waves of nausea roll through me as I fly over the carnage, the stench of death already thick in the air, the ground stained red. Phanes has unleashed monsters of his creation upon us—creatures even worse than my own. The field below me, once a beautiful forest in the realm of the living, a quiet sanctuary, is now nothing but ash and death.

I look ahead to where Lilith is still fighting. Her last stand.

I push myself harder, even as exhaustion and pain from my open wounds scream at me to stop. But I can't. I must get to Lilith before it's too late—we can escape back to Hell and hide behind the wards she created. Let my father and I live out our existences in a stalemate.

Soaring through the dark skies, I rush to her, her magic like a beacon of light.

Phanes has finally reached her.

Panic overrides my fatigue and agony. I tunnel into my magic, rallying it to strike him down.

Not to kill, but to give Lilith enough time to run.

She won't, though. She wants them all dead, including my father.

We've spent too much time arguing over Phanes's fate, but she won't listen. We just recently learned that he cannot be killed without taking everything down with him, and it has caused us to argue constantly. *There must be another way,* she'd claim. *I feel it in my soul.*

Her rage and unending need for revenge are driving her now.

My magic shoots out of me, barreling towards him as he prowls toward her. His attention turns to me too slowly, and he's knocked backward, landing with a boom against the earth.

I descend upon my worst nightmare.

Lilith is lying on the ground, wounded, struggling to rise. She's gripping her stomach with pain etched into her face.

I quickly land next to her, my shadows swirling around her, assessing the damage.

Her entire stomach is cut open. Blood gushes out from underneath her hand.

"We have to leave," I rasp, my voice strained. I go to grab her, but she tries to move away from me.

"Lilith," I say, pleading. "You're going to die if we don't move *now*."

Her face switches from pain to pure, undiluted anger. "It isn't over. He isn't dead."

Gritting my teeth, I snarl, "There's no time to argue!"

I hear him stir behind me, alerting me that he's coming towards us. I move to scoop Lilith up, but her wound is too severe. She lets out a whimper, her arm tightening around herself.

We're stuck.

I steel myself and turn to face him, putting myself between my love and my enemy.

My father looks worse for wear; his white armor is covered in blood and mud, his long hair matted, his dark eyes wild as he takes us in. He limps toward me and smiles, his mouth full of blood.

"My dearest daughter," he laughs, "how kind of you to join us. I was just about to kill your precious witch."

My shadows vibrate around me menacingly.

"It's a pity it had to end this way," he muses as he drags himself forward.

Our magic reacts at the same time, colliding with one another. I grit my teeth against the force, trying to push forward, to weaken him even more. I hear him grunt as he staggers back. I send another blast of magic into him, but he's quick, meeting me with another surge of his power. Fighting to keep upright, to keep him from Lilith, I tunnel into every bit of power I have.

But it isn't enough. His magic breaks through, knocking me back.

My vision blacks out for a moment as my body hits the ground. Pain radiates through me, my lungs unable to get any air.

This can't be how it ends, I think to myself.

With a scream of agony, I roll myself over to see my father grab Lilith by the neck, place his other hand on her chest, and drag her soul, her very essence, out of her.

Her body goes limp immediately, her skin turning gray as he discards her, her body crumpling on the ground.

No no no—

I pull myself up, crawling to her, hoping in vain that he hasn't done the one thing that would keep her from me forever.

I reach her body, panicking with desperation.

I turn her over and recoil.

It isn't Lilith.

The red hair has transformed into blonde locks and green eyes have molded into hazel.

Vivian's dead eyes stare up at me.

"You thought I would stop with Lilith?" my father asks from behind me, laughing.

No, no, this can't be—

An earth-shattering scream erupts from my body.

And then the nightmare begins again.

Chapter One
Vivian

I can't sleep without my bird noises.

There is no noise in this castle. No movement of any kind except for Phanes and me. His booming voice. His even breathing when he sleeps, plastered to me.

The same nightmare repeats over and over and over again. Phanes dresses me like his own life-size doll in a white, flowing dress. He escorts me to my meals, where I'm required to sit and eat silently as he talks at me. I used to pay attention, searching for any slip-ups that might give away some weakness of his, but I no longer care enough.

He doesn't seem to notice I'm not listening.

Some days, he will leave me alone to wander the halls like a spirit stuck in this perpetual Hell. I'm never sure where he goes, but he always seems to have a renewed energy buzzing from him when he returns. It makes him even more unbearable.

And on other days, he will do what can only be described as experiments on me. He's grown paranoid that my magic is tricking him, pretending to be weak so he will lower his guard.

He hurts me, again and again, trying to force my magic to retaliate.

It never does.

I wonder if my magic has completely left me.

I would be better off if it did.

He apologizes profusely and soothes me afterwards, pouring honey in my ear about how he simply hates hurting me, but that it's a necessary evil. *We must know how much magic our future children will possess,* he tells me. That this is the last time, that he knows for certain that my magic is too weak to withstand him.

But he continues to hurt me, again and again.

What happens after is the part I dread the most.

He bathes me, refusing to let me lift a finger. His hands have explored every inch of my body with no shame, stroking between my legs, trying to get a response from me.

My body never does, to his increasing annoyance. He tells me it is only a matter of time before I feel for him what he feels for me. That my body will react appropriately.

Sometimes, he'll threaten to break into my mind and command me to enjoy it, enjoy him.

I used to cry at this point, but I think my tears have finally run out.

After this, he takes me to bed, where we lie next to each other with no clothing between us. He runs his hands over my skin, keeping me pressed against him.

He hasn't violated me in the way he ultimately plans to—not yet.

But it's only a matter of time before he does. He's a ticking time bomb, just barely keeping himself from destroying me. I wonder if my self-preservation will kick in. If I'll fight him or if I'll cry and scream and beg him not to.

I don't bother wondering if my magic will help.

So, I lie here every night, hoping my time will run out before his does.

Chapter Two
Venus

"P hanes is defenseless. He has no allies, no army. We must strike him now."

"But with Vivian in his grasp, he will surely destroy her soul. We must tread carefully."

"Treading carefully is precisely the reason we are in this mess in the first place. If you witches hadn't dallied about remaking the wards, we wouldn't even be having this discussion," I hear an archdemon snarl.

"Do not dare blame us for this," a High Priestess hisses.

"The issues of the realm always seem to come back to the witches," another archdemon retorts haughtily.

"You seem to forget yourself, demon," a different witch growls.

My council continues to squabble behind me as I stare out the large windows that overlook the city below.

I was in and out of sleep for weeks, healing from the near-fatal injuries, reliving nightmares of my past and fears of my future, blending to make me witness the most un-thinkable things.

Today is the first day I am finally healed enough to be plotting Vivian's rescue, although my body still aches and my wings are still too weak to carry me through the skies.

Weeks. That is how long Vivian has been in my father's prison of a home.

I have thought of nothing but fighting my way to her, even if that means my father destroys everything. I would happily hand over everything in exchange for her.

She isn't dead—I know she isn't. Even if her soul doesn't belong to me, I would know it in my bones, in my blood, if her soul had been destroyed.

Besides, my father can't pass up an opportunity to boast his winnings, to take from me and mock me with what he has stolen.

No, he would rather lure me to his castle, where he will murder Vivian in front of me.

I know I'm walking right into his trap, but I don't care. I will get Vivian to safety, even if it's the last thing I do with my miserable existence.

"Permission to speak out of turn?" I hear Marie ask, clearly directing her question at me.

"I believe asking defeats the purpose of the intent," Luke quips.

Turning from the windows, my eyes land on Marie and I dip my head to her.

She swallows nervously but continues. "We understand Phanes has no true defenses but himself. He has no children to protect him. But we must not forget that he is a powerful entity—along with his...pet."

The room grows somber as we remember my father's serpent destroying the city streets.

"In the last war, he created his own armies and monsters. We must consider the entire realm before we attack," Marie presses. "All those in the city must be evacuated to a safer location, with demons and witches on alert to protect the realm, if necessary."

"And where shall we put everyone?" Grigor asks, his black eyes narrowing, his green-tinted skin nearly glowing in the dim candlelight.

Marie does not back down from his look. "Phanes will try to attack the castle, so they are not safe in the city. The souls should be moved to the forest that surrounds us."

"The forest is uninhabitable," Luke argues. "Besides, demons do not enter the forest."

"They will simply have to, for their own safety," Marie pushes.

"Luke is right," Azrael interjects, his light blue skin seeming to pale at the mention of entering Hell's wilderness. "Demons and the forest's beasts do not get along, as you well know. No demon will step into the forest; the beasts will do anything to get their claws into one of us."

Marie quickly tweaks her plan. "Then only witches will work to keep the peace between the souls and the forest beasts. Demons should be protected by other forces. Perhaps they can be kept close to our demon soldiers that reside on the edge of the city."

An olive branch.

Luke seems taken aback by this. He clears his throat and grumbles, "There is...potential with that idea."

Marie cannot hide the beam she radiates.

None of this is my primary concern. I grow impatient, pinching the bridge of my nose and closing my eyes for a moment. "I will not leave Vivian in his clutches for a moment longer. She has already been there too long."

Waiting for me.

"You were gravely injured, Your Grace," Isobel reminds me quietly, as if that is an acceptable excuse.

I bite back the snarl building in my throat.

"It would be unwise to approach your father in his home," Aradia adds. "He will work to protect his palace by any means necessary—including hurting Vivian."

My shadows cast around the room angrily, causing everyone to hold their breath. "He is most likely already hurting her," I growl.

"He could destroy her soul," Aradia reminds me.

My magic rumbles throughout the room in agitation. She's right. As long as he has Vivian, Phanes has the upper hand.

And he knows it.

My father and I have been at a stalemate ever since Lilith's death, erecting magical wards around our realms, never advancing into the other's territory. While I harbor such strong hate for him, I was content to live out our existences the way we had: him residing over the living and I the dead.

Until this.

"I am going to get Vivian," I declare to the council. The room falls into tense silence. "But," I sigh, feeling deflated, "I must be strategic. Saving Vivian is my priority. I don't want to do anything that could jeopardize her safety."

The High Priestesses have a glimmer of pride in their eyes at my words but wisely decide against saying anything.

I roll my own. "Perhaps I could be shielded in some way. I already shield myself when flying in the realm of the living, but I fear he'll detect me." Being his daughter, he seems to sense my magic. "We had planned to use a concealment spell for Vivian. Could the same be applied to me?"

"Potentially," Isobel replies. "But you would still have to destroy his wards to get to him. While you might have the strength to, it will alert him to your presence."

"That is too risky," I counter.

"There's also the possibility that his wards are failing like ours were. We don't know how he made them, but he must have made them himself," Marie guesses.

Luke picks up the thread. "So, you could try to find a hole in the ward. Slip through with the concealment spell and, hopefully, find Vivian without much interference from Phanes."

"You could always kill him," Aradia offers, making it clear she believes I should simply kill my father and take his place.

Gritting my teeth, I reply, "This is not the conversation we need to be having right now."

She shuts her mouth and looks down at the table.

"We should discuss your strength," Luke interrupts. "The healers say your wings won't carry you. Not yet any-way. They expect you to rest."

How can I rest when the woman I love is being held hostage?

But I know he's right. I'll only get Vivian killed if I'm not at my strongest. My wings rustle in agitation, causing my muscles to groan in protest.

"Thank you for the reminder, Nurse Luke," I sneer.

He clears his throat awkwardly, knowing everyone is on thin ice with me until Vivian is back.

"I will go when my wings are ready," I tell the room.

The High Priestesses share quick glances among themselves before Aradia says, "We will be ready to conceal you."

I nod at my council. "Then I will be prepared to take back what is mine."

Chapter Three
Vivian

"Do you know why my children came to be, my little flower?" Phanes asks me one morning as we lie in bed, his front still pressed into me. He rarely stays long after he wakes. There is something different about today.

The pet name he has chosen for me makes me sick.

One of his hands draws idle circles on my stomach. I fight the urge to shudder under his touch.

He chuckles into my hair as his hand on my stomach floats downward. "When I arrived here, I found myself to be so lonely. I thought, what good is making this earth if I do not have someone to share it with? So, I made my own lover."

Ew.

"She was the first being of night. Not Venus. Her night was quite different—quiet, soothing, gentle. Nothing at all like the destruction and horror that my daughter has created." His grip tightens on me angrily as he speaks. "She was named Venus after love and light, hoping it would keep her from leaning into the horrors of the darkness, but the name is simply ironic now." He sighs. "But she did love Venus, perhaps even more than our other children, and that was her downfall."

Venus told me, alongside the demons and witches, that she destroyed all the gods and goddesses except for Phanes. Did that mean she killed her mother too?

I don't ask. I don't think I want to know. It wouldn't make a difference anyway.

Venus has forgotten me and has moved on to figuring out another way to keep her realm safe.

"But together," he continues, seemingly unaware of the depressing turn my mind has taken, "we shall replenish this earth with our offspring, to make this world anew." His hand now rests right above my center, making it clear he can touch me wherever he likes, whenever he likes.

He stops speaking, giving me a bit of respite. I'm wondering when he's going to get up, to leave me be—at least until tonight, to see if he'll decide to touch and torture me.

But he doesn't get up. "Say my name," he growls into my hair.

I blink in surprise.

"Say it," he demands more urgently. "Say my name."

"Phanes," I whisper, unable to speak any louder.

He shudders against me. His cock twitches against my backside and it makes me flinch.

"Touch me, Vivian."

I freeze. He's always touched me; he's never demanded I do the same. The most I touch him is when I remove his robes every night, but I'm careful to avoid his skin as much as possible.

"I want you to touch me," he breathes into my neck. My hair stands on end.

Slowly, I twist my body to face him.

He's grinning down at me, a near-feral look crossing his face as his dark eyes take me in greedily.

Calculating the safest option, I raise my hands to touch his face, but he aggressively grabs my wrists. I cringe away from the contact, which only makes him grip tighter. He rolls on top of me, pushing himself between my legs. He towers over me, crowding me, trapping me underneath him, pinning my wrists to the bed.

"No," he says roughly. "Touch me as if I were a lover. Touch me as you wish to touch my daughter."

Bile begins to gather in my throat, and I freeze, teetering between fighting with all my might to free myself and to keep perfectly still. For a split second, it looks like the veins in his neck are...moving. Like something dark is crawling through them. I blink and it disappears.

Surprise enters his gaze as he releases his grip on me. Clearing his throat, he has the audacity to look sheepish. "Forgive me. I'm not sure what came over me."

I close my eyes to avoid looking at him and to avoid him seeing the disgust and hatred I know is written all over my face.

"I think it best we leave this for another time," he declares as he removes himself from the bed. "But I am not a patient god."

Chapter Four
Venus

*E*verything is white—the floor, the walls, the furniture. *Sterile.*

Void of life.

It's ironic. My father meant for his castle to signify purity and new beginnings.

But he has managed to twist it and make it into something cold and lifeless.

I hate when I must come here. My siblings either sneer at me or ignore me completely. My father demands my attendance but only has judgmental words to throw at me.

The only one I want to see is my mother.

I stop outside her chambers which are strategically placed on the opposite side of the palace from my father's. Her door is ajar, so I push it open and let myself in.

My mother's room is a splash of color in this dreary castle.

Murals stretch across the entirety of the walls and the ceiling, depicting the story of creation and this world's many wonders.

As a child, I used to marvel at them, peppering her with questions about each one and what they symbolize.

It fueled my brief obsession with the living realm, which quickly turned sour once my true purpose was revealed.

Now I hate it.

My mother is seated at her desk, bent over what I'm assuming is her beloved sketchbook that's filled with smaller versions of the murals spread throughout the space. Her long, inky black hair is pulled back into an intricate braid, with a few hairs having wrestled their way out of confinement and sticking up in various directions.

I make my way over to her, sliding my feet gently on the marble floor to alert her to my approach. Her head snaps up and she turns to look at me.

My mother and I look nearly identical with the same dark hair, golden skin, and graced with the same writhing shadows. Mine are much wilier than hers; while mine slither and vibrate when distressed, hers always seem at ease, float- ing lazily around her lithe frame.

Her warm blue eyes crinkle at the corners when she sees me, a beautiful smile blooming across her mouth.

"Venus," she breathes, rising from her chair and meeting me in the middle of her chambers. Her hands reach forward to gently cup my face. My shadows, ever ornery, swirl more

tightly around my wings at the approach, but my mother and her shadows pay them no mind.

"I'm so happy you could come to visit me." She smiles.

"You know I only come here to see you," I reply, relaxing into her touch and reaching to hold her hand to my face for longer.

She sighs as she steps back, breaking contact. "I wish that were not the case."

She doesn't have to elaborate. I know she resents my father nearly as much as I do.

My mother is darkness, much like I am, but a different form altogether. Her darkness soothes while mine frightens; hers lulls to sleep while mine wakes one from nightmares. I always assumed that's why our dispositions are so opposite. She has always seemed settled in herself, while I have never felt comfortable anywhere.

One thing we have in common, though, is our hatred for my father and what he has created. Even if that includes us.

"Come, sit with me," she says as she makes her way to her seating area. She sits on the dark, plush chair in front of the fireplace, one leg crossed over the other. I sit on the chair opposite her, letting my wings drape over the chair's back.

The room, as always, is a mess. There are buckets of paints, drawings ripped from her sketchbook and tacked onto the wall, and a large tarp is settled on the floor.

"And what was it you were working on before I so rudely interrupted you?" I jest.

Her smile falters a bit. "Just my next piece, of course. It will go right over there." She points to the only blank space on the wall.

"What is it of?" I ask.

Confusingly, her face grows serious. "It will be of the truth."

"The truth of what?"

She chews on her lip in contemplation. Even her shadows appear more alert than they were a few moments ago.

My mother is rarely not smiling; we spend our time laughing and talking about only pleasant things.

"Has something happened?" I ask. "Has Father..." I trail off, unsure of what I want to ask or how I want to ask it.

She shakes her head. "No, no, nothing of that sort," she placates me. "Would you like to see?"

I nod, hoping my agreement to share her art will get rid of this change in her demeanor. We both extract ourselves from our seats and walk over to her desk. My mother scoops up her sketchbook before I can lay eyes on the open page, holding it to her chest. She eyes me with a mixture of wariness and anxiety.

"Promise that you will not speak of what this is."

I shake my head. "I do not understand," I admit.

"One day you will, but until then, this shall remain our secret."

"Why is it that what you paint is now a secret?"

"This is unlike the others," she replies. "Once it is painted on this wall, I worry about the repercussions."

"You mean by Father?" I ask, my wings rustling angrily. If he dares to hurt her—

"Everything will be as it needs to be," she evades, making my stomach churn. "Promise me."

I swallow the uncomfortable feeling, the strange energy that has entered the room. I nod my agreement.

She sags in relief and hands me the sketchbook.

It's a rudimentary sketch of a large circle with a white oval in the center, lines crisscrossing through the center and into the larger circle.

"Mother, I don't know what this is," I tell her.

"Not yet. Now is not the time. But when you are ready, the answer will make itself known to you. Just as it has been made known to me." Her voice deepens. I look up and see her eyebrows furrowed in anger. A moment passes and she blinks, her features smoothing out, and an easy smile graces her lips. "No more talking in riddles." She laughs gently, grabbing the sketchbook from me and shoving it into a drawer of her desk. "Now, let's have some pastries sent to *us while we play a game. You've gotten quite good at the card game I showed you last time you were here."*

Chapter Five

Vivian

Phanes has demanded we lounge in his despondent throne room, making me sit on his lap as he sprawls on the throne. A king with no subjects. My back hurts from sitting ramrod straight, trying to avoid leaning back into him.

"Something you said has weighed heavily on me," he says. I haven't spoken in days. When I don't respond, he continues, "You said no one has even heard of me."

He's talking about when I found the mural, I realize. The mural that depicts the true nature of this world, that he's a pretender and that it's actually my magic that created everything until he came along and stole it. "They do not know my name, it's true. Some worship a god, but they aren't aware that it is me." He's clearly irritated by this. I don't doubt he'll use my words as another excuse to hurt me.

I keep silent, not sure what he wants me to say. A few moments of quiet pass by before he changes the subject, nearly giving me whiplash. "Do you wonder why I do not simply slip into your mind?"

I shake my head at his question, terror working its way up my spine.

"It would be so easy to do it, to make you do whatever I wanted." He sighs, running his fingers up and down my arm. I bite my lip to stop myself from squirming away. "But I like seeing you obedient of your own free will. To see you become more subservient with every passing moment." I'm biting my lip so hard, I'm sure I'll break the skin.

He presses his nose to my neck and inhales. "Denying myself that is the sweetest torture."

Nausea builds in my throat.

"But," he goes on, gliding his nose up and down my neck, "it does take considerable effort to take over one's mind, even for a moment. I was bedridden for weeks after entering yours, too weak to do much of anything."

Surprise flickers in me before I snuff it out. It doesn't matter.

Nothing matters.

"But soon..." he says against my skin. "Soon, I will have everything I want."

He pulls back, no longer crowding me. "And then our subjects will fill this castle." His voice echoes in the emptiness. "Our subjects and our children, together, just as it was meant to be."

Chapter Six

Venus

Healing is taking too much time.

I shift my wings, feeling soreness radiate through my body as I expand them to their full width.

The healer's cool hands poke and prod at the muscles. I grit my teeth, not wanting to show any weakness.

"Still tender?" she asks, seeing right through me. I grunt my response. "Have you attempted flying?"

Yes. It ended in disaster. I had taken a running start, unfurled my wings, and flapped hard. The pain had been excruciating, but I kept going.

I only got a few feet off the ground before my wings had given out completely.

"We can try a healing spell again," the healer offers. "But, as you know, the magic can only do so much. Your wings still need rest."

Irritation worms through me, but I bite my tongue. Berating this healer for my own shortcomings won't speed my recovery along.

Her nimble fingers continue pressing gently along my wings. "I'd say, with another week of rest, you could be airborne again."

A week. Another week of Vivian stuck with that monster.

I twist to look at her. "Are you sure?"

She nods, her gray hair slipping from the bun at the nape of her neck. "You have healed quite well in a short amount of time."

Not short enough.

After my disastrous meeting with the healer, I must tend to something else that requires my attention.

The newly departed souls are kept separate from most of the realm while they transition to Hell. It helps prepare them for the next phase of their existence while allowing for the memories they've lost to resurface.

Many souls forget everything once they die and come here with no understanding of who or where they are. As time passes, their memories return, but it can be quite disorienting.

I rarely make an appearance in this phase, but these are unprecedented times.

I arrive at the tall gates, nodding my greeting to two demons standing post. They bow their heads nervously. "Your Grace," one responds, "the spirit you wish to visit is ready."

"Very well," I respond gruffly.

They turn in unison and the gates open. Inside is a smaller replica of the city: a few shops manned by experienced spirits and demons, buildings that mirror the ones just outside the gates so as to acclimate them to what they will soon see.

I send my shadows away but keep my wings out as I trail behind. My wings need practice, and spiriting them away without healing properly could reverse any progress. It has been a bitch sleeping on my stomach—not that I've gotten much sleep since Vivian was taken.

The demons lead me through to a quiet garden where a spirit floats alone.

"Your Grace," they both say before scurrying away.

I approach the spirit and try to hide the pang of sadness I feel upon looking at her.

Vivian's aunt.

She resembles Vivian so much that it hurts to look at her. When I met Vivian's mother, I saw the physical resemblance, but their souls were completely at odds. As I approach Judith, I can sense the same energy that I do with Vivian—the same brightness emanating from within.

Then it dawns on me, who this woman truly is.

Looking up at me, her eyes widen in shock. "The Dark Lady," she breathes before bowing her head.

I try to hide my pain at seeing a mirror of Vivian, instead replacing it with my cool exterior. "Judith."

"I suppose you are here to talk about my niece," she states.

My wings shift in surprise. "And how would you know such a thing?"

She chuckles—like a mother talking about her child she loved dearly. "I could never forget her, or her magic."

"You know of her magic?" I ask.

"I do."

"And you kept it from me—created a concealment spell to hide her."

"I did." No remorse.

"Why?" I demand, trying to rein in my irritation. Must all women in this particular family disobey me?

She looks me square in the eyes. "Her magic is unlike anything I had ever seen. I knew my darling girl was special, but she is truly beyond my wildest imagination. One night, fifteen years ago, I suddenly had the urge to check on her. I knew she was upstairs, asleep in her room, but something told me to go see her. So I did. She was fast asleep, just like I knew she would be. As I was turning to leave, her magic simply...jumped out at me." Judith smiles at the memory. "I thought I had gone mad, seeing her magic's past lives. Her magic was the earth, was the beginning and middle and end. Vivian was the child of the earth, just like the witches before her with the same magic. I knew I had to protect her—I saw how each life ended. I began combing through any ancient texts I could get my hands on, to see if I could prevent her from having the same fate." She looks down at her hands. "But I couldn't find anything. I knew it was inevitable: Phanes destroying the witch holding this magic."

"You certainly remember quite a lot," I murmur.

She shrugs. "Truthfully, I remember very little. I'm not sure why *this* is what stuck with me. Maybe because it is too important."

"Does Vivian know the truth about who you are?" I ask.

Judith's eyes go wide. "My lady, I'm not sure—"

I wave my hand flippantly. "Don't bother lying. If you remember Vivian's magic, then you would surely remember who you truly are to her. Why would you hand Vivian, *your* child, over to your sister?"

"I—" She gulps. "My sister was concerned about pleasing you. She realized she couldn't carry her own children and worried you would strip her of her matron title. I don't remember the details, but I do remember my lover was a non-magic wielder. I was blessed with a child, but my sister and I decided to switch places until the baby was born. She wanted an heir, and I wanted to help her—"

"I don't demand witches have offspring." I can't help my harsh tone.

No wonder Vivian's 'mother' acted the way she did towards her.

I fight the urge to rip someone's head from their shoulders, gritting my teeth as I spit, "Thank you for dropping another problem into my lap."

"Are you going to tell her?" Her voice shakes.

I don't have her, I nearly admit. "When the time is right," I evade. Without any reassurances, I stalk out of the garden, the feeling of the world pressing down on me, the clock counting down too quickly.

Chapter Seven
Vivian

"I believe tonight shall be the night, my little flower."

Chewing on the pineapple chunk in my mouth, I simply furrow my brows in confusion.

We sit in his large, empty dining room, a spread of various delicacies laid out before us. I can barely stomach to eat more than a few bites.

Phanes continues, "I have tested your magic in every way, and not once did it attempt to shield you. You have not lashed out or attempted to harm me. Perhaps it is finally time for me to truly believe your magic is weak." He smiles, making my stomach sour. "It means the balance still tips in the way it is meant to. Now, we must come together. To bind ourselves together."

The fruit in my mouth tastes like dirt.

"I have been patient," he goes on. "I have not pushed you, nor have I infiltrated your mind. You finally seem amenable to our destiny of bringing new celestial beings into this world."

My throat is closing. I can't swallow—I spit the pineapple out onto my plate instead of choking. "I—we're going to…tonight?"

No, no, no—

He smiles at me, a predatory gleam in his eye. "I will give you today to prepare," he states.

Understanding that's a dismissal, I rise on shaky legs from the table. I fight the urge to hyperventilate as I turn to leave this room and enter my own personal Hell.

"Oh, and Vivian," he calls to my retreating back. I stop and look over my shoulder at him. "I do not like to be kept waiting."

The threat is obvious.

Swiftly, my bare feet slap against the cold marble floor as I hustle back to our shared room.

I knew this day would come. I had just hoped he would take his little experiments on me too far and accidentally kill me first.

I'm in a daze as I open the bedroom door. My vision is dark around the edges and blood is pounding in my ears. My head swims as the room starts to tilt sideways.

I land on the cold floor, my panic causing my legs to finally give out. My body is wracked with tremors, adrenaline flowing through me, causing my vision to blur even more and for my teeth to chatter so hard I'm worried I'll accidentally bite my tongue off.

Curling into a ball, I succumb to my body's response, letting it rip me apart from the inside. Maybe this will be the way I die.

I hope so.

Chapter Eight

Venus

Something is wrong. An unshakeable sense of dread plagues me throughout the day. I drill the council on any shifts they can sense in the world, but they report that all seems normal.

It doesn't soothe my nerves.

It's nearly unbearable by the time I'm sitting with the healer, her cool hands gently pressing into my wings. "They look nearly healed," she informs me as she continues prodding them. "How has flying been?"

Taking a deep breath to try to steady myself, I grunt out, "Fine."

She hums, clearly dissatisfied with my response but thinks better of pushing me.

Suddenly, a wave of nausea hits me. I double over, grabbing at my midsection.

"Your Grace?"

I don't respond out of fear that I'll vomit all over the floor. The anxiety is suffocating me. Something is very, very wrong.

What is happening? What is—

The scent of cherry blossoms and pomegranates floods me.

Surely, I'm hallucinating, I try to reason. She isn't here, she's still—

Horror washes over me, mixing with my nerves. I don't know what's happening to me, but something must be happening to Vivian.

I spring up and race out of the room, ignoring the healer's yelp of surprise. Demons and witches waltzing through the halls dart out of my path, letting me race to the first open pair of windows I can fly from.

I need to get to Vivian—now. Whether my wings are ready, I don't know, but I can't wait any longer.

I launch myself from the window and unfurl my wings, forcing them to beat hard. Pain spiderwebs through my veins, but I grit my teeth and flap harder, pushing myself to stay airborne. I'm falling, the city below getting closer and closer with each breath.

I can't fail now. Vivian needs me. I've done wrong by her so many times in so many ways, but I will gladly sacrifice myself if it means she's safe.

Just as it feels inevitable that my wings will give out, a burst of strength radiates through me, and I glide along the wind.

I'm staying airborne.

A triumphant shout bellows from me as I fly higher and higher, Hell's city getting smaller in the distance as I prepare my rescue.

Chapter Nine
Vivian

I 'm rooted to the spot, sprawled out on the cold floor. I can't bring myself to move, to prepare myself for what will be the worst of this torture.

"Get up."

I didn't even hear him enter the room. My vision is blurred and I scramble to right myself, facing the direction his voice came from.

"Now, now, my little flower," he tsks, "I thought you were past the hysterics."

Tremors wrack my body as he prowls toward me. A forgotten feeling begins to stir in my stomach. I can't place what it is—is it another panic attack? Another rush of adrenaline when faced with an opponent?

"Must I force you?" He sounds disappointed. "I would prefer not to, but I will. The question is, how should I?"

His blurry figure stops directly in front of me, and I feel his hand grab my hair, yanking me up. A cry passes my lips as he pulls.

"It would bring me no joy to break into your pathetic, little mind." He's lying, I know he is—he'd love to do it.

He aggressively spins me around and pushes me back, forcing me to bend over the bed, my toes barely touching the floor.

I feel him pawing at the dress he forced me to wear, knowing I've run out of time. As he pushes the dress up past my hips, exposing me to him, his magic slithers up my body, worming its way into my ear. I scream and thrash as it prowls into my mind.

My little flower, his voice floats into my head. *I won't fit if you aren't ready.*

A wave of arousal spreads through me, easing my muscles and making me pliant. Welcoming him into my body.

No, not this—

His chuckle bounces around in my mind. *I knew I could make you enjoy it.*

I'm going to be sick. My stomach begins to churn as the desire his magic is forcing on me and that forgotten feeling spreads through my body, seeming to war with each other.

I'm not sure if I'm going to pass out or vomit on the floor.

Waves of these battling feelings cause my insides to twist to the point of pain. A low, pained moan escapes my lips before a voice that is not wholly mine shrieks, *"Get off us!"*

I hear Phanes gasp, his hands hesitating against my skin. He releases my hair and steps back from me, his hold on my mind slipping. It feels like cold water is dumped over me, extinguishing the pleasure and leaving only my disgust and pain. Shocked, I twist and look up at him to find his face is slack, his eyes wide. "Vivian, stop this."

I'm not doing anything, I want to say, but my mouth won't work. I feel something building inside me, like I'm a pressure cooker about to explode, my skin stretching, feeling too tight—

I collapse onto the floor. A wave of something bursts from me, throwing Phanes and everything around us back.

My magic.

My magic has finally responded.

It burrows into the castle's foundation with a fury I've never felt before, frothing at the mouth for retribution.

It begins to alter the very stone we are standing on, twisting it, breaking it apart, making it into something else entirely.

"Vivian!" Phanes shouts.

I look up and see him approaching, his dark eyes sinister, his white hair disheveled. "I knew you were hiding this from me!"

My magic lashes out again, barreling into him, throwing him clean across the room and into the door. His body sags like a doll as he falls to the floor in a crumpled heap. My magic seems to laugh maniacally at that.

It continues altering the stone, shaping it into...

Into a summing monolith.

"Stop," I try to shout but my voice only comes out as a whisper.

Creating a summoning monolith here would give Phanes direct access to Hell. To Venus.

Dooming everyone in the process.

"Stop!" I whisper-scream again, trying to get some form of control over this situation. I grit my teeth, demanding my magic to stop, stop, stop—

A fissure forms in the floor under me, across the room, up the wall, and into the ceiling. Marble begins to break apart, the walls cracking open as the ceiling caves in on itself.

The floor under me falls away, and suddenly, I'm free-falling.

I feel weightless. The wind cradles my body as the descent to my death continues.

A euphoric feeling flows through me and a laugh passes my lips. *No one can hurt me now,* I think, closing my eyes in relief. No one can hurt me if I'm dead.

Just as the calm overtakes my body, something barrels into me, causing me to shriek in terror.

Phanes won't let me go that easily.

My eyes fly open and I flail, trying to dislodge him, trying to get free—

Something familiar brushes against my cheek. Focusing my gaze, I see feathers—an array of colored feathers, black, silver, brown, shimmering in the dim sunlight.

I choke back a sob.

Venus.

Her powerful arms wrap around me, pressing me to her body. I grab her, clinging to her, sobs shaking me as I look into her face. Her midnight eyes are wild, roving over me as she shouts against the wind, but I can't make out the words.

It doesn't matter. She's here. She came for me.

She's more beautiful than I remember.

One of my hands reaches upwards, my fingertips lightly tracing her face in wonder.

She's here.

Her mouth continues to move but I hear no words. I'm laughing and crying, inspecting every inch of her face, of her wings. She's here.

Her wings beat powerfully as she steers us, but I'm not looking at where we're going. I simply can't take my eyes off her.

It isn't until we're in a quiet, dark room that I realize...we're back in Hell.

The last place she should have brought me.

Chapter Ten
Venus

Vivian is here. Back in my arms. Back in Hell. Exactly where she belongs.

But she seems to be acting panicked instead of relieved. She scrambles from my arms and begins pacing and pulling at her hair from the scalp.

"He can't come here, he can't come here," she repeats urgently.

"Vivian, we need to erect the wards," I urge. "You and your magic need to remake them."

She stops pacing and looks at me with a slightly deranged look in her eye—I've never seen this look from her before. Her scent reaches me and I wrinkle my nose. It's as if her scent has...rotted. Rotten pomegranates and wilted cherry blossoms.

She rushes to me and grips the front of my top in her fists, her knuckles white and her eyes still wide. "He cannot come here," she says again.

"You destroyed most of Phanes's castle," I inform her. She flinches at the sound of his name. "He won't be able to attack us—not yet. But we shouldn't wait. The High Priestesses are ready to help you channel your magic for the wards."

"No magic. Not mine. It can't be trusted." Her face contorts in anger.

This version of Vivian is foreign to me. Something akin to...fear sits in my stomach.

"Vivian," I try again, "I know my father. I know he will lick his wounds before retaliating. We have time, but not much."

"His snake," she groans.

"Did you see it?" I ask, my heart lurching.

She shakes her head. "It will come back."

I gently extract her hands from my shirt. "We need to get the High Priestesses," I say, not interested in leaving her for one millisecond.

She cradles her hands to her chest and nods limply.

I had flown up to his castle, searching for a crack in his wards, when the entire castle began to rumble and groan as if under immense pressure. Then, a blast of power swept through, disintegrating the wards and sending me flying backward.

That's when I saw part of the palace crumble, with Vivian's limp body careening towards the earth below.

The fear I felt in that moment was unlike anything I had ever experienced before. I raced for her, pushing my wings past their limit as they screamed at me to stop. I couldn't—not when she was plummeting to her certain death.

It was horrifying.

I can't be away from Vivian now, so I send my shadows after the High Priestesses. Vivian will never leave my sight again.

Not after this.

Her eyes are blank, a shocked expression on her face, as she curls in on herself, lowering herself to the ground, staring at nothing.

"Vivian?" I want to touch her, to tell her how much I missed her, how I'm so glad she's back, and what I will do to Phanes the moment—

The High Priestesses burst into the room and rush to Vivian, causing her to yelp and scramble away from them, her eyes wide with terror. I flare my wings out, one of them separating Vivian from them.

"Careful," I snarl.

The three halt immediately, their faces a mixture of concern and relief. I look over my shoulder and see Vivian breathing rapidly, struggling to acclimate.

It feels like my heart was ripped from my chest. I pull my wings back in and approach her slowly. "The High Priestesses are ready, Vivian."

She gulps down some air before pushing herself into a standing position.

A sharp intake of breath comes from one of the other witches, and I would strangle them if I didn't see it myself.

She's thin, a hideous white dress swallowing her entire frame. She has large half-moons under her eyes and her hair hangs limply down her back. She looks like she hasn't eaten or slept since I last saw her.

This is a shell of who Vivian is.

The High Priestesses slowly walk to her, Marie offering her hand for Vivian to take, which she refuses.

"Vivian," Aradia says gently, trying to keep a warm and welcoming smile on her face, "we will need to remake the wards now, with your magic." Vivian lets out a small, hysterical laugh, which confuses and concerns the witches, but Aradia continues. "When they were last erected, it occurred right outside Hell's forest. Would you like to go there?"

Vivian doesn't respond—she simply picks herself up and trudges towards the door.

The High Priestesses and I share an alarmed look before we follow her out.

Chapter Eleven
Vivian

The city is unbearably loud.

I don't remember it being this way. When I visited with Venus, I was in awe of the beautiful city, its people, and its architecture. Now, the buildings are too tall and too close together. The demons and witches and spirits make too much noise, carrying it down the streets, echoing through me.

The High Priestesses guide Venus and me through the streets, covered by Venus's shadows.

I'm overstimulated, struggling to keep myself together when all I have the urge to do is fold myself into a ball on the ground. Being in his silent castle has made every noise seem much louder.

The three witches walk us to the outskirts of the city, the vast forest looming ahead.

My vision is going cloudy and I'm struggling to breathe. I know my magic won't show up to help—it certainly didn't show up for me when I needed it most, only waking up to create another potential disaster.

We are separated and will never come back together.

But *he'll* come back. He won't stop until he has me under his thumb again.

I don't realize I've stopped walking until I see four sets of eyes staring at me. Venus's mouth is moving, but I can't hear anything, like my ears are full of water.

I shake my head like a dog trying to dry off. "Can't hear," I grunt.

Venus approaches me slowly, like I'm some wounded animal, and it sets my teeth on edge.

Her melodic voice finally filters through my ears. "It's time, Vivian."

The High Priestesses move towards me, standing in front of me. "We will need your blood for this, Vivian," says the one with dark curls framing her face—Aradia. "A simple cut on your palm will do."

I thrust my arm out, palm up to the sky. "It won't come out." My magic won't come out, but they don't understand.

The four in front of me share a concerned look before Venus summons a knife and hands it to the witch. "Can we try?" Venus asks.

Aradia approaches me, reaching to touch me.

"No!" I scream, my heart lurching at the simple idea of being touched. "I'll do it."

If I have to demonstrate that nothing will happen, then I will. I grab the dagger before anyone can object and slice my own palm open.

I don't even feel the sting.

"Place your palm on the grass," the one with icy blue eyes commands—Marie.

I do as I'm told, getting on my hands and knees, my blood hot against my skin as it drips onto the grass beneath.

Placing my hand on the ground, I feel nothing for several seconds. I would almost feel smug at being right if we weren't in such a dire situation. I'm about to stand when suddenly, my magic sprints out of me, pulling from me and channeling into the ground beneath me. I feel the three witches around me shouting words I can't hear.

My magic reacted. It's working to rebuild the wards.

I think this might be the thing that truly breaks me. My magic chose not to help me when *he* was doing those horrible things to me. It left me to suffer.

It feels like the ground is opening its mouth, swallowing me whole. So I let it.

Chapter Twelve
Venus

I do not know who this Vivian is.

It's heartbreaking. The light she has always exuded seems to have been snuffed out.

By my father.

My rage feels like a separate being living inside of me, ripping me apart to avenge her even when she physically is here in the room.

The warding ceremony was horrifying.

Vivian places her bleeding palm upon the earth, shrieking loud enough to nearly rupture my ear drums. Her back arches, her face contorting in a look of pure pain. Then her magic causes the ground to shake beneath our feet, the giant trees of the forest trembling and groaning under the pres-sure.

Vivian tries to tug her arm back, trying to dislodge her palm from the earth, but it is no use—as if it's glued down.

I lunge for her, gripping her arms as she screams and screams, tears rolling down her cheeks, her eyes screwed shut. The High Priestesses are a flurry of activity around us, shouting that this is not the way a warding spell should be. We all try to remove Vivian's hand from the ground, but it doesn't budge—she is fused by the magic roiling in her veins.

"It's okay, it's almost over," I repeat again and again to her, wiping her tears, brushing her hair back as she rages on, feeling lost as her voice gives out and her screams become silent.

Lifetimes later, her magic releases her, and she collapses. I wind my arms around her, feeling protective but helpless, unable to get her screams out of my head.

The High Priestesses look as horrified as I feel.

"That...that was unlike anything I've ever witnessed," Isobel whispers.

I don't have it in me to be angry.

"When Lilith made the wards," Marie croaks, "it was powerful, but it did not seem painful."

Vivian's head is cradled in the crook of my shoulder, her breathing even, her face smoothed out, as if she had not let out bloodcurdling screams just moments ago.

"Perhaps her connection to her magic is more fraught than Lilith's was," Aradia murmurs. "We apologize, Your Grace, we didn't—"

I shake my head, too tired to argue. Without another word, I unfurl my wings and fly my precious Vivian to our chambers.

She did not wake for two days. Healers attempted to console me, to tell me she seemed healthy, albeit a bit dehydrated, and that she was just replenishing herself. That she would wake soon and be right as rain.

But the Vivian who woke up seems to have deteriorated even further. Her hazel eyes are flat, her hair is limp, and her skin remains a sickly pallor. I've never seen her this way.

I usher her into the bathing chamber, urging her to bathe, but she nearly gouges my eyes out when I go in there with her. I hold my hands up in a show of surrender, backing out of the room without another word. She rushes to the door, a look of ire splashed across her face before she slams it shut.

Ten minutes later, Vivian unlocks the door and tiptoes out, wearing a pair of my black pants and a top that is too large, her wet hair soaking her back.

"Black?" I ask. "I'd assume you would like some of your more...brighter ensembles."

She shakes her head profusely and I snap my mouth shut. The pain in her face, in her movements, nearly brings me to my knees. I want to know what happened, what

Phanes did to her, to my beautiful, courageous, bright witch, to make her act so skittish and afraid.

"Vivian," I say helplessly, rising from my seat to approach her, "what do you need? Please, tell me and I will do it."

She simply shakes her head again and walks to the floor-to-ceiling windows, seating herself on the edge of them. It gives me a nervous feeling in my stomach to see her so close to the edge.

I slowly and loudly approach, seating myself next to her but stopping myself from being too close. Her body tenses and it sends me spiraling into despair. "I'm concerned about you being alone," I admit.

She doesn't look at me—just stares straight ahead.

"Vivian," I try again to get her attention, "what happened with Phanes?"

Her head whips to face me. "Don't say his name," she snarls.

I fight the urge to snap back at her. "I just want to help you."

No response.

"Would you like me to go?" My body screams at me not to offer this. I can't be away from her—not again.

She nods, and it feels like I'm breaking apart, but I don't want to ignore her needs, so I force myself to get up and walk out, feeling like my entire world has just collapsed.

Chapter Thirteen
Vivian

Time seems to pass me by, but I struggle to move with it. It feels like I'm unable to grasp where I am or how long I've been here.

Sometimes, I think I'm back in his castle. That I never escaped.

I try telling myself where I am, but it never seems to stick.

Venus comes in and out multiple times a day to check on me, only leaving to attend to whatever Dark Lady duties she has. She usually finds me in the same place: sitting on the floor by the open windows, letting the fresh air keep me rooted to the spot.

In his castle, fresh air never flowed through, probably by some form of magic, but these windows allow for the breeze to filter through me.

She doesn't know what to do with me, I can tell. I don't know what to do with me either. She tries to nudge my old self out, offering me coffee I'd like or random pink items you'd find in the five-dollar section at Target, but I think that part of me has died.

Every now and again, she'll urge me to bathe. I constantly teeter between wanting to wash my skin raw to get any trace of him off me and never setting foot in a tub ever again.

Venus doesn't sleep next to me, but has chosen to sit in a chair next to the bed, monitoring me in my sleep. I struggled with someone—anyone—being so close while I was unconscious, but my body eventually gives in, throwing me into a restless sleep each night.

I wear Venus's clothes that are too big for me, but the constant black feels safe to wear. She repeatedly mentions my old clothes, but I can't even bring myself to look at them.

How can she care for someone like me? Someone so weak, so disgusting? How can she possibly look at me without knowing it was her own father who did such horrifying and invasive things to me?

I don't blame her for what happened. No, that is his fault—and mine.

I see the hurt and devastation on her face every time I don't interact with her. I hate it. I hate her concern, I hate how she cares for me, I hate it all.

But most of all, I hate myself.

Chapter Fourteen

Venus

Weeks have passed since Vivian returned home, and she has not improved. She rarely speaks and must be encouraged to eat or to bathe or to do much of anything.

I've found that anger is the only emotion she can show. Otherwise, she is stoic, sitting in the window, panicking whenever I get too close. I rile her up on purpose, solely to see some light in her eyes. Irritation seems to be the only emotion she expresses anymore. If she isn't reacting to me needling her, she's just a shell.

Empty.

It terrifies me. I'm not equipped to handle this, to bring her back. So I just keep trying to irritate her, which seems to come naturally to me.

I don't like leaving her for long, but some things cannot wait. I soar through the air, beating my wings against the winds as I slip through the realms towards my father's castle. I've been monitoring his home every day, just to see if he's recovered.

Each day is the same: no wards, no repaired castle. Just a crumbling tomb.

It takes every ounce of self-control I have to not fly through and destroy him. Slowly. Painfully.

As I soar through the skies, I can't help but notice the stark difference between my reaction to Vivian's well-being and Lilith's death. Lilith's death and destruction of her soul caused me to spiral through grief, closing my realm's borders and refusing to do more than necessary—which included ignoring my father's existence, even after everything he did.

I felt defeated. He had taken everything from me, and I could no longer cope with losing her.

Perhaps that's why I am prepared to destroy myself if it means Vivian gets to live.

I steel myself as I get closer to my father's home. This happens every day, this anxiety—memories of growing up here, of having to endure him and my siblings, of losing my mother, all flood my senses as I approach.

It's over, I remind myself. My siblings are dead. My mother is dead. I don't have to experience those hardships anymore.

My anxiety turns to shock as I fly outside the palace grounds.

Strong wards are back in place, barring entrance.

The magical wards feel...wrong. A dark energy I've never felt from his wards radiates in the air.

How can this be? From what I've seen each day, Phanes shouldn't have been able to erect these wards again.

Not on his own.

A gasp escapes my lips as I tuck in my wings and barrel down toward the earth below, needing to get back to Hell immediately.

I wasted no time, sending my shadows to fetch the council. As everyone sits and stares at me with confusion, I loose a breath. "Phanes has been able to erect wards around his palace."

A beat of stunned silence.

"How?" Aradia says, shaking her head in disbelief.

"I don't know," I admit, hating myself for not knowing. "But I fear he may not be working alone."

My words cause panicked murmurings to float through the room.

I swallow my nerves and say quietly, "I do not know this for certain, but we must not rule out that he has created another god to assist him."

The room erupts into questions and theories, trying to understand if it's possible and what we can do.

"Why create a new one now?" Isobel asks. "He hasn't made one since losing nearly all of his children. Why now?"

"I don't know," I answer honestly. "But his wards feel different than they have before. They feel...darker. This isn't his magic. I can only assume another being created them."

"We must protect ourselves," Marie says. "Call every demon in the realm of the living home; alert every coven of this potential new god. We must be prepared for an attack."

I bristle at the command in her tone, but she's right. Turning to the archdemons, I instruct them, "Contact all demons in the other realm and order them back here."

"Is it necessary to prepare for another attack?" Kali asks. "Why can't we live as we did: both within the confines of our wards, without provoking the other?"

"Of course it's necessary," Marie argues angrily. "He took what was ours, and we retrieved her. He will try to have her again."

Aradia steps in. "Especially because the Dark Lady took Vivian from his own home."

"I remember what it was like during the War," Luke adds. "We can't go back to that."

"Enough," I sigh wearily. Everyone immediately quiets. "Has there been any activity on our wards?"

"None—no sign of Phanes attempting to tamper with them," Aradia replies.

"It is unusual for Phanes not to retaliate," Luke muses. "He has always had a vendetta against you, Your Grace. He will definitely try to strike us. Perhaps he is waiting for us to let our guard down."

I nod. "Station more witches around the perimeter. We must know if he tries."

"Has Vivian considered handing her soul over to you?" Isobel asks.

I grind my teeth together. "No. That has not changed."

Her soul has always been a sensitive subject. Vivian handing her soul over to me would bind us together and make us both more powerful, but she has never wanted that. I fear bringing it up now will just make everything worse.

They all nod in understanding, even though I notice the concern in their eyes.

I stand from the table, everyone following suit.

"My father will pay for what he did," I promise.

I round the table, exiting the room without another word, desperate to get back to Vivian.

She sits in the window, stoic like a gargoyle, her damp hair wetting the back of the shirt she's wearing.

Another one of mine.

I clear my throat and Vivian tenses but doesn't turn.

"Come, Vivian," I instruct. "We have things to do today." She looks over her shoulder at me, her brows narrowed. I continue, "I have something I must do, and you're coming with."

Her eyes flare, showing her irritation. It causes relief to flood my mind. *Come on, Vivian. Play with me.*

She seems to sense what I'm doing, because she stands and walks over to me, throwing me a look as if to say, *I'm not doing this because you told me to, but because I'm choosing to.*

I bite back the grin that wants to spread across my lips. Walking side-by-side, I try not to get blinded by the overwhelming sense of panic and hopelessness I feel at seeing her flinch when she sees others mingling in the halls. I remember how eerily silent my father's castle was, even when my siblings were alive. I can only imagine how jarring it must be to hear noise again.

One of my wings curls around her, shepherding her closer. She gives me a startled look; I simply raise my eyebrows in challenge.

She stares me down as we navigate the halls, her mind now trained solely on me as I send my shadows to chase everyone out of our way. Vivian doesn't seem to notice everyone has cleared out as we navigate our way to the archives, her gaze ensnared by mine. She gives me a small growl and stomps out of my grasp, her shoulders bunched by her ears as she storms toward the doors to the archives.

Her angry little footsteps thud against the floor as she descends the grand staircase, heading to a destination she doesn't even know yet. I stop and observe her, a chuckle slipping past me.

Vivian halts on one of the steps and whirls to me, her body nearly vibrating with agitation.

Crossing my arms over my chest, I tilt my head. "Oh, I assumed you knew the way, seeing as you so confidently strode in here."

I'm pushing her, but I can't stop. I need her to come back to me.

She bares her teeth, a feral beast ready to rip out my throat.

"Would you like to ask me something, Vivian?" I croon. "All you have to do is ask. *Use your words.*" It's nearly a plea on my lips; I'm desperate to hear her voice again.

Straightening her spine, she glowers up at me as she spits out, "Where are we going?" Her voice is rough from lack of use the past few weeks.

It's music to my ears.

I give her a smirk as I uncross my arms and saunter down the stairs right past her. I throw over my shoulder, "We're going to meet the head archivist. She's been pulling texts for me."

I hear Vivian huff and follow after me. She can be angry at me for the rest of her life; I got to hear her voice, and that's all that matters.

Arya, the head archivist, floats over to us, bowing her head to us both. "Dark Lady. And Lady Vivian. I've pulled what you asked for. Shall we?"

I nod, and Arya guides us to a seating area, a small table covered in ancient texts nestled among aisles of books. Floating candles dance in the air, illuminating the space with warm light. I pull one of the table's chairs out for Vivian before I turn back to the spirit. "Thank you, Arya.

I will call for you if we need any further assistance." As she flits away, I round the table and sit across from Vivian.

She eyes the texts curiously but says nothing.

"Words, Vivian," I remind her.

Her eyes snap up to mine, a bit of flame igniting in them, as she sneers, "Are you forcing me to join a book club or something?"

I nearly clap my hands in glee, but rein myself in, giving her a lazy smile instead. "We are going to read about how to kill a god."

Chapter Fifteen

Vivian

I'm not sure I heard her right. Maybe I have something in my ears. "We're going to read about *what*?"

She leans back in her chair, an annoying smirk on her face. "We're going to read about how to kill a god," she repeats, as if speaking to a small child.

"Why would I need to read about something like that?"

"Because Phanes has most likely created a new one, and we all need to be prepared."

My mind goes blank. "What?" I whisper, my voice trembling. No, that can't be; she has to be mistaken.

"I've been flying up to his palace every day to see how he's faring after you destroyed part of it." She's trying to play it off like this doesn't faze her, but her words are laced with anger. "Each day, it appeared the same: no wards, and a section of it is completely crumbled. When I went today, however, new wards had been erected. It's possible, of course, that he's working alone, but we can't rule out the possibility of him creating a new god to assist him."

"He can't," I argue, memories flashing through my mind. "He told me…" Panic begins slithering through my veins. Was he telling me things to trick me, to make me think he was weak when he actually wasn't?

My head starts to spin. "When he had me, he said entering my mind had left him bedridden for weeks." I nearly choke on the words, on the horrible memory of him forcing me to sit on his lap. "I thought it meant he was getting weaker."

Venus's dark eyes flash, an unreadable expression on her face before it smooths out into mild curiosity. "I wouldn't put it past him to lie." White-hot anger flares in me. "But," she continues, "I don't see a reason for him to lie to *you*. What purpose would that serve? It was just you and him." She seems to be musing to herself now. "He never confided in anyone how much magic it took to do anything. I was surprised a new god might have been created."

Images of him on top of me cloud my mind. I force the words out before they can clog my throat. "He said he made your mother himself."

Venus's shadows lurk around the table. "What else did he say?"

"I know what you're doing," I snarl, ignoring her question.

She holds up her hands. "And what is that?"

"You're prying me for information, *using* me for intel." The words taste like dirt on my tongue.

The room gets darker as her power starts to leak from her. She leans forward, her body thrumming. "I'm trying to get you to *share* with me so that you can get better." Her words are clipped. "You've barely spoken about what happened."

"I can't tell you what happened," I seethe. I can't tell anyone.

"Why not?"

"Because you'll think I'm disgusting!" I screech. "You'll know what he did to me and look at me differently, like I'm some repulsive, weak girl who couldn't save herself when she needed to." Angry tears pool in my eyes, and I wipe them away furiously. "You'll judge me and think less of me, and I won't be able to deal with that."

Venus blinks, her agitation leeching away. I want to reach across the table and gouge her eyes out. *I can't take this anymore,* I think as I rise from the table.

A shadow wraps around my wrist, making me pause, and I look over at Venus.

She seems to be at a loss for words, staring at me like she's never seen me before. "Vivian," she breathes. "I'm sorry, I thought I was helping—"

"Save it," I snap, shaking the shadow from me and darting through the archives.

I make it back to our room before I fold in on myself, my arms wrapped around me, as I quietly cry alone.

Chapter Sixteen

Vivian

His hands caress me, touching me everywhere and nowhere. My body won't move, unable to get away from his wandering touches.

I try to cry out, but he covers my mouth and presses himself on top of me. His giant serpent coils around the bed, making any hope of escaping impossible.

I can't take it. I scream against his hand. I thrash, trying to dislodge him, trying to throw his weight off me.

"My little flower," he tsks playfully, settling himself, forcing my legs apart with his enormous frame. "You are finally going to be mine."

Chapter Seventeen

Venus

Clearly my attempts to help have only made things worse. I spent the rest of the evening in the archives, simply to give Vivian time away, but also to grapple with my own shortcomings.

I don't know what I'm doing; I don't know how to help. I want her to get better, but it feels like everything I do is wrong. I thought giving her a task would keep her mind occupied, that it would push her past her despair and spur her into action.

Unfortunately, all I've done is make it worse.

It makes me feel like I have no control, and I hate it.

As I'm dragging myself back to our room, I feel the ground rumble beneath my feet. I freeze, trying to sense what power this is. Has Phanes broken through our wards, undetected?

My shadows dart around me, sensing, testing, as another rumble of power spreads through the castle. Panic overrides all critical thinking as I race to our bedroom. If

Phanes is here, I'll destroy him without hesitation. I don't care if it damns everything—I'll drag Vivian's soul from her and spirit us away to avoid the destruction if I have to.

Ripping the bedroom door open, her name on my lips, I'm hit with a surge of power and stumble backward.

I realize with a start that Phanes isn't here.

The power is coming from Vivian.

Righting myself, I dart into the room and see Vivian lying on the bed, body arched, mouth open in a scream, tears leaking from the corners of her eyes. Another surge of magic threatens to knock me back. My own answers, shielding me from the onslaught.

I quickly climb onto the bed and grip her shoulders before I can think clearly.

"Vivian!" I shout.

She screams again and flails, trapped in the throes of her fears. Her magic wraps around us, as if trying to protect her from danger.

I shout her name again and again and again.

Her magic pauses, as if also waking from a nightmare, and it eases back.

Vivian's eyes fly open, wide and frightened, and she scrambles into a seated position, looking around frantically.

"You were having a nightmare. Do you know where you are?" I pant, sweat beading on my skin.

She starts hyperventilating, grabbing fistfuls of her hair and yanking as she gulps down air. The magic within her seems to growl, but retreats completely, seeming to understand the threat is imaginary. The world around us quiets.

I try again, fighting the urge to pull her into my arms. "Where are you, Vivian?"

"In Hell," she gasps out.

"That's right." I nod patiently. "That's right."

Slowly, so slowly, her breathing evens out and she releases her hair. She stares at me, eyes wide, as if she's remembering who I am.

"Vivian," I whisper, my voice breaking.

A tear rolls down her cheek and she nods, seeming to understand the desperation I feel.

"I want to help you. I will do anything to do that, but you must let me."

She nods again, her face crumpling.

"Can I hold you?" I ask, feeling like I've ripped my heart out of my chest and handed it to her.

She begins crying in earnest, but to my utter shock, she whispers, "Yes."

My heart stops beating. Swallowing my nerves, feeling like I'm approaching a wounded animal, I shuffle towards her and scoop her into my lap, pressing my back against the headboard. She immediately wraps her arms around my neck and presses her face into me, her tears quickly soaking the fabric of my shirt.

I rub her back soothingly as she cries into me, purging emotions that are finally ready to be expressed. I whisper soft words to her, telling her how I missed her, how my life means nothing without her, how brave and brilliant and beautiful she is. I don't know if this is what she wants to hear, but she eventually stops crying.

Pulling back, we lock eyes.

So much hurt and anguish sits between us, her scent tinged with decay. I hold her gaze, refusing to look away, weathering all the hurt she has, as if I could take it from her.

We stay like this for lifetimes, arms locked around each other, looking into each other's eyes, neither of us willing to turn away from each other.

This is what love is, I realize. Love is holding the broken pieces of someone and waiting for them to put them back together, even when all you want to do is force the pieces back in place yourself.

I can't force her to get better, as much as I want to. All I can do is weather the storm and hope she lets me be there when it clears.

Chapter Eighteen
Vivian

I don't want to live like this anymore. I just don't know how to stop it.

I'm underwater, swimming hard to reach the surface, to get air in my lungs, but it's as if something is tied to my ankle and keeps dragging me down. No matter how hard I fight, I'm still drowning.

Venus doesn't stop trying to pull me out of the water. She drags me from place to place, meeting to meeting, all because she doesn't want to leave me on my own. I think my nightmare last night freaked her out and she wants to monitor me even more than before. She irritates me on purpose, just to get a reaction out of me.

I find that I actually enjoy feeling annoyed with her. It's one of the few times I feel anything but unending emptiness.

The only other emotion that rears its ugly head is hatred. Hatred for *him*.

Now that he might have made a new god, it feels like my hatred for him has grown exponentially. My wrath is a living thing inside me, both feeding from me and fueling me.

Venus and I sit across from one another in the archives, a pile of books sitting between us on the table. "Why do I need to read about how to kill a god?" I ask her. "You could just tell me how to do it."

"I can't do everything around here, Vivian," she scolds.

I roll my eyes. "It's literally your realm, so yes, you can."

She examines her nails. "I want you to do it yourself. Once you find the answer, we'll have to prepare you to enact your revenge."

"My revenge?" I blink in surprise.

"Isn't that what you want?" Venus replies as she looks over at me, tilting her head. "Don't you want to get back at him for whatever he did to you?"

I do, I think. I'd do anything to make sure he suffers.

She seems to sense my thoughts, or she can scent it on me, because she nods knowingly. "Killing a god he's created is a perfect way to do that."

It's not enough, I nearly say. It's not enough because he'd still be alive.

I might just have to settle for this avenue instead. Turning back to the text in front of me, I vow to figure out how to get that revenge.

A god can be killed by decapitation, apparently.

They can heal themselves against nearly all other fatal injuries, but losing their head proves too difficult for their magic to repair.

So basically, I need to get close enough to cut their head off.

Venus left the archives a few hours ago, nearly dragging me along, but I was too engrossed in my new task to be torn away.

Now, as I sit here with the answer, I can't help but get pissed off. How in the Hell am I going to be able to kill a god? I'm a witch with a disconnect to my unique magic. I haven't signed my soul over to Venus, so I'm not strong enough or quick enough to heal if one attacked me.

I'm basically a sitting duck, and I fucking hate it. I hate how weak I am, how pathetic I've become.

A nagging sensation starts poking my stomach, feeling like something is sloshing around, causing me to wince with pain.

My nails dig into the wood of the table. Why would Venus make me figure this out? To remind me that I'm useless? Fury burns in me, looking for a way out, for an opponent to eviscerate.

My stomach spasms, making me gasp. I grit my teeth and get up from the table, trying to ignore it. Is my anger making me feel physically sick?

Another spasm rocks me and I pause, leaning against the closest bookshelf. I breathe deeply through my nose and out my mouth, but the pain doesn't subside.

No, it can't be.

I haven't felt my magic since the creation of the wards. I damned it to Hell, telling it to never bother me again. I don't want it anymore—I am tired of harboring it inside my body, letting it put me in the middle of its messes.

My magic throws itself around in me as if it's having a tantrum.

"Stop it," I whisper as I continue down the hall towards the stairs. I need to get out of here. I need to go back to the sanctuary of my bedroom.

It kicks my stomach, and I clutch at my midsection.

"Stop," I grunt. "Leave me alone."

It doesn't. It keeps moving through me, pressing into my skin, making me feel like I'm going to explode.

Images of my magic destroying *his* castle flash across my mind.

"Stop!" I scream, my panic overwhelming my body. "Just stop it, stop it, *stop it*!"

My sight gets cloudy and I feel faint. I wrap my arms around myself and crouch on the carpeted floor. "Why won't you just leave me alone like you did when *he* did all of those things to me?" I yell. "Just *get out of me and leave me alone.*"

I'm not sure if my magic is reacting to my words—I can't feel anything but my overwhelming feeling of anxiety. I press my hands hard against my eyes and begin rocking back and forth. I know I must look insane to the entire archives, to everyone simply going about their business while I have a loud mental breakdown in the middle of the day.

"Vivian?" I hear my name being called like I'm stuck underwater. I can't remove my hands from my eyes or stop rocking. I can't pull myself together.

"Everybody out!" a dark, foreboding voice demands, making me tremble.

Gentle hands grip my wrists and pry them from my face. I blink my eyes open slowly to see Venus on her knees, her wings bent around me, shielding me from view.

"It's alright," she soothes, her hands still holding my wrists. Her tattoo slowly dips its tongue out—for some reason, it registers as a sympathetic gesture.

I'm sucking in air, trying to calm myself down. I can't even bring myself to be embarrassed at everyone seeing me like this, about Venus finding me like this.

"I don't want to be like this," I whisper as hot tears roll down my cheeks. "I don't want to be weak. My magic chose me and then abandoned me when I needed it," I whisper, my voice cracking. "My magic didn't protect me. I can't trust it ever again."

"I know," she replies softly.

I keep going, as if a dam has burst inside me. "And when it finally bothered to help, all it did was try to make a summoning monolith in the middle of his castle, making a direct line between you and him. All it does is fuck everything up in my life."

Venus strokes the inside of my wrists, letting me cry it out for an eternity. When it feels like I have no more tears left, Venus hesitantly releases one of my wrists and swipes her thumb across my cheek. "Talk to me," she murmurs. "Tell me something."

"Like what?" My voice is thick.

"Anything. Anything about your time with...him. Whatever you share, I will carry it for you."

I can't tell her what he did to me, I think in a panic. She must already think I'm horrible and gross; knowing what he did will only make her think even worse things about me.

Taking a deep breath, I settle on something that won't make her think less of me. "When he would leave me unattended, I once stumbled upon a mural. It was the only color in the entire place."

Venus goes rigid and releases me. I keep going. "It showed my magic. That my magic was here before he was, before you were. That it's the earth itself, the original creator—until he came and tried to get rid of it." I swallow the anxiety rising in my throat. "He won't stop until he has me again, Venus."

"The mural," Venus responds hoarsely, "Tell me about the mural."

I explain what it showed me in detail, the magic at the core of the planet. Venus sucks in a breath and says, "That was my mother's mural. She painted it in her chambers. She showed it to me and told me my father had her paint it."

I blink. "That was your mother's room?"

Venus's expression is a mixture of pain and sorrow. "Yes. I...I didn't care to visit him or my siblings, but my mother..." She trails off, her eyes closing for a moment. "My mother was the reason I even bothered to go home."

"Did you kill her?" I ask, unable to stop the question from crossing my lips.

She recoils as if I've slapped her. "Of course not. My mother was the only one I loved unconditionally."

I chew on my bottom lip. "When you told me you killed all your siblings, I just..."

"You assume I meant my mother as well?" she finishes for me.

I nod and she blows out a breath. "I never would have harmed her. My father was the one to murder her." Her voice deepens with barely contained rage. "I came to visit her one last time, to convince her to come to Hell with me. We were ready to attack, and I needed her safe here, but I found her chambers empty. Her handmaidens informed me that she had passed suddenly in the night. He never admitted it, but I know he killed her.

"I believe my mother was meant to be the ruler of Hell, but my father has always been selfish and didn't want her too far away. Didn't want her to be corrupted by darkness either. So, instead of her getting to live out her true purpose, they had me, and my mother was stuck in his castle."

My heart aches—her fate would have been mine, was too close to being mine.

Returning to the topic of the mural, Venus says, "I didn't know that the mural portrayed your magic. It makes sense, I suppose—your magic is connected to the earth around it and, as we've seen, can bring it back to life." Her eyebrows furrow in thought. "It is...interesting."

I should ask what she means and what this all might mean for *me*, but I don't. I can't. So instead, I whisper, "Your mother was the first Night Goddess."

Venus lets out a sigh. "She was. And I was their first child."

"He talked incessantly about having more," I choke out. Her shadows snake around me, checking on me, trying to protect me.

Venus clears her throat as if to dislodge anger from rendering her speechless. "He no longer had a need for my mother after my siblings were born, but he kept her around." Her tone shows her disgust. "Cloistered in her chambers."

Memories flash before my eyes and I close them, trying to get them to go away.

"She was the one who named me Venus," she continues, her tone softening, turning wistful. It catches me by surprise, this shift. I open my eyes and find her scrutinizing me, as if trying to see if her memories are helping or harming me. "She would always tell me how it meant 'lightbringer.'" She scoffs at the irony. Even my mouth tugs upwards.

"Maybe because you're sunny," I try to joke, but it falls flat.

Venus tilts her head curiously, registering my attempt at humor. I know it sucked, but she's being a good sport because she throws her head back and laughs, her inky black hair shifting with the movement.

She is ethereal when she laughs. It takes my breath away as I take in the crinkles around her eyes, the curve of her lips, and the column of her throat as her tattoo shifts with her movements.

I'm struck by her.

Onyx eyes meet mine and I realize I've just been gawking at her. I quickly avert my gaze, my cheeks heating. "Sorry," I mumble.

Venus's fingers lightly grip my chin and turn my head to look at her. "Don't apologize," she murmurs, her eyes dipping to my mouth.

Need ravages through me like a wildfire, but it's quickly doused by disgust at myself.

Venus seems to sense the shift from me, looking like she might push but thinks better of it. I hate that she thinks better of it. "I take it you found out how to kill a god," she assumes, dropping my chin.

Oh right, that's why I was so pissed off. "Yeah, I did. What the Hell, Venus?"

She grimaces. "I thought it would help you to have something to do."

I gape at her. "You think I'm like this simply because I'm *bored*?"

"No," she says fiercely. "I just..." For once, she seems to be struggling with finding the right words. "I thought it would help you move forward, maybe harness your feelings better. I realize I've made everything worse." Her shoulders slump a bit. "Even your magic would agree with me."

"I don't know what my magic was responding to," I admit. "Maybe getting angry made it react."

"Then why did it nearly bring the entire palace down last night?"

I blink at her. "What?"

Her face is a mirror of my own confusion. "Don't you remember? You were having a nightmare."

"Yes, I definitely remember," I say slowly.

"Before I was able to wake you, your magic had reacted. It nearly knocked me on my ass."

"I..." I remember the nightmare, but I don't remember feeling my magic at all.

Venus continues, "Maybe it was letting its own anxiety out."

Her words make me pause. My magic, feeling anxiety? Feeling fear like I did in my dream last night? The thought makes me feel...incredibly unhappy. A deep, aching sadness, even when a tiny voice in my head tells me that my magic doesn't deserve my sympathy.

Venus's dark eyes scrutinize me, letting me think through my warring feelings, before she holds out her hand to me. "I need to meet with the council. Will you be joining me?"

I'm shocked she's asking instead of simply telling me—it shocks me enough that I hesitate. Of all the meetings she has, she doesn't take me to sit in with the council. I don't even know where they meet. After a few moments, I shake my head. She looks momentarily disappointed but doesn't push me as I tentatively slip my hand into hers. As she stands and helps me up, I find myself not wanting to let go, even when she pulls away.

Licking my lips, I promise her, "I'm not sure how to move through this, but I want to. I don't want to be this way."

Her eyes soften. "I know, Vivian. There is no rush."

But there is, I want to argue. He'll be back for me, and he'll stop at nothing until he has me again.

Chapter Nineteen
Venus

My mother summoning me to visit is not new. She calls upon me quite often, in fact. I think it's because she's lonely—I know my siblings visit her, but not as much as she'd like.

While I love her dearly, it is always a struggle to get myself to go.

Even now, as I swiftly walk through the halls, my unease grows.

The witch, Lilith, and I have finally agreed to be allies. To destroy my father and my siblings, so we can live free of their tyrannical ways.

The only one we will spare is my mother. She isn't like the others; she has no interest in harming anyone or anything. But I can't tell her yet. Not until the witches and my loyal demons are ready to strike.

As I make a turn down the hallway, I nearly run into two of my siblings.

Aether and Pontus both halt, sinister grins marring their faces as they realize who stands before them. Pontus is the God of the Sea, while Aether is the God of the Sky. Both gods delight in torturing mortals.

They'll be the first ones to go.

"Venus," Aether drawls, the two circling me like predators eyeing prey. "It has been too long. Tell me, what brings you before us?"

"I'm not here for either of you." I keep my back straight, not letting them sense any fear. I send my shadows away, not allowing my brothers access to them—last time, they tried trapping them in jars. "Now, if you'll excuse me—"

I go to step out of the circle, but Pontus blocks me. "Pity. We have all missed seeing you at court. Especially Father."

"A pity, indeed," I reply snarkily.

"How is your little cesspool of a realm fairing, Sister?" Aether asks behind me, the two of them now blocking me between them.

"Come sometime and you'll find out," I purr.

"As if we'd ever step foot in that horrid place," Pontus sneers. "Father says I'm welcome to flood your realm whenever I please." My brother puffs out his chest, acting like a preening peacock.

"Father says a lot of things," I growl.

Pontus picks up a lock of my hair, curling it around his finger while Aether steps closer to my back. I can feel the heat radiating from them both, making me nauseous at the proximity. "You would do well to respect him. He created us, after all."

I don't respond.

"Besides," he continues, "I'll be the one to take over once he deems me ready, and I'll make sure you stay in your place."

Aether snorts. "I doubt that, Brother—Father says I'll be the next in line."

Pontus's beady eyes shift to our sibling and he drops my hair. "Lies."

"It's true."

The two begin squabbling with me still stuck in the middle, their voices quickly raising to shouts about who is best to lead. Silently, I tap on my serpent tattoo three times, letting it slither across my skin and transport me out from between them.

I arrive outside my mother's door, thanking Hell I am able to move further and further each time I use my magic. I can usually only move a few feet at a time, rendering this completely useless, but it looks like my magical ability to transport myself is getting stronger.

Loosing a tense breath, I let myself into my mother's chambers.

She sits in front of a raging fire, her feet curled under her and a mug of something steaming cupped in both hands as she gazes into the flames.

My shadows reappear and dart for hers, circling them like an excited puppy. My mother smiles fondly at them before turning her head and giving me a warm smile. "Venus," she says in greeting, "I've just had tea made."

Seating myself on the chair adjacent to hers, I nod at her mug. "Looks like it will burn your tongue."

Her eyes twinkle. "It's the best way to drink it." She raises the mug to her lips and takes a sip before she brings it to her lap again. "You look uneasy. What troubles you?"

I shake my head. "I ran into Aether and Pontus on my way here."

She gives me a concerned look. "I know they enjoy teasing you."

"They all enjoy teasing me."

"Next time they do, send them to me and I'll set them right."

No, thanks, I nearly say. I can't have my mother fighting my battles for me. It'll make the relentless bullying from my siblings worse.

Besides, I must deal with it for only a little while longer.

Color at the corner of my eye catches my attention, and I turn to look at the mural my mother is painting. The one she's convinced holds the truth—the truth that she evades sharing every time I ask.

"Your mural seems to be coming along," I note.

"Indeed, it is."

"Why are you painting this?" I try every time to get something out of her.

"Your father asked me to."

"Ah." He wants her to paint this in her own chambers? How strange.

"Venus," my mother says, her tone serious. I turn to look at her and find her blue eyes boring into me. "I fear something has shifted in the world."

I still. "What do you mean?"

"I sense something is amiss. Promise me that, no matter what happens, you will stay in your realm and not involve yourself."

I clear my throat. "Mother...perhaps you'd like to come visit me in Hell sometime soon? You haven't been in such a long time."

"I cannot leave now. Things are being set into motion," she states matter-of-factly.

My brows narrow. "What is set into motion?"

Is she referring to my meeting with Lilith and our discussions to overthrow my father and siblings? How would she even know about that? She never leaves the castle.

I glance at her shadows suspiciously. Perhaps they are better informants than I realized.

She shakes her head, her dark hair shifting with the movement. "Once the mural is done, everything will make sense."

I try to clamp down on the irritation rising in me. This fucking mural is the least of our problems.

My shadows vibrate, sensing my agitation, and slither over to me. I'll keep trying to get her to leave, I decide. I won't attack until she's safe.

So I plaster on a smile and say, "I'd like some of your scalding hot tea."

Chapter Twenty

Venus

After bringing Vivian back to the bedroom, I quickly called the council together to discuss what she revealed. That her magic—not my father's—created this world. Everyone was struck by this revelation, our minds silently churning about what this means, and if it is helpful or harmful to us.

"If what you say is true, Your Grace, if Lady Vivian's magic is the true magic of this earth, Phanes will stop at nothing to take her again." Marie shakes her head, her white-blonde hair gliding with the movement, her icy blue eyes closing for a moment before landing on me. "She will need to practice her magic. Seeing as her magic has made itself known in Hell, we should work with her now."

"She still isn't ready," I point out.

The High Priestesses don't respond, but I sense their urge to push. I can't tell them that I'm trying—and failing—to get Vivian to come back to herself, hopefully leading her to connect with her magic. They'll think I'm a failure for being unable to get her there, and I can't have that.

"This does also bring up another item to discuss." Aradia shifts. "We have discussed a new God of Life. First, we considered you as the appropriate being to destroy your father and step into his role. But now...perhaps we have another who is more suited."

Shock overtakes me for a moment. "No," I growl.

"Please, Your Grace," she begs. "Lady Vivian's magic may become strong enough to defeat him. We must not turn a blind eye to the possibility."

"She cannot go up against Phanes."

"She will have help—from you, from our armies."

"Just like Lilith did?" I spit.

The room goes silent.

My anger radiates through me as my magic reverberates around the room. "Lilith had the same magic that flows through Vivian's veins and Phanes had no trouble destroying her. What makes you think this time would be different?"

"Lady Vivian could give you her soul," Isobel interjects quietly. "It would strengthen both of you. It could be the difference—it could tip the scales in our favor."

"I said no." I rise from the table. "This council has always been the most loyal and powerful this realm has seen.

But I am noticing more dissent than ever before." I make eye contact with each individual in the room.

Only Aradia dares to hold my gaze.

"My word is law. You would all do well to remember that."

I hold Aradia's eyes as I step away. She finally lowers them to the table, to my satisfaction.

Even as a seed of doubt starts to sprout in my mind. The correct path has made itself known: strengthen Vivian's connection with her magic, get her soul, and prepare us to defeat Phanes.

But at what cost? Could Vivian ever come back from this?

I feel I must choose between her and the sanctity of the realms.

Before, I would have pushed her into making the decision I wanted, but now? Now, all I am concerned with is her getting better, her healing from this.

I just wish I knew how to help her. Lacking clarity has always made me agitated—not having a plan or a trick up my sleeve. It makes me feel out of control.

A feeling I can't handle.

I find Vivian in her usual spot by the window, her long blonde locks gently carried by the breeze. My approach doesn't seem to startle her as she looks over her shoulder and gives me a small smile that nearly knocks me over.

Seating myself next to her, I hold her gaze for a few moments, taking in the kaleidoscope of colors that dance in her irises. "I have something I need to speak with you about," I tell her.

She seems to brace herself.

"I discussed what you shared with my council. They have expressed...concern over it." She tilts her head in confusion. "We believe connecting with your magic is crucial."

The sheer panic on her face makes my heart lurch.

"I don't know if I can do that," she tells me.

"It might help with what happened today. You and I both know that a witch refusing to release her magic can become uncomfortable—even painful. It's dangerous to bury it."

She looks down at her lap for a moment. "I don't want my magic anymore."

I nod, her scent decaying rapidly. I try to hide my disappointment that she's put in this position. "The High

Priestesses have agreed to assist you with connecting you with your magic again. Just...consider it. For me."

She licks her lips nervously before responding, "Okay."

I nearly sag with relief. It's a starting point.

The other topics discussed with my council—that they want Vivian to hand over her soul, to defeat Phanes, and to take his place—are on the tip of my tongue but I swallow them. *She isn't ready,* I think to myself. She can't even say his name and gets panicked at the mere mention of him.

Does Vivian even want to go down this path? She has fought tooth and nail to keep her mortal life—why would she want to ascend into a goddess?

Ascending to godhood has never happened. I don't even know if it is possible. I don't want to offer this to her, all for it to be for naught.

She deserves to heal first. Heal herself and her magic before she's thrust into another situation where she has no choice.

So I keep it to myself, struggling with the guilt that snakes its way through my body.

Vivian catches me staring at her and asks, "What is it?"

I plaster a smile on my face and tell her, "Nothing. Just thinking about how aggravating it is to not simply boss someone around."

She rolls her eyes, but one side of her mouth quirks up. "Your life is so difficult," she sighs sarcastically.

"It is."

That earns me a full smile before her face softens in contemplation, her eyes shifting to the sprawling city beyond. "I want to be able to go into the city again. I loved it the first time; I want to love it again."

I grit my teeth against the overwhelming heartache that threatens to knock me over at her words. "I want nothing more than that for you. I promise that you will come to love it again."

Tears well in her eyes. "You think?"

I nod solemnly. "I know."

We fall into a comfortable silence, letting our words settle between us, when Vivian says, "When I was there, with...him," she shudders but presses on, "it felt like my magic and I completely separated. I couldn't feel it the way I could before. Today was the first time I felt it again."

Swallowing my shock, I ask, "How did that feel?"

She purses her lips in thought before answering. "It felt like a reminder...of how it left me to defend myself." Her voice cracks and she closes her eyes for a beat. When she opens them, she looks directly at me, and I fight the urge to destroy the entire world at the devastation in them.

"Perhaps you and your magic will be able to forgive one another. Forgiveness is your greatest strength," I remind her, thinking back to our conversation at her childhood home, where she forgave me for all my misdeeds.

Her eyes go distant. "I'm not sure that is true anymore."

Chapter Twenty-One
Vivian

"Why are demons the ones in charge of souls? Don't they eat those?"

Venus shoots me a look that says, *could you say that any louder?*

I snap my mouth shut. Venus decided a trip to see the newly departed souls would be a good idea—she has work to do there and wanted me to tag along. I was hesitant at first, unsure of how I'd handle it, but something in me wanted to go.

It's like a smaller version of the city but with less hustle and bustle, less noise. It feels like a safer place for me to walk around without getting overwhelmed.

"Demons are heavily vetted before they can work with souls," she replies in a hushed tone so as to not freak anyone out. "Only those proven to be past the point of insatiable hunger are ready. They mostly prefer the souls of demons to humans or witches, for whatever reason."

"Cannibals," I mutter under my breath, which elicits a snort from Venus. It feels foreign to make jokes, to even think about humor, but Venus's easy laugh warms my stomach.

One of her wings curls around me, keeping me close but is mindful not to touch me too much. "So demons are always hungry for souls?" I ask.

"Up until a certain point in their development," she replies. "Many of the demons will be kept under close surveillance during that time, to make sure they don't go on a killing spree, as it is bloody and violent."

I shudder. "It sounds complicated."

"It is," she agrees, "I've tried many things to alter it, but it seems out of my control. So I simply have to put up with it."

Which she clearly hates.

We walk in silence as we pass a small garden. I pause, shocked to see a thriving garden in a place with no sun. "How?" I ask.

"Magic," she replies simply. I roll my eyes. "It's a different magic than yours. It is more of an illusion than an actual, living garden," she explains.

"So what about Hell's forest? Is that an illusion too?"

"No," she answers, "but it isn't alive."

I'm about to press her on that when my eyes land on a lone spirit, floating along and admiring the flowers.

Shock reverberates through me.

"Aunt Judith?" I gasp.

The spirit turns to me, and it feels like I've been hit in the chest. It's her—she's transparent, floating above the ground, but her features...it's her.

"Vivian?" she asks.

I run over to her, worried she'll disappear, a mirage taunting me. I go to throw my arms around her, but I'm met only with air.

Stunned, we both retreat slightly.

A sob works its way up my throat as I take her in but can't touch her.

My loving, warm, vibrant aunt, the one who loved me like I was her own, is here because of my mother.

Because I left.

"I'm so sorry," I blubber, my heart cracking as I realize the gravity of what I've done and how I'm responsible. "I'm so sorry," I repeat over and over, covering my face with my hands, unable to look at what I've caused.

"Vivian," my aunt says gently, "look at me."

I can't. I just sob harder.

"Vivian," she tries again, her voice soft but firm now.

I wipe my eyes and put my hands down, but the emotions are overwhelming, like they're too big for my body.

"Come, child, let's sit for a moment."

Obediently, I follow behind her, seating myself on a bench in the little garden. She sits beside me, although she hovers just above her seat.

"I know what happened," I say, my voice thick. "I went back to the coven—it's a long story—and *she* was there. She told me what happened after I left, what she did to you."

My aunt looks at me with nothing but love and patience in her expression and it makes me feel even worse. "I'm sorry, my dear, but I'm not sure I follow."

I furrow my brows at her. "You—you don't remember what happened?"

She shrugs her delicate shoulders. "I remember having a sister who acted as matron of a coven and having a niece that I loved more than anything. And I remember the extraordinary magic she had."

Shit. I forgot souls temporarily lose their memories once they die.

"I have so much I need to ask you," I tell her sadly.

"I'm sure you do," she chuckles. "I remember you were quite a curious child."

My mouth lifts at that. "You were the only one who ever indulged me."

She sighs. "Your mother has always been a cunning spider, determined to do whatever must be done to help herself. Why else do you think she was the matron?"

"She's in the dungeons," I tell her quietly.

My aunt blinks in surprise. "I take it the Dark Lady had an issue with her. She must have deemed it a grave offense if your mother is down there."

I grimace. "She told me I could have her removed from her cell, but...I don't think I want that. I think I want her to stay down there, to suffer."

Judith seems to consider me a moment. "The Dark Lady came to visit me not too long ago, to speak about you."

My brows narrow. "About me? Why?"

"She wanted to know what I knew about your magic."

Memories of me finding my aunt's grimoire, of her note to me to be careful because someone was coming for me.

"Child of the earth," my aunt says in a fond tone.

"How did you know?" I ask, leaning forward intently.

"Your magic is quite talkative with the right person," she chuckles.

I fight the instinct to reach inside myself and ask my magic. My stomach drops at the reminder that we will never get to that point—not again.

"So you know then. You know what it is."

Judith nods. "I do, and I know who took you." Her face softens in sympathy. "I cannot imagine what you have been through, my darling girl."

"I wanted to die," I admit, shame leaking out of me at the ugliness inside, the feeling of hopelessness and how it tore through me.

My aunt's face crumples at my words. She reaches for me but seems to remember she physically can't and pulls back. One of Venus's shadows burrows into my hair and sits on my shoulder in comfort, reminding me she's close by.

"He's still alive, I assume," my aunt states.

I cock my head. "Of course he is. He has to be," I tell her.

My aunt looks around the garden for listening ears; no one is around except for us and Venus, pretending not to listen in. She drops her voice to a near-whisper as she says, "There is another way."

Shaking my head, I argue, "No, there isn't. If he's dead, there's no one to take his place."

She throws a look in Venus's direction and takes a deep breath. "It is best if you speak with your magic about what can be done."

"I don't understand. Why can't I ever get a straight answer out of anyone?" I grumble, fighting the urge to stamp my foot in annoyance.

She smiles at me. "I am glad to see you still have your fire."

"Is that why you always let me spend time in the wilderness—because you knew about my magic?"

"At first," she answers, "but over time it was clear you loved it too. In a way, it was for both of you."

"What does that...nickname mean?" I ask, thinking back to when I spotted it in her notes.

"Your magic did not choose witches willy-nilly to carry it. It sought out only those it believed strong enough, not only to withstand its power, but to combat him. Unfortunately, none proved to be strong enough. Child of the earth is the name of all the witches that have held your magic."

"So, I'm meant to die, just like all of them." I scowl.

She gives me a sympathetic look. "All of their lives ended the same way."

My magic, harboring itself inside poor, unsuspecting witches, just to be the cause of their demise.

I swallow my irritation, not wanting it to ruin our reunion. "I have missed you so much. There's so much I need to tell you."

"And I to you."

I realize something. "Can't witches switch into a physical form here?" My hopeful tone borders on desperation.

"So I've been told." My aunt sighs. "But it can take some time. I'm afraid I'm not there yet."

My shoulders slump, but a kernel of hope settles in my stomach. I'll get to hug her eventually. "Can I come see you again?"

"You are welcome here anytime, my love." She smiles.

We both stand and say our goodbyes, her floating out of the garden, and me walking over to Venus.

"How did it go?" Venus asks, pretending like she didn't hear the entire conversation.

"Good." I sigh. "I missed her."

"I know. I wasn't sure when she would be ready to see you, but I felt you needed it."

I look up into her dark eyes. "Thank you," I rasp before she slowly leans forward and presses a kiss to my forehead. My stomach tightens and I hold my breath, trying to fight the conflicting feelings flitting around of wanting her closer and never wanting her to touch me again. I pull back and plaster a smile on my face. "I need to go back," I tell her, my anxiety creeping up my throat. I need the safety of my room.

She scrutinizes me for a moment before nodding and ushering me out, leaving my aunt's spirit behind.

Something about seeing my aunt, dead but existing here in Hell, has fueled a fire within me. Seeing her, and all the other spirits, working to acclimate to their new normal made me realize: healing is a marathon and not a sprint. What he did to me has fucked me up, and I might never fully recover from it.

But I can't let it overtake me. I need to figure out how to push forward, how to fight back.

The problem is, I have no idea how to go about that.

My aunt told me to ask my magic, but I clearly can't. I doubt I'll ever be able to.

Maybe there's another avenue.

The High Priestesses—they must know something. They're the most powerful witches in existence, ruling over all witches from Hell; they have to have some insight into all this. They must know *something* about my magic and a way to finish this. Maybe they can even help me connect with my magic again, even if that isn't what I want.

The next morning, I asked Venus to escort me to wherever it is they stay, and she jumped at the chance to do so.

As I finish getting ready, I exit the bathing room to find a creature in the bedroom that Venus looks close to smiting with her magic. An all-black cat is perched on Venus's desk, its tail slowly swishing back and forth as its orange eyes size us up, ignoring Venus's attempts at getting rid of it.

"A cat," I say dumbly. "A cat is in here."

Venus sighs, sounding irritated. "Cats are one of the creatures that can pass from realm to realm. They straddle the line between the two, passing through whenever they please."

"So this cat is alive?"

She nods as the cat begins licking its paws. "They come here to wreak havoc in the city—and on my paperwork."

I tilt my head. "This one doesn't seem like a troublemaker."

"Tell that to my now-disorganized desk."

Approaching slowly, I bend towards the cat. It raises its eyes to me before prowling across loose pages. I stretch out a hand for the cat to sniff, and it does, then immediately rubs its face against my skin, purrs making its body vibrate.

"Are you someone's pet in the other realm?" I ask playfully.

The cat meows in response.

"I'll take that as a no," I say before gently scooping it into my arms. The cat doesn't hesitate to nuzzle into me. A grin graces my lips as I give it a little squeeze. "Who knew that the fearsome Dark Lady would be thwarted by a house cat."

Venus grumbles something about personally destroying all felines under her breath.

I give the cat in my arms a look before stating, "His name is now Steve."

With Steve nestled in my arms, I turn to Venus. She's staring at me with a blank expression, as if my words haven't quite registered in her brain yet. After a few beats of silence, she furrows her brows in confusion. "Steve? You want to name the cat...Steve?"

"He looks like a Steve," I argue.

"Not, oh, I don't know, Nightwalker? Demon Slayer? Not even something as generic as Salem? You want to go with *Steve*?"

"He *looks* like a *Steve*," I repeat.

My little man looks up at me and begins kneading into my—Venus's—dark sweater.

That settles that.

Venus shakes her head, disbelief replacing her confusion, but her grin makes it clear she thinks this is hilarious.

I don't get what's funny. He's giving off 'Steve' vibes.

Taking my new best friend in my arms, we head out of the room and into the hall. I walk beside Venus, unable to stop sneaking glances her way.

Maybe it was seeing my aunt, or having a purring cat in my arms, but I feel more like myself than I have in a long time. Which is maybe why I can't help but notice how gorgeous Venus looks. Her golden skin is illuminated in the candlelight of the halls. Her dark eyes are focused forward, the intensity never leaving them as she scans the space.

The realization that I want to touch her nearly knocks me sideways. I want her to touch me. I—

Venus throws me a curious glance before stopping in front of a door, and I try to wipe away the look of longing I'm sure is written all over my face. Can she tell what I was thinking?

Then I remember she can scent me, my emotions.

Humiliation washes over me.

Steve yowls and leaps from my arms, landing on the ground and sauntering away, seeming offended that my attention was taken from him.

Venus chuckles. "Please, don't stop on my account. I was quite enjoying the game of guessing what caught your attention."

Her words keep me from spiraling into a pit of self-loathing, stoking the flames of my irritation instead. "I was thinking about this demon I saw the other day," I lie smoothly, trying to piss her off.

It works. She stops walking and turns to me. Her eyes darken, towering over me as I face her.

My breath catches, but not from fear. Funny how she was the one who frightened me the most, but now...I don't want anyone but her.

"You dare look at someone else?" Her voice is dangerously low, making my blood heat.

I swallow the feeling, not wanting to lose this little battle we've engaged in. "Is that not allowed?" I bat my eyelashes.

While she looks ready to rip someone's head off, I can see the hint of mischief twinkling in her eye. I know she's doing this on purpose, riling me up for a reaction, but I can't help falling for it every time.

Venus opens her mouth to reply but is interrupted by the door swinging open.

Aradia stands on the other side.

"Your Grace." She bows her head to Venus, then turns to me, her face warming as she smiles widely at me. "And Lady Vivian. We are happy you have decided to speak with us."

I nod to her, unsure of how to respond, thrown by my own emotions.

"Well," Venus says as she straightens to her full height, "I shall leave you both to it." With another intense look at me, she swaggers away, her wings shifting with the movement as her shadows dart after her.

"Shall we?" Aradia says to me, stepping back to let me in.

The room is large, with three desks equidistant from one another and a wall of shelves holding books as well as various trinkets and jars full of things I definitely do not want a closer look at. In the center of the floor is a large pentagram, permanently etched into the floor. Lit candles float in place above our heads, giving everything an eerie glow.

"The Dark Lady has informed me that you have questions and has given my sisters and me an update on your current connection to your magic," Aradia says to me, walking about the room. My eyes track her as she grabs a chair and pulls it over to a desk. "Please, sit," she tells me before seating herself on the other side.

I tentatively make my way over, throwing wary looks around the room. I learned to fear witchcraft when I ran from Venus, going so far as to even hate it. Being surrounded by memorabilia is the last place I'd ever think to find myself.

Then again, so was Hell, and here I am.

Aradia leans her elbows on the desk and clasps her hands together. "I understand you have a strained relationship with your magic—I saw it myself when the wards were remade."

I squirm in my seat, feeling like a specimen under a microscope. My playful mood from flirting with Venus is gone, with only agitation left in its wake. What am I doing here? "Having magic meant the Dark Lady demanding my soul, so you're right, we aren't exactly BFFs." I'm being defensive, I know I am, but I can't stop.

She can tell too. Her eyes travel over me carefully. "Your magic is extraordinary."

I want to crawl out of my skin. "That's what everyone keeps telling me, but it's not like it's done anything good for me lately—or ever," I snarl. I've completely forgotten why I'm here, what I even want to know. All that fills my head is my anger, my resentment at the problems my magic has caused.

Her eyes narrow. "Your magic is not your enemy."

A hysterical laugh bubbles out of me. "Oh, yeah, it *definitely* wasn't my enemy when it didn't stop him from hurting or touching me."

"If what you've uncovered is true, then your magic is the lifeblood of this world."

"So it can sacrifice me for whatever reason it wants?" I'm like a volcano that's been dormant for too long, its lava ready to flow and destroy everything in its path. I stand up and lean over the desk. Fuck this—fuck getting help, fuck working with my magic, fuck everything. "You know nothing about what happened to me. About what he did to me, all because of something I didn't ask for. Something I don't even want."

"I hate to break it to you, Vivian," Aradia says with unnerving patience, her deep brown eyes searing into me, "but that is the cost of living."

I've heard enough. I pull back and swipe my arm across the table, clearing the desk of books and keepsakes just because it feels good. Aradia rears back in surprise, but I can't hear her, my ears roaring as I storm out.

I fling the door open and run down the halls, not really seeing, not even sure where I'm going. All I know is that I need to be far from here.

My wrath, my hatred, is guiding me, not letting me stop until I'm a few yards into Hell's wilderness. I burst through the trees, desperate to be alone, desperate to not be *here* anymore.

I'm hyperventilating, my body not slowing down until I'm swallowed by the dark forest, just as a scream erupts from me.

I scream out my fury, my despair, my self-hatred and pity. I hate this, I hate him, I hate that my life has never been anything more than collateral damage for the universe. My screams echo through the trees, bouncing around, carrying me further and further away from myself. I scream until tears stream from my eyes and my voice goes out. I scream until I have no air left in my lungs and I fall to my knees. Panting for breath, I slowly curl into a ball on the ground, letting the emotions take me further and further away.

Chapter Twenty-Two
Venus

I scented arousal. I know I did.

The Vivian I know is still in there somewhere. I play with her, goad her into arguing with me, just so I can catch a glimpse of who she once was.

It makes me hopeful that I'll see her again.

As I navigate the halls to meet with Marie and Luke to discuss how the wards are fairing, Vivian's decaying scent flits past me. Halting, I try to locate where it was coming from, confused about why I can scent her at all. Aradia had said she would meet with Vivian to answer her questions—she didn't mention leaving the royal grounds.

Following her altered scent, I'm shocked to realize she's heading further and further away on her own. I spot her blonde hair whipping around as she races away from the castle...towards the wilderness.

I keep a healthy distance away as I trail her, wanting to see what she's doing, but concerned about why she's doing it—and why the wilderness seems to be her destination.

The forest is not for mortals. I doubt it has ever witnessed someone living.

She doesn't even hesitate when she reaches the trees; she simply runs into the thicket. Panic floods my veins as I race through the trees shortly after, her screams reaching my ears. My heart lurches and I break into a sprint, using her rotten scent and screams to guide me to her. If a beast has attacked, this forest will cease to exist immediately.

I race through the large trees, my breath sawing in and out of me, when I finally spot her.

Vivian is standing among the trees without any interruption from the wilderness or its inhabitants. Her screams carry through the forest—rage, anguish, and shame all mingle together in the noise. The forest waits silently while she rages on as if absorbing it, taking it from her, withstanding it for her.

I stand back, frozen, as I witness the broken pieces of this woman being exposed to the wilderness around us. My heart is splintering with each moment, making it difficult to breathe.

My bold, courageous, lively witch, ripping herself apart makes me want to destroy this world and start anew, with only her and me and no one who can ever hurt us.

An eternity passes before her screams quiet down into cries and gasps of air. She slowly lowers herself to the forest floor, her back still to me as she curls into a ball.

No beasts prowl forward for what would be an easy target. As if the beasts know to stay away.

Slowly, I approach her and murmur, "Vivian?"

No response. I crouch down without another word and gather her into my arms. Her eyes are open, but she doesn't seem to register what is happening. Cradling her body to mine, carrying her as if she's made of glass, we exit the forest. As soon as we clear the trees, we're airborne, flying towards the safety of our home.

"And why, exactly, did you feel it was appropriate to approach her in such a way?" I snap at Aradia. After depositing Vivian in her bed, I stormed through the castle to the High Priestesses' workroom and demand to know what happened. I nearly ripped the entire room to shreds before I bothered to ask a question. Luke, for some reason, was ready to join me as soon as I found the witch. "I entrusted you with assisting Vivian and her magic, not to rile her up."

Aradia dares to hold my gaze. "Vivian does not understand the first thing about her magic. She is too engrossed in her pain from whatever happened. I believe that must be addressed first before she can even consider the power she has."

"That's enough," I snarl at her.

"She is broken, Your Grace, and I do not know if she wants to be put back together."

My power shakes the room, books falling from the bookshelf and the castle groaning in protest. Aradia averts her gaze. "Need I remind you of what I tasked you with and who I am?"

"No, Your Grace," she replies quietly.

My anger is spiraling out of control, too quickly for me to leash it. I need to get out of here before I do something I regret.

"I should strip you of your title," I threaten. "Do not question me so brazenly again," I warn her before stalking out, Luke on my heels.

"Why is my council so quick to defy me as of late?" I demand as we leave the room, stalking through the halls.

Luke prowls next to me. "Everyone is frightened. The weeks you were healing..." He shudders. "Phanes had never set foot in this realm until now. They feel your priorities have shifted, leaving the realm vulnerable."

I forgot that Luke is a gossip.

"My council has been conspiring against me?" I growl, my shadows slithering around me.

"No," he replies quickly. "We are still loyal to you—and will remain loyal, but you must admit, Your Grace, that Vivian has clouded your judgment."

I halt in the hallway and turn to the archdemon. I fight the urge to strike him down where he stands.

He weathers it, though, as he always has. His pitless eyes do not flinch as my shadows swarm around us. He continues, "We understand how important Vivian is—"

"No, you do not," I interrupt. "This is not simply about her soul or her magic. This is about *her*." Luke seems to scrutinize me but makes the wise choice not to voice his conclusions. "My father is still a threat, I know. Do not misunderstand that I want him brought to justice. It is just..." I can't believe I am going to express my concerns, to be vulnerable this way. "I'm not sure how," I admit. "We have been in a stalemate for centuries. Neither of us can die without damning this world. I doubt he has anything he cares enough about for me to take from him."

"Take his place," Luke urges. "In a way, it *is* your birthright."

"You just confided in me that my council doubts me," I scoff. "You expect me to then take on the responsibility of managing the living realm too?"

Luke's shoulders slump wearily. "It's a terrible position we are in, it's true."

My aggravation lodges in my throat. Taking my father's place is not what I envisioned for myself. When Lilith and I rallied to destroy him, we did not understand the gravity of his necessary existence. But now I do.

And now, with the origin of Vivian's magic making itself known, it complicates things further.

Control is slipping through my fingers.

I shake my head, trying to dislodge the irritation, the worry, the fear. "Taking his place cannot be our only option."

"You know what the High Priestesses believe."

"If they truly believe Vivian can ascend to a god-like being, then maybe they need to be replaced with witches who are less fanatic."

Luke's mouth tightens as if he wants to defend them but thinks better of doing so to me.

I've had enough of this for today. I'm losing my grasp on everything—my realm, my sanity. It makes me want to grip harder to whatever power I do have, which is crumbling the tighter I try to hold onto it.

Trying to shake this crushing sensation from me, I stalk towards where I left Vivian tucked into bed. She needs me and I need her. I leave Luke in the hallway, feeling worse than before.

⁂

Vivian hasn't moved from the spot I left her. I approach and sit on the edge of the bed, slowly removing my boots before spiriting my wings away and climbing up. I settle in next to her, close enough to reach her. To my surprise, Vivian doesn't object—she simply lies on her side, facing me, as I stare up at nothing.

"I spoke to Aradia," I tell her. Her breathing hitches, showing me that she's listening, but doesn't reply.

I lick my lips and keep going. "I catch glimpses of you. I see your courage, your wit, your self-preservation peek out from behind the curtain. But, in a blink of an eye, it's gone again." Emotions I can't face build in me. "No one can help you if you don't share what happened, Vivian. I imagine it's difficult to do so, but I want to help. I don't want you to waste away into yourself." My voice cracks, my biggest fear finally being voiced. I can't lose Vivian. Losing her would make my existence pointless. I don't think I could recover from that. "But I will do anything to make sure you don't."

Tears burn in my eyes, and I grit my teeth against them as if that will stop them from spilling. I can't handle this, this feeling of being so helpless, of not knowing what to do or how to assist her. The emotions roll through me too quickly, and I fear panic is going to overtake me.

"I want that, too."

I swivel my head to the sound of her voice. She's staring at me, her eyes wide—and clear.

"Then tell me how we do it," I rasp.

Vivian eyes me curiously. "We?"

"We're in this together," I say slowly, as if it's the most obvious thing in the world.

She seems to consider it for a moment before admitting, "I don't know."

"Please," I whisper, sheer desperation pouring from me. Silence.

"Please, Vivian," I try again.

She blinks, her face going blank, before she gets up and drags herself into the bathing chamber, the door clicking shut behind her.

Chapter Twenty-Three

Vivian

Speaking with Venus has me realizing I can't keep living like this, thrown into a spiral of despair at every turn.

No, sadness will get me nowhere. I need to act instead of sitting on the sidelines.

Which means I need to work with my magic.

After my spat with Aradia, I didn't want to meet with any of them ever again. I've had enough of bitchy witches bossing me around for many lifetimes.

Unfortunately, I think working with the High Priestesses is the only option.

Deep down, I know what has to happen. I will have to face him again, and I will be helpless if my magic and I do not resolve our issues.

My resentment is in direct opposition to my fate.

After spending a few hours in the bathroom sitting on the cold floor, gathering myself together after Venus begged me to divulge what her father did to me, I went back out there and told Venus I was open to meeting with the High Priestesses again. She simply nodded and made sure Isobel met me outside the castle entrance the next morning.

Now, I walk next to Isobel as we make our way through the city's cobblestone streets. She's as on edge as I am, but that's because Venus decided she didn't want to leave me alone with the High Priestesses, just in case we have another blowout.

So she sent Luke to tag along.

Luke walks a few paces behind us, but it's difficult to ignore the presence of a ginormous archdemon. Isobel walks stiffly beside me, not uttering a word.

Isobel is arguably the most beautiful of the three High Priestesses. Her stick-straight hair is a shiny, rich, dark brown that flows down her back, accentuating her sepia skin tone and amber eyes. She has flawless dark eyebrows that I keep peeking at, wondering how she got them so thick but so symmetrical, and large, naturally pouty lips—which I've rarely seen open to speak.

Venus explained Isobel is also the quietest of the three, only speaking when there's something important to be said. She told me Isobel possesses elemental magic like me, but hers is the manipulation of water.

After the fifth time of sneaking glances at her, she shoots me a disgruntled look. I startle a bit and keep my eyes ahead. I swear I hear Luke chuckle behind us.

We reach the tree line and Isobel stops abruptly. I halt and turn to her, waiting for instructions, but she doesn't say anything. She just stands there, scrutinizing me, her dark eyes narrowing. It feels like she's dissecting me with her gaze, staring right into me and where my magic currently slumbers beneath the surface. I bounce from foot to foot, unsure of how to proceed. Being so close to any form of nature usually awakens my magic, but I feel nothing. No hint of interest.

Isobel and I continue to just stand here, her staring at me and me awkwardly fidgeting, until Luke's booming voice says, "Would it be possible to speed this along? I have more important things to do. Like watch paint dry."

Isobel's head whips to him and she snarls, "You should keep your mouth shut, demon."

Luke turns his lethal attention to the witch. "You were instructed to train Vivian in connecting with her magic, not to stand here in silence and stare at her."

I want to kiss Luke right now.

Isobel's lip curls at him. "The Dark Lady did not give specifics on how this should be handled—just that it be done." She turns to me. "I am waiting for her magic to react to our surroundings, to see what her magic's first instincts are."

I wring my hands together nervously. "I don't feel it at all," I admit.

She doesn't seem surprised. She simply nods and muses, "It might not recognize this realm in the way it recognizes the realm of the living, simply due to the differences between the two. It will take time, I assume, to get your magic to react to this wilderness in the same manner."

"That's annoying," I mutter.

"When I was alive," Isobel says softly, "my magic would react to any form of water—a lake, a stream, even a glass of water. It would demand my attention, will me to manipulate the liquid, but once I passed on to this realm, my magic went silent for quite a time."

I tilt my head in curiosity. "Really?"

She nods, her shiny hair floating on the breeze that passes by.

Even though I know being in Hell isn't my magic's problem, her words bring me some comfort. I roll my shoulders back and ask, "How did you get your magic to react to Hell?"

She looks away and takes in the wilderness beyond as she gets a distant look in her eye, as if recalling memories from long ago. "It came forth when it was needed."

I wait for her to extrapolate, but she doesn't; she simply continues staring off into the distance. I follow her gaze and turn to the trees. They're truly larger than any I've seen before, the tops so high in the sky that they're invisible from down here. Silence radiates from the trees—an ignorant person's mistake would be to believe predators aren't lurking in the darkness, able to move about without creating any sounds.

When I ran here, I hadn't noticed how eerily silent the forest seems.

"Should we keep walking?" I ask, the hairs on my arms standing. "I'm not sure why, but this place is giving me the creeps."

Luke seems to agree with me as he begins walking parallel to the trees. I spin and follow suit, until I realize Isobel hasn't moved a muscle.

"Isobel?" I call over my shoulder. "Aren't you coming?"

"Yes, witch," Luke drawls, "time is of the essence. It's nearly time for supper." He looks out into the wilderness. "And I do not care for this place."

I narrow my brows at him. "Why not? Aren't you, like, one of the most powerful archdemons?"

"Demons do not go into Hell's forest. It is a dangerous place, even for us."

"Why?"

He shakes his head, something akin to nervousness beginning to radiate from him. "It is not to be spoken of—not so close."

I drop it as Isobel catches up to us, not saying a word. Luke and I share a glance before we continue along. None of us say anything else for the rest of the time we're out here, as silent as my magic, stuck in our own thoughts. Luke gets increasingly agitated the longer we're out here, muttering something under his breath that I can't quite hear. After a few hours of walking, Isobel decides to call it a day, essentially telling us that this session is over. All three of us start our way back to the castle, but Luke seems preoccupied.

As if he's sensed something in the wilderness that has left him speechless.

Chapter Twenty-Four
Venus

Cats have roamed Hell for as long as they've existed. I had considered blocking their entrance, worried they were finding cracks in our wards, sent here by my father to exert his control over me, but when I went to investigate, I found no such evidence. Somehow, they manage to travel between the realms without any issue. I'm not even sure how they get here—one day, one just appeared, alive and unbothered. None of Hell's residents seem interested in eating them or bothering them. The witches seem to encourage their visits, cooing over them whenever they pass one grooming itself in the middle of the streets.

Still, they've become a bit of a nuisance, showing up in places uninvited, pissing wherever they please, and apparently, stealing Vivian's attention from me.

As we sit in my dining room, Vivian is fixing a plate for the cat, for crying out loud. She scoops some eggs from her plate onto one for him, and he sits in his own seat beside hers.

I press my temple into my propped-up hand, observing this strange turn of events with exasperation. "I'm not keen to allow *him* at the table, Vivian."

Both my guests turn to look at me, Vivian looking bemused while the cat eyes me with a look that I swear says, *tough shit*.

"He needs to eat too. It's not like Hell has a cat food store."

I narrow my eyes suspiciously. "How are we certain he doesn't have a family?"

She purses her lips as she puts a sausage link on his plate. "I guess we don't," she admits. "But he seems quite attached to me already."

"Because you keep feeding him from your plate."

"He loves me," she states matter-of-factly.

I fight the urge to roll my eyes. "Cats are incapable of loving anyone but themselves."

Vivian tsks at me. "Don't speak such a way in front of him."

"He can't understand me," I argue. Steve keeps staring at me, unblinking—unnerving me.

Vivian points her fork at him while raising her eyebrows at me. "See? He knows and can pick up on your vibes."

"Must we discuss this over our food?"

Vivian shrugs, a smile tugging at the corner of her lips before she looks down at her plate. We eat in comfortable silence for a few beats before I ask, "How was your session with Isobel yesterday?"

Of course, I already know how it went. I demanded a full report from both Isobel and Luke afterward. Their reports were the same: Vivian's magic didn't appear.

Steve begins slurping down his eggs and Vivian looks over at me. "My magic isn't interested in Hell's forest."

I tilt my head. "What makes you say that?" I ask, feigning ignorance.

She looks down and begins pushing her food around with her fork. "It didn't come out at all during my time with Isobel—didn't even make itself known. Usually, I feel like a pressure inside me when it wants to come out. But I felt nothing."

I hum. "Do you not want it to come out?"

"Yes? No? I don't know," she admits with a sigh before looking at me again. "Isobel told me about her magic not responding to Hell for a while after coming here, but I don't think that's the issue. My magic and I have never trusted each other. I stuffed it away inside me when I ran from you, and it basically left me for dead when I really needed it."

My fury ignites in me, seeping into my bones. I try to calm myself, not wanting Vivian to think I'm angry at *her*. She still hasn't divulged the details about what happened, but I know her magic did not work to protect her from whatever my father did to her. I send my shadows away, worried they'll tip her off to the shift in my emotions.

She goes back to her plate, finally lifting her fork to her mouth and chewing slowly. The only sound is the scraping of silverware and Steve loudly chewing for a few moments.

"You are welcome to share what happened," I finally say for what feels like the millionth time. "It will change nothing between us."

Her fork freezes halfway to her mouth. Her eyes dart to me, and it makes me regret saying anything. The look in her eyes is one of pure, unrelenting fear. Not of me, but of divulging the trauma. I lean forward, lightly placing my hand upon her wrist in a gesture of comfort, but she recoils, snatching her arm away. The fork drops, clattering on the table and splattering food. Steve looks perturbed by the disturbance, his ears going flat against his head.

"I'm sorry," I mutter, feeling completely at a loss. No matter what I think is right, I keep sending her spiraling into her fear and shame.

"No, it's alright," she says in an attempt to soothe me while her tone shows her worry. "I *think* I want to tell you,

I just..." Her scent turns sour. Shaking her head, as if to dislodge whatever thoughts she's having, she continues, "I'm worried."

"Of me thinking differently about you."

She nods.

Shoving my chair back, I rise from the table and walk over to her, my eyes never leaving hers. I kneel at the side of her chair and grip the arm. "That could never happen," I breathe. "I would never look at you any differently for what happened to you or for anything you were forced to do."

Her eyes are guarded and suspicious. It makes it hard to breathe, that look.

I can't blame her for it, truly. I have not always been trustworthy—I've kept things from her and lied to her before, betrayed her trust in more ways than one.

I will spend eternity showing her I have changed for her. I stand and go back to my own seat, fighting the urge to grab her and demand she trust me, demand she believe my words now.

The cat is the only one still eating, unbothered by us. Vivian stares at the table, eyes unseeing, her teeth digging into her bottom lip. I open my mouth to apologize, to tell her it doesn't matter, that I'll leave her alone if that's what she prefers—

"I appreciate you trying so hard," she whispers. She looks at me out of the corner of her eye. "I've never had anyone..." She trails off, squeezing her eyes shut. "I've never had anyone care enough to fight so hard for me. My aunt tried, sure, but I still had to deal with my mother." When she opens her eyes, vulnerability shines in her hazel irises. "I feel like I'm at the edge of a cliff, feeling the urge to jump, but you're the voice I hear that tells me not to. Like your voice is trying to bring me back to you."

I've lost the ability to think.

"Why do you try so hard?" she asks. "Not even for trying to help me, but for all of it—for hunting me down for a decade. Why bother?"

Because I love you. Because my heart belonged to you the second you appeared before me, and I didn't even know it.

I can't tell her that—not yet. I can't spring my deepest emotions on her when she's struggling with her own. I lick my lips nervously. "At first, it was because you slighted me, denied me, and I don't like to lose. I quickly became obsessed with the chase, but once I finally had you, I became obsessed with *you*."

She searches my face for a moment, making me wonder if she can hear what I really want to say. If she does, she doesn't demand I profess my love. She simply nods and says, "Okay," softly. "Okay."

Chapter Twenty-Five
Vivian

Every day feels like I'm hiking up a mountain; I manage to drag my exhausted body to the top, only to realize the actual top is hidden behind clouds, and it's as if I'll never get there. Today is especially hard to climb.

I was awake all night, struggling to settle down enough to sleep. Ever since Venus told me that my magic tried to take her out during my nightmare, it's been difficult to feel safe sleeping.

I tried to distract myself by going down to the archives, but there were too many noises, too much movement, and I left as quickly as I arrived.

I dragged myself back to our room, pulling myself back into bed. I've been staring up at the ceiling since then until I hear the door open.

I know it's Venus—for one, she doesn't let just anyone in here, and second, I know the cadence of her steps so well that I would know she's approaching me as soon as she's within earshot.

When she enters the room, she has a giant grin on her face. "I got you something," she announces.

Her smile is contagious, causing one of my own to lift my lips until I look at what's in her arms.

It's a bright pink silk robe with pink feather cuffs and hems. The neckline dips into a V, and pink jewels are encrusted on the sash that cuts across the waist.

If I wasn't so broken, I would've squealed and immediately put the beautiful thing on.

All I do now is burst into tears.

I'm too disgusting to wear something so beautiful, so vibrant, so lively.

And for Venus, the one who only wears black and would never be caught dead in any other color, to think of me and want me to have this...

I can't bear it.

My chest heaves as sobs break free, making it difficult to breathe and hold myself together. It feels like my body is cracking open from the inside.

Through my blurred vision, I can tell I've startled her with my reaction. She rushes over to me, dropping the garment on the floor and reaching for me, her eyes scanning my face in bewilderment and concern.

I don't want her looking at me. I throw my hands up to cover my face, curving myself inward, as I cry and cry.

"Vivian," she rasps, her voice alarmed, "I'm sorry, I thought you might enjoy this. You haven't worn any of your own clothes—"

I'm hyperventilating now; my breath won't pull into my lungs. Panic is overwhelming me.

"Where are you, Vivian? Tell me where you are," she instructs, her tone authoritative.

"I—I'm with you," I gasp into my hands. "I'm with you. In Hell."

"Yes," she breathes, her fingers running soft, soothing circles along my skin.

"I'm sorry," I sputter. "I'm sorry."

"You have nothing to apologize for."

"I didn't think you'd come for me." My voice cracks at my confession. "I thought you were going to leave me there."

"Listen to me," she demands fiercely. Her hands peel my own from my face, forcing me to look at her as she lightly tilts my chin up with her fingers. "I will never abandon you. No matter what happens, I will always find you."

"He did such horrible things to me," I cry, my shame and sadness flowing out with my tears. I'm dirty and disgusting and I can't believe Venus would ever want someone like me.

A shadow scurries up my arm and dips into my hair, nestling against me.

Venus looks at me with a mixture of pure rage and deep, unrelenting sadness. "Vivian." She says my name so gently, so reverently, that it makes me want to throw up. "Give this burden over to me. I can bear it. I want to."

Her words just make me cry harder. I want to hide, but she keeps her hold on my face firm.

"I can't, I can't," I sob. "It will disgust you; it will make you think horrible things about me." *It will show you everything that is wrong with me.*

She flinches like I've slapped her. Good. I need her away from me, I need her to see how broken I am.

Her midnight eyes darken, and she grips my face harder. "How dare you say such a thing to me."

Her words confuse me enough to stop me from crying and puzzle over the meaning. She takes that opportunity to bring her forehead to mine.

"Nothing he did to you will ever make me think less of you. It doesn't matter what he did or what he forced you to do—I will never see you as anything but the strong, brave, and courageous woman you are. Now," she says, blowing out a breath, "tell me."

I search her dark eyes and find that she's telling the truth. She doesn't see me as this tarnished, broken shell of a person.

So I tell her everything.

Chapter Twenty-Six
Venus

Many times during Vivian's story, I wanted to fly myself up to my father's castle and flay the skin from his bones.

And then let Vivian grind those bones to dust.

But I knew my anger was not what Vivian needed from me—not while she was being so vulnerable and brave by sharing every horrific thing he did to her.

Her body seemed to relax after she shared, her scent returning to its regular cherry blossom and pomegranate aroma. It's as if holding onto the burden of what happened to her was tainting it, and her letting me in has released the rot and decay.

I wasn't going to waste that.

I refuse to let her out of my sight for the rest of the day, some part of me always touching some part of her: my hand around her waist, a shadow perched on her shoulder, my wing folded in to keep her close. I worry that even allowing myself to blink is too long to have her out of my sight.

She doesn't seem upset or angry at the constant touch, which is at odds with how she was even this morning; she seems to seek it out, always shuffling closer, as if to merge herself into me.

Later that evening, Vivian stands in front of the mirror, the pink robe hugging her body. Seeing her in some color makes my heart feel like it's going to burst.

All that happened between her and my father has changed her irrevocably. He tried to break her, over and over, and did horrifying things to her. She will never be the same.

But my love for her will not change.

She examines the garment. She turns this way and that, seeing how it sits on her body. In the mirror, her eyes raise to mine, a look of doubt clouding them.

"Is it too much?" she asks.

My heart cracks at her question. "Never," I reply fiercely. Vivian has never been 'too much.' I don't want her thinking this now. I walk up behind her, pressing my front into her back. She melts into me immediately as I wrap my arms around her waist. "It's perfect," I murmur as one of my shadows climbs over to tickle her earlobe.

She smiles and squirms in my arms but I hold fast. "I love seeing this color on you again," I tell her.

Her smile falters and she squeezes her eyes shut. "It didn't feel...right to wear what I used to. Like those clothes belong to someone else. Like maybe I couldn't wear them anymore, but I don't want to think like that anymore."

I lean forward, placing my chin on the top of her head. She sinks further into my touch.

Vivian quickly grows somber, chewing on her bottom lip for a moment before saying, "I just can't forgive what he did to me."

Her words make me rear back. "Forgive him? Why would you ever forgive him?"

She sniffles and opens her eyes. "If I forgive him, then I can move on from what he did. But I just can't—I can't forgive him. I hate him. I hate him with my entire being, not just for what he did to me, but what he's done to all of those before me too."

"Don't," I growl. "Don't forgive him."

She blinks in surprise. "You told me that it was a strength to forgive."

"He doesn't deserve it—he will never deserve it. You do not need to forgive him to heal. Use your anger, use your hatred. Hone it and wield it like a blade."

She seems to consider my words for a moment, her hazel eyes scouring my face as she takes a deep breath and blows it out before nodding. "Okay. Okay, yes, you're right. I want to become the weapon I deserve to be."

"We will take it one day at a time," I promise. "For now, I'd love for you to simply parade around our room in this stunning ensemble."

She giggles—actually giggles—and it's like a melody I haven't heard in a long time.

I spin her in my arms, her chest pressing against mine. "Will you do that for me?"

"If you insist." Her eyes dip to my lips and her breath hitches before she pulls herself out of my grasp, her scent souring slightly.

"Vivian?" I ask, surprised by the change in demeanor.

"Sorry," she mumbles, looking down at our feet. "It's just..." She takes a deep breath, then another, then another. She takes eight breaths before she continues, "I don't think I'm ready for...that yet."

I blink at her. "I don't follow."

Her cheeks turn bright pink. "I missed your touch so much, but I can't do anything else—I can't go further than that. Not yet. I understand if that's a problem, and if you need release, I'm sure there are many that would love to help you with that—"

She continues rambling as I try to piece what she's say-ing together. Then shock ripples through me. "Stop," I tell her, and her words cease. I almost want to laugh at how ridiculous this conversation is, that she thinks I will even consider touching someone that isn't her. "Listen to me when I say this. I will never demand that from you. Even if you never wanted to be touched in that way again, I would never begrudge you for it or look for another to provide me that pleasure." I'm so shocked I even have to say the words aloud. Is she so unaware of how deeply I care for her?

Her eyes look doubtful.

"Never," I repeat.

Her eyes well with tears as she whispers, "Thank you."

I give her a feline grin. "Although, I'm sure it will be difficult for you to resist me. I mean, just look at me."

She snorts, but she smiles again, her tears drying.

I place a chaste kiss to the top of her head before reluc-tantly pulling away. "Now, as you promised." I take her hand, step back, and twirl her, eliciting a soft laugh from her. "Show me how beautiful you look in this garment."

Chapter Twenty-Seven
Vivian

Venus decided that Aradia needed to apologize to me.

I'm fine without an apology, I'd told her. I just don't want to ever see or speak to her for the rest of eternity, let alone work with her again.

Venus had rolled her eyes and said it was required.

So now the three of us sit around a table, Aradia and I awkwardly avoiding eye contact.

"I don't want your fake apology," I finally tell her, tired of wasting my time sitting here.

"It is not fake," she retorts.

"You're only doing it because Venus told you to."

"Be that as it may, I do feel remorse for my words causing you pain."

"Do you?" I push before turning to Venus. "I think you should leave."

"And why is that?" she asks, and I swear I see amusement dancing in her midnight eyes.

"Because she's not going to be honest if you're sitting here, breathing down her neck."

Venus narrows her eyes, looking between Aradia and myself, assessing, weighing the options. After a beat, she sighs, resigned, and pushes back from the table to stand. "I don't care how this is resolved—just that it is, somehow." She gives us each a warning look. Aradia bows her head while I curl my lip at her. Venus snorts and exits the room, leaving the two of us to lock eyes.

We size each other up. "I'm perfectly content to sit here in awkward silence for a few minutes and then pretend we're all cool if you are," I inform her.

Aradia purses her lips before saying, "You are angry."

"Yeah, no shit."

She shakes her head, her luscious curls bouncing. "You are angry, deep within yourself. It has always been there, this anger, but now...now it festers."

I grit my teeth against the emotions moving through me. I will not cry, I will not cry. "I don't need you to psychoanalyze me."

"I thought I was being helpful," she offers, "but it is clear I wasn't. I apologize for upsetting you."

Gripping the chair handles, nails digging into the wood, I choke out, "Thank you. Are we good to leave now?"

The look on Aradia's face is one of pure pity. It ignites my anger so quickly that I could destroy this entire realm with my rage.

Sensing my agitation, the High Priestess wipes the pity from her face and replaces it with a look of openness and understanding. "It took me many years to move through my hurt, my anger, and fear. I would help you if you let me."

"Thanks for the offer, but I'll pass," I retort, sarcasm dripping from each word. I need out of here, I can't deal with her, I can't deal with anyone—

The walls feel like they're closing in. I try to stand, but my limbs feel heavy and my head feels light, like I'm going to faint.

Everything is alright, Vivian.

I jolt at the sweet voice in my head. Was that my magic speaking to me?

"Vivian," the voice says again, but this time, it comes from Aradia's mouth. Did she just speak to me in my mind?

The last time that happened was when *he* did it.

I must be hallucinating from lack of oxygen. I sink further into my seat and pull my knees to my chest, rocking slightly. I'm not in his castle, he isn't here. I'm in Hell, with

Venus—who is most likely sitting on the other side of that door.

That thought alone helps crack the wall of panic that is sealing me in. A breathy laugh passes through my lips as I picture it: Venus, leaning against the wall just outside the door, her shadows pressed against the wood, reporting on every word we're saying in here.

My limbs start to tingle as I become aware of them again, as I see the room around me and the High Priestess I'm stuck here with, who is now kneeling on the floor next to my chair. Her eyes rove over me, assessing, before she nods and stands, seeming to notice I'm no longer in the throes of panic.

As she walks back to her seat, I pant, "You ever have a panic attack before?"

The corner of her mouth quirks up. "I used to have them quite often."

"How did you get them to stop?"

Sitting back down and splaying her hands on the table, she replies, "A lot of patience with myself."

I hum. "I used to do breathing exercises—still do sometimes, but they don't seem to work as well, after...well, you know."

She observes me for a few moments silently before offering, "I used to be angry with myself whenever they would happen. Especially when time from my own…traumas had passed but the panic didn't. Now, when I find myself feeling one come on, I will remind myself that it is okay—it is okay to feel panicked, or upset, or angry. It is your body or your mind's way of protecting you. Do not begrudge them for doing what they are intended, but keep yourself grounded so your emotions do not control you."

I mull over her words. Letting myself move through my feelings but keeping myself grounded enough that they don't carry me away. I suppose that's what Venus does when she asks me where I am while I'm spiraling—she's helping me ground myself in reality.

My heart feels warm at that realization. Venus has her flaws, but she's trying to help me in her own way.

I look over at Aradia and give her a hesitant smile. "I like that."

Her answering smile is bright. "I'm glad I could be of service."

"I'm good with a truce," I tell her honestly. "I have no real issue with you, and we'll need to work together, so I'm happy to put it behind us. And…I'm sorry for the way I acted."

Aradia nearly sags in relief. "Thank the depths of Hell. I worried the Dark Lady would force me to live in exile."

My eyebrows raise. "Would she do that?"

She shrugs as we both get up from our seats and head towards the door. "She never has, but when it comes to you, I am sure she would go to extreme lengths. If you wished for something, I'm sure she would grant it."

I can't stop the goofy grin that spreads across my face at that.

Aradia opens the door, and as I imagined, Venus's shadows zip right to Venus's shoulders, where she is examining her nails as she leans against the wall, pretending to be nonchalant. I roll my eyes at what an amateur eavesdropper she is.

She looks up at us as we enter the hall and shoves her hands in her pockets. "All settled?"

"Yep," I say with a saccharine smile.

"Good." Venus turns to the High Priestess and dismisses her with a nod.

As Aradia's footsteps disappear down the hall, I cross my arms over my chest. "Hear anything interesting?"

Venus's wings rustle, giving her away even further. "I'm not sure what you're speaking of."

I snort and head towards the bedroom, ready to spend for some quiet time. My body has reached its limits for the day after my adrenaline rose and fell so quickly just moments ago. Venus walks silently next to me, her shadows sweeping along the floor as we go.

"How did Aradia die?" I ask, my mind snagging on her mention of working through her own traumas.

Venus gives me a guarded look. "I'm not sure if I should share that with you."

I blink. "Why not?"

"Because it is not my story to tell. Would you like it if I went around and told everyone what has happened to you?"

That's an excellent point. "No, I wouldn't," I state. "Although, some of my issues are from you chasing me down." I shoot her a smile to communicate that I'm joking about our shared past and not about her father.

She narrows her eyes at me but her wings shift, one of them closing around me, bringing me closer. "Tell me, Vivian—did you secretly like the chase?"

A thrill runs down my spine at her sultry tone. "That depends," I reply.

"On what?"

On what you would have really liked to have done once you caught me, I think, startling myself. Arousal blooms in my body, catching me off-guard.

I try to tamp it down, worried about the self-hatred that will soon follow.

When he forced his way into my mind, it felt like my ability to feel pleasure was tainted. Like my body's reactions were no longer my own. I'm not ready to feel that way...and I might never be ready again.

But Venus flirting with me should be harmless, I decide. We don't have to take it any further than that.

"If you're going to come across the new god, you need to know how to fight."

"I think I get the basics; the pointy end of my sword goes into their neck."

Venus gives me an exasperated look. We're standing in a large room made of stone with various weapons mounted on the wall. A combat training room of sorts. This morning, Venus dragged me here, telling me I need to know how to defend myself—and to know how to kill if and when the time comes. "Without the benefits of giving me your soul, you'll be dead before you can even think to cut their head off."

I want to roll my eyes, but I know she's right. I have to be prepared.

This is the first time Venus has mentioned my soul since I've been back. Butterflies flutter in my stomach at the mere mention of it. It's clear to me how hard Venus is working to give me choices, which includes not badgering me for my soul. Given she's such a control freak, I know she hates handing over the reins to someone else.

It makes me wonder...do I want to give Venus my soul?

Venus is still talking, instructing me on something, and I shake my head. "Sorry, what?"

"If you aren't paying attention, you'll be dead in an instant." She prowls towards me until we're nearly chest-to-chest. Without looking away from me, her hand extends to the side and a dagger materializes into her awaiting palm. The same dagger that I used to slice my skin open ten years ago. "Take this." I grab it, looking down at it. "Now try to stab me."

My head snaps up. "What?"

"You heard me. Try to stab me." She holds her arms out to her sides. "I'm right here, within reach. Just try it."

I know this is a trick. She is clearly faster and stronger than me. I shake my head in disbelief. "I can't stab you, Venus," I chuckle.

She tilts her head. "Why not? Are you afraid?"

"What? No, I'm not afraid. Well, I'm not a big fan of blood, but—"

"Are you afraid you can't do it?"

"I *know* I can't do it."

"Of course, you can't. You're just a weak mortal."

She's right, but it still irks me. "There's no need for name-calling," I grumble.

But she keeps going. "A weak mortal with magic she doesn't understand," she sighs dramatically.

I grit my teeth. "Cut it out, Venus."

She doesn't. "Or maybe your magic is the weak one."

Blood pounds in my ears as white-hot fury moves through my veins. For some reason, hearing someone else talk shit about my magic is what pushes me over the edge.

Only I'm allowed to do that.

Venus is still spouting shit, but I don't hear her. I lift my arm holding the dagger and swipe at her.

She doesn't even flinch—an irritating smirk is on her face as her hand whips out and wraps around my wrist, stopping the dagger from hitting its target. She tsks, "You'll have to do better than that, Vivian."

I bare my teeth at her as I wrangle my wrist free, staggering back once she finally releases me. Venus shifts into a fighting stance, bending her knees slightly, her smirk widening into a feral grin. It pisses me off even more. I lunge, gripping the dagger tightly as I try to make contact.

I don't actually want to hurt her, so I'm not aiming for any vital organs. Just drawing some blood will do.

She blocks my attack, dancing out of the way. A little shriek of agitation works its way out of my throat as I advance again, again, and again.

Each time, she blocks my attack. She grabs hold of my wrist and drags me close, causing me to nearly lose my footing as we stand nose-to-nose. "This is pathetic," she sneers.

"Stop," I growl, nearly losing my grip on myself in my anger, my frustration. A feeling I've grown to resent builds in me, fury that isn't completely mine, is pressing against my skin. "Venus—"

"Do you want to die? Because this makes me think you do."

I erupt. My magic lashes out, throwing Venus across the room where she lands with a loud thud. A wave of power sweeps through the room, shaking the entire structure. The wrath is mine and my magic's mingling together, ready to destroy everyone and everything.

Take back what is ours, it seems to whisper to me. *Erase it all and start anew.*

Yes, I nearly say, a giddiness mixing with the rage. I feel unstoppable, invincible. It feels like my magic and I are weaving together, binding ourselves into one being.

No one will survive me.

"Vivian."

The sound of my name makes me pause my descent into my magic. I blink, focusing on where I heard it.

Venus is on the ground, propped up on her arms, staring at me.

Immediately, my magic winks out, shrinking back to hide in the darkness of me. Once my body feels like its own again, I gasp and race over to Venus.

"Unholy shit, Venus, I'm so sorry. I just got so angry, and—"

"That was magnificent," she breathes, her onyx eyes wide with awe.

I kneel next to her, trying to find any injuries. "Are you okay? I didn't mean to hurt you."

"Yes, you did," she argues. "And you should have. I was provoking you to act, but I didn't expect *that* to happen." She shakes her head in disbelief as she chuckles.

It's then that I look around the room and see it's in complete disarray. All the various weaponry has been discarded on the floor, with windows blown out and chunks of the stone walls completely missing. I'm shocked the room is even still standing.

Venus is babbling on, "Your magic reacted to the potential threat and lashed out, sending shockwaves throughout the room." Her eyes are a bit wild as she assesses me. "How did it feel?"

Like I was going to destroy everything—and enjoy it. I shrug, trying to play it off. "I didn't feel much of anything," I lie.

She doesn't press me on it as I help her stand, even though she isn't injured. She throws her arm around my shoulders as she guides us out, already planning our next training session.

The High Priestesses take turns trying to awaken my magic, to get some sort of answers out of it. It feels like a waste of everyone's time. My magic has no interest in the wilderness in this realm.

The witches are patient though.

Aradia joins me today on the outskirts of the city, walking along the tree line. Her hope is that being so close to the wilderness will urge my magic's action.

"What lives out there?" I ask, jerking my chin to the tall trees.

"Various nightmares," she responds. "Creatures with no conscience, made of death and decay, feasting on anything that dares to disturb them."

I shudder. "I'll stay out here then."

She smiles at me, a dimple appearing on her cheek. "You would make a delicious snack for them."

I bark out a laugh and startle myself with the foreign sound. Slowly, it feels like I'm returning to myself—I speak more each day, I started introducing color into my wardrobe, and I even *laugh* sometimes.

Aradia gives me a smile, as if she, too, knows what that's like. I don't know much about the High Priestesses or their pasts. All we are told is they are the most powerful witches to ever live. Them and Lilith—and any other witch that had my magic before me.

"I will say, though, I'm confused why we keep coming out here. My magic still hasn't responded to Hell's forest yet. Why would it decide to today?"

Aradia shrugs. "Each day may provide us new opportunities. We must not waste them."

I want to grumble that I don't want any new opportunities, but I keep it to myself. Taking a deep breath, I plant my feet and widen my stance like Aradia showed me, relax my shoulders, and close my eyes.

Go ahead, I say internally to my magic.

Nothing.

I grit my teeth. *Come on, don't be annoying.*

Not even a faint flicker of my magic inside me.

I let out a huff of air, already irritated.

"It takes patience." Aradia's gentle voice floats to my ears, making me even more annoyed.

My eyes open and I glare at the Priestess before me. "It's just so impossible. I don't feel anything. It's like my magic is punishing me, which is ridiculous. *I* should be the one punishing *it*, not the other way around."

"Perhaps you are, and this is why it does not come forward."

I let out a laugh that sounds a bit deranged. "Oh, right, *I'm* the one punishing it. Silly me!"

"I will not argue with you, Vivian."

Her words hit me like a slap. I know I'm goading her into an argument unnecessarily. Maybe because she's snapped at me once before.

I know she won't again—Venus made sure of that.

"Fine," I sigh, guilt worming its way through me. I shouldn't put her in a shit position with Venus just because I'm upset. "I'm sorry."

She gives me a relieved smile. "We will keep trying. Eventually, your magic will build up and need to release."

Her words make me think back to the times it would spiral out of me while I was on the run, always alerting Venus to my whereabouts, or when it apparently showed itself during a nightmare.

"Shall we head back?" she asks me, and we silently fall into step next to one another.

The archdemon, Kali, is accompanying us today, as Luke was apparently unavailable. I figured he was just spooked by the forest and didn't want to be so close to it anymore, and from the way Kali warily observes the tree line, I get the sense that he feels the same.

"We're leaving," I announce, to which he gives an answering grunt and begins to speed walk back to the castle. "I'm not running to catch up with him," I grumble to Aradia, who shoots me a look as if to say, *neither am I.*

The more I walk through the city, the less it overwhelms me. I'm learning to tune out the noise, to let it become a buzzing in the background of my mind. Luckily, everyone still gives me a wide berth—either because of the vibe I give off or because I'm with an archdemon and a High Priestess, I'm not sure.

Aradia walks closely to me, her dark curls bouncing with each step. "There is something I have been meaning to discuss with you."

"Oh?" I ask.

Aradia glances at Kali's retreating back ahead of us and lowers her voice. "It must be decided how we will move forward, once you and your magic are in alignment."

"Move forward with what?" I ask.

"We cannot expect Phanes to stay in power," she states. "We must decide on what will happen once he is gone."

I fight the urge to cringe at hearing his name. "Well, considering he can't be killed, it's moot to consider the 'what-ifs' of it all."

Aradia bites her lip, a look of hesitancy in her eye.

"What is it?" I ask.

She seems to consider her words carefully. "It is possible another could take his throne."

Her words hit me like a ton of bricks. "Who?"

"Who is the only surviving goddess in this world?"

Venus.

As if I said my realization out loud, Aradia nods. "Our Dark Lady does not want to take his place."

I halt. Venus could kill him and take his place, but hasn't because *she doesn't want to*? I feel like I've been kicked in the chest. I'm struggling to breathe, and I take big gulping breaths, trying to get my lungs to work.

Venus could have killed her father and taken his place this whole time. She could have prevented this, could have prevented me from being taken—

"Vivian, it's alright," Aradia says firmly, but her voice sounds far away. I put my hands on my knees to steady myself, suddenly feeling lightheaded. I'm going to throw up. My mind is racing with the thought that Venus could have killed him and didn't.

Aradia touches my back, rubbing soothing circles against me. Breathe in for four, out for four. In for four, out for four. I look up and lock eyes with her, and she is staring at me intensely. "I know you are struggling with this information, but you must know she may not be the only one who could take his place," she says in a hushed tone, tilting her head closer to mine.

"What?" I gasp out.

She opens her mouth to tell me, but a shuffling of feet interrupts. Aradia rears back, smoothing out her features as Kali approaches.

Kali looks between us and addresses Aradia, "What is going on here?"

She opens her mouth to respond, but I interrupt. "Nothing," I pant. "Just not feeling well. Must have been something I ate."

He narrows his pitless eyes at me, then at Aradia, before stalking away, grumbling something about *babysitting duty* under his breath.

I push myself back to standing and grab Aradia by the shoulders, bringing us nose-to-nose. Shock is in her dark eyes, but I don't care, I don't care—

"Why?" I growl, anger and panic now warring with each other inside me, trying to become the dominant feeling.

Aradia bites her lip, clearly rethinking what she's said, but it's too late now.

"Why hasn't she done it?" I cry. It feels like the world is collapsing beneath me.

"Vivian—"

I release her and stumble my way back to the palace through tear-filled eyes.

Venus never told me. I suppose she wouldn't want to, especially after all that's happened. How could she do this—see me like this and *not* do it?

Because she doesn't want to, a voice in the back of my head snickers. *You aren't worth the trouble.*

Angry tears stream down my cheeks. Of course I'm not worth it. Why would Venus sacrifice everything for me? I'm just a witch with broken magic and a fucked up brain. I wipe my tears, but it doesn't stop new ones from falling. I make my way through the castle gates, the demon guards giving me startled looks as I approach, clearly looking worse for wear. Another embarrassment for the mighty ruler of Hell, the only goddess left. The one who could have killed her father and saved everyone—even me.

My heart pounds in my ears as my fury and tears nearly blind me. I wind through the hallways like a bat out of

Hell, running on my memory of the castle layout. Spirits and demons shuffle out of my way, murmurs following me as I weave around. At this point, they should all be used to seeing me like this. Just everyone in the realm, knowing what an absolute disaster I am, probably laughing at me when I have yet another breakdown.

I finally reach the bedroom doors, and I'm so angry that I'm nearly foaming at the mouth. I shove the door open and burst through, ready to fight.

Chapter Twenty-Eight
Venus

The scent of Vivian's anger reaches me before she does. She rushes into our room, her face splotchy and wet from crying.

"Vivian, what's wrong?" I move quickly across the space, reaching for her, but she slaps my hands away.

"Why haven't you done it?" she demands.

I shake my head in confusion. "I'm not sure what you are referring to."

"*Why haven't you killed him!*" Her shriek echoes through the room, and I feel the ground beneath our feet shift—her magic reacting to her rage.

I nearly fall to my knees.

She knows.

Somehow, she knows that I may be capable of stripping my father of his existence and taking over. She's panting, thick tears rolling down her cheeks as she looks at me with venom. I've never seen her look at me like this before, even when I crashed into her life again.

She hates me.

I turn from her, walking over to my desk, unable to look at the hatred in her gaze. I brace my hands on the desk, bowing my head. "Vivian, please. This isn't even worth a conversation."

"Excuse me?" she snaps. I hear her feet stomp towards me. "Ridding him of this world should be the *only* conversation."

"You aren't even ready to have it," I retort. "You can't even say his name."

Her silence is deafening. I raise my head and look over my shoulder. She looks like I've slapped her.

Instant shame washes over me. Spinning to her, I rush over but she steps out of reach. Fresh tears well in her eyes as her face contorts with anger. "*Phanes* deserves to die." She spits his name out with such vitriol. It's the first time I've heard her dare to say his name. "Not just for what he's done to you and this world, but to me. If you won't kill him for yourself or your realm, then do it for *me*."

"It isn't that simple," I sigh.

"Aradia told me. She told me there's potential for a new God of Life."

I swallow. "It is simply a theory. I do not know if I am strong enough to defeat him. Besides, you know as well as

I do that I'm barely capable of ruling my own realm, let alone taking over his rule too."

"I'm here to help you with Hell," she sniffles.

"Vivian, you aren't ready. You've just started showing signs of yourself since you've been back."

Angry tears roll down her cheeks. I reach a hand towards her to wipe them, but she slaps me away again. "I want to be better." Her voice sounds so small.

My heart cracks at her confession. "I know," I say gently.

"Why am I not better?" she shouts, a sob working its way through her body.

"It will take time," I say, trying to calm her. "I'm not telling you how to heal. I'm not trying to rush you. I'm just being realistic; the responsibility of helping me isn't what you need right now."

"Don't tell me what I need!" Her shout echoes through the room.

I hold my hands up in surrender. "I am not your enemy," I murmur.

Her face crumples. "Aren't you?" she cries, her shoulders curving inward. "You could get rid of him, and you won't."

"It is all I want," I argue fiercely. "I want to carve out his eyes for looking at you, to slowly remove his hands for daring to touch you. I want to kill him, over and over, in the most creative ways possible. I dream about how he will hurt for what he's done."

"I dream of that too," she admits quietly.

Approaching her like a scared doe, I cup her face, running my thumbs across her tear-stained cheeks. "We must think of the consequences and not let bloodlust take over. I know that's incredibly ironic, coming from me." She lets out a huff of a laugh. "We will get our revenge, I promise, but we must be strategic. I have always been rash and short-sighted when it comes to what I want, but I will not allow myself to get in the way of what is best, especially when it comes to you. I will not operate off mere hypotheticals when it comes to your safety."

"If you had killed him, he never would have taken me."

I nod, the truth of her words stinging, like I'm swimming in the ocean with a gaping wound. "I wanted to get you the moment you were gone, but I couldn't. I'm not strong enough to defeat him, and I may never be," I admit.

"Why not?"

I suck in a breath, debating if I should tell her that I need her soul. I'm no longer sure what is best kept secret and what will help her. She's looking at me expectantly, and I decide to just tell her the truth. "I may need your soul, to tip the scales in our favor. It will make us both formidable, unstoppable."

"You need my soul," she echoes, searching my face.

I nod, unsure of how she's taking this information.

"Do you want it?" she asks.

What kind of a question is that? I nearly laugh at how ridiculous it is that I would ever pass on the opportunity to have her bound to me, to keep her soul as mine for eternity.

It is all I want.

But something stops me from demanding it like I once did.

"Only if you wish to give it to me," I answer.

Something shifts in her expression then, but it's gone so fast that I miss it. "But I've been baptized in a church."

I blink. "You *what*?"

Her cheeks redden. "When I ran, I got baptized in a church," she mutters.

I'm fighting the urge to laugh. All witches know organized religion is unnecessary—all souls come to me, regardless of their denomination. I'm not sure why Vivian wasted her time.

"I can't believe this," I sigh dramatically, releasing her face to pinch the bridge of my nose. "How shall I ever possess your soul now?"

"Alright," she scoffs, clearly disinterested in my sarcasm.

"Your soul shall never truly belong to me now that it—"
I look at her and whisper, "Was it a Catholic church?"

"Yes," she grumbles, her face beet red.

"—Now that it belongs to the Catholic church!" I wail hysterically.

Vivian narrows her eyes at me. "I was panicked when I did it, okay? I wasn't thinking clearly, and I had hoped it would put some distance between us."

"My darling witch," I chuckle, "you know all souls go to Hell, regardless of their religion during their life." She squirms a bit, clearly uncomfortable with the spotlight on her. I decide to show her mercy and say, "I would still accept your soul, even though you're a devout Catholic."

"Shut up."

I can't help the grin that spreads across my lips, but I sober quickly. "I am *really* fighting the urge to not demand it from you, Vivian. As I'm sure you've noticed, I'm trying this new thing where I let you decide what you'd like to do."

That earns me a grin as she rolls her eyes. "I know. I can tell it's been a difficult journey for you."

My shoulders relax. The storm seems to have passed. For now.

Chapter Twenty-Nine

Vivian

Trying to get my magic to react to Hell's wilderness is becoming annoying. Not even a whisper of it comes forward.

Venus and I continue to train together, helping me get physically stronger, but my magic doesn't bother to come out again. It's as if it now understands what we're doing and it won't cooperate.

Maybe I need to force my magic's hand.

My magic and I need to go back to my forest, I realize—to train, to finally work together in the way we're meant to. If my magic was here before he was, then it's time for my magic to get itself together and fight back.

The thought makes me feel conflicted and like a coward. I'm terrified of stepping out of Hell's wards for fear of him coming to steal me away again, but...I think this might be what I need. Coming face-to-face with him makes me want to throw up, but I fear it's inevitable. It's what has happened every single time. It is meant to be him against me, and I can't hide in Hell forever.

Would Venus take me to my forest if I asked? Let's be real, when has Venus ever truly let go of control when it comes to me? She hunted me like an animal for ten years, never stopping until she finally caught me. She's kept important things from me, things about her father that I deserved to know. Keeping the fact that she could take his place, and that she may need my soul to do it, is the most difficult pill to swallow.

As I walk beside Marie after another failed training session and enter the castle gates, I've made up my mind.

"When does the Dark Lady's council meet?" I ask the witch.

Her icy blue eyes swing to me. "And for what purpose do you need to know?"

I shrug, pretending to not give a shit. "Just curious. Venus seems to be gone a lot recently, and I worry if she's maybe seeing someone on the side," I lie smoothly.

It's total bullshit, but Marie's eyes grow wide in surprise. "Oh, Lady Vivian, she would never do such a thing." She hooks her arm with mine and brings her head closer. "She is quite taken with you," she says in a hushed tone.

I pretend to not believe her. "It's just..." I sigh dramatically. "She's always away. Perhaps she's grown bored of me."

Marie shakes her head, her white-blonde locks moving like a lion's mane. "That is nonsense. The Dark Lady would never forsake you—I'm certain of this." She pauses, assessing my expression, and whispers, "We have been meeting more often than usual. It is up to nearly every other day, sometimes going on for hours," she groans.

"And she is present the whole time?" I ask.

She nods. "Oh, yes. The council never meets without her."

I pretend to digest this information. "Where does the council meet?" Her eyes grow suspicious, so I quickly add, "Just so I can see her for myself. It's not that I don't believe you, but I have been hurt by lovers in the past."

Marie's eyes darken as she listens. "I know that exact feeling," she confides.

Shit. Now I feel bad about spinning this story. I pat her hand on my arm in what I hope is a comforting gesture.

Marie takes a deep breath and says, "We meet in the east wing of the castle, third door from the grand staircase. Our next meeting is in an hour."

I try to control my reaction, acting like it isn't that interesting. "Thank you," I tell her, feeling guilty at having to trick this information out of her. "And whoever hurt you in the past, I hope they rot in Hell."

Her answering smile makes me shiver. "Do not worry about that. I've already seen to it."

A little over an hour later, I'm standing outside the doors Marie told me lead to the council room. The two doors have handles shaped like snakes, with their heads looking downward. Images of his castle come into my vision and I shake them away before I lose my nerve. I grab the handles with a newfound resolve and shove them open.

The room is massive. The walls are covered with maps, all annotated with different colors and pins. Sconces hold little flames to keep the room bright. A large, rectangular oak table sits in the center with eight chairs, four on one side, three on the other, and one at the head, facing the door.

Each seat is filled, except for Venus's. She's standing with her hands on the table, leaning forward, her wings flared out to her sides.

Eight pairs of eyes all look at me. I stop in my tracks, suddenly coming to realize maybe this was a terrible idea.

Around the table, sit four archdemons with colorful skin shades—Kali and Luke I've already met, but one has greenish skin and the other has a violet hue. They all have identical pitless eyes, but their horns range in size. Across from them sit the High Priestesses, who all stare at me with shock—except for Marie, who looks like she's trying not to throw up.

Venus looks so bewildered to see me that I might actually start laughing. I swallow down the urge and say, "Hello, esteemed council."

Crickets.

No one dares say a word, and Venus is still too shocked, so I continue. "I wanted to discuss something important with you all." I approach the giant table, looking only at Venus as I speak. "I know I am safest within the wards of Hell that I graciously helped recreate, but my magic refuses to work with the forest here. I propose that I be taken back to the realm of the living to see if it will respond there instead."

All eyes shift nervously to Venus. The tension is thick in the air, a charged energy encompassing everyone. Her shadows spill out of her, swiping across the table, across the floor, circling my ankles, wondering why the Hell I'm here doing this. I don't avert my attention.

"And why, exactly, did you feel the need to bring this before my council?" she asks, her voice foreboding.

"Because I'm tired of letting decisions be made on my behalf. I don't want to sit idly by anymore—I want to do what it is I'm meant to do."

"What are you meant to do, Vivian?" she asks, her tone clipped.

"I'm meant to stop Phanes," I reply, nearly choking on his name. "With my magic, I'm meant to end him, so that you can take his place." I don't look at the High Priestesses, for fear of getting them into any trouble.

"You believe you are ready for such a thing?" she snarls.

I raise my chin. "Not yet," I admit. "But I will be—if I can work to revive the forest from my childhood. The one you destroyed," I say, not to throw it in her face, but to remind her.

Her jaw clenches. "It is too dangerous."

"It's the only option we have," I argue. "The longer we wait, the higher the chance is that he'll come looking for me—stronger than he was before."

"You do not know of what you speak."

"Of course I do," I spit. "I was his prisoner. I know exactly what he is and what he is capable of. Our best chance is to prepare me, to *truly* prepare me to destroy him."

The eyes of the council ping-pong back and forth between me and Venus as we verbally spar.

A few beats of silence sit between us.

"The lady does make a good point, Your Grace," Luke interjects. Venus looks at him like she cannot believe he has the audacity to speak. "It is best to strike sooner rather than later."

Venus ignores him, dismissive, as she looks back at me. "This is not something to discuss in front of the council."

"Why?" I push. "Because they're beneath you?"

Venus bares her teeth at me. I refuse to lower my chin, and my back starts to feel stiff. My anger is building in me, too quickly for me to stop my words. "So you'd rather keep me locked away in this castle than have me fix the fucked up situation we're all in?"

"If that's what it takes to keep you safe, then yes."

His white castle, his empty throne room, the horrible white bedroom, dart across my mind. Panic grips my throat at feeling trapped, feeling stuck here. I stare into her eyes—into *his* eyes—and whisper, "You are just like him."

I regret saying the words the moment they leave my mouth.

Someone takes a sharp breath as Venus's face goes slack with shock. Even her shadows stop vibrating and seem to stare directly at me.

The ground beneath us rumbles, a power awakening to destroy.

I open my mouth to backpedal, but a cloud passes across Venus's face, now contorting with undiluted rage. "And you are nothing but a broken, naïve, little girl who doesn't understand the magnitude of what is happening."

"Do not speak to me like that," I warn her with quiet venom.

The castle groans beneath us, struggling to withstand the magic she's exuding. My own magic yawns awake in answer, pressing against my skin to meet the challenge in front of us.

I don't see the others in the room anymore. It is just Venus and I, unable to stop ourselves from squaring up, from spiraling out of control.

She seems to sense this too, because Venus straightens and gives me a cold look I've never seen from her before. "If that is what you wish, then so it shall be. But do not be shocked when it ends tragically."

Her words hit like a slap across the face. My magic winks out, curling inside me, releasing my anger. All that it leaves is the realization that I've royally fucked up.

Venus swiftly stalks around the table, everyone rising hastily as she crosses the room without another look at me.

"Venus—" I try, watching her leave, but she doesn't turn. She simply exits without another word.

Everyone else begins to silently file out, avoiding eye contact. Except for one.

"You could have told me what your true intentions were," Marie says as she stops next to me, her eyes like ice.

"I'm sorry I lied," I say quietly.

Her cold eyes narrow. "I do not believe you are sorry—not truly."

I open my mouth to argue, but she walks steadily out of the council room, leaving me alone.

Chapter Thirty

Venus

My wings shift as the current pushes me forward, the cool sky chilling me to the bone, but I don't stop—stopping means I'll have to go home and deal with the nightmare waiting for me.

You are just like him.

Those words roll around in my mind, getting louder and louder until it is the only thing I can hear.

How dare she? How dare she compare me to that monster? I have been nothing but gracious with her—I have not pushed her to get better before she is ready; I will gleefully accept any part of her that she wishes to give me.

And yet, she feels he and I are one and the same.

The one who has destroyed us both.

Unease blooms in my stomach, swirling with the anger already residing there. I have spent my entire existence hating my father, that hatred only growing each day until it almost exists as its own living thing inside me, ready to devour me completely.

For Vivian to say we are alike...it feels like my entire world is crumbling.

I glide on the wind, letting the crisp air in the dark sky chill my face, embracing the bit of bite it has on my fingers, my feathers. My back, my wings, moan in protest as I push them harder, soaring against the wind trying to send me in the opposite direction, as if it wants to escort me back home.

I know I have to face this, but I don't want to. I don't even know if I can without making things worse.

I can't talk to her, I decide. Not yet. Not until I know I won't level the entire palace out of anger.

Despite my body screaming at me not to, I turn myself around, hoping that she isn't there waiting for me.

Dipping through the window, Vivian is sitting at my desk, her fingers twisting her hair around anxiously. A sense of dread washes over me as I see her, clearly waiting for me.

I can't speak to her.

She stands as I land on my feet. "Venus," she starts, but I ignore her, heading into the bathing room and shutting the door—shutting her out. "Venus," I hear her muffled voice on the other side of the door. "I'm sorry. I didn't mean what I said..."

An incredulous laugh bubbles out of me. I rip the door open and see her shuffle away, as if her ear was pressed to it. "You thought coming before my council, unannounced, to declare your grand plan was a good idea. Then you have the nerve to tell me I am just like *him*?"

"You can't keep me locked in here," she murmurs.

"I don't do that, and you know it. Just because you went through something traumatic does not give you the right to drag everyone down with you." My wings splay out in aggravation.

Her eyes widen in disbelief. "Say that again," she breathes.

"I have been trying to help you—the High Priestesses have all been trying to help you. You're smarter than this. What happened to the woman who managed to outrun me for a decade?"

"She's dead!" she shrieks.

I still.

"She's dead," she repeats, quieter this time. "She died when Phanes took me and tortured me and touched me however he pleased." Her entire body trembles. "I'm trapped. My magic might be the only thing that can destroy him, but we aren't strong enough. We need to work together. I've wasted so much time already; I can't afford to lose anymore— none of us can."

My shoulders droop. "Why would you say such a thing to me?" I realize, in this moment, that I'm not truly angry with her.

I'm *hurt*. I'm hurt that she felt the need to go around me, to not come to me. To tell me I am just like the being who tried to break her.

Her hazel eyes shimmer with tears. "I wasn't thinking clearly. I felt trapped in that moment and lashed out. I'm sorry—I didn't mean it."

"How long must I endure hurt from you?" My voice cracks.

She sniffles. "I don't know," she sobs. "Everything is just so, *so* hard. I don't want to argue with you. I don't want to hurt you, especially when we might not have a lot of time left."

Her words feel like a fist wrapped around my lungs. "Do not speak like that."

"We can't fight fate," she says softly, her eyes holding no anger, no resentment. "I'm tired of trying anyway. All the witches before me died. There's no guarantee it will be different for me. My life has never been my own. Why should it be now?"

"I can't be without you," I admit, my voice hoarse.

"You have to come to terms with the fact that I need to do this, and that you might lose me in the process."

I can't, I want to scream. My instincts are roaring at me to hide her, to keep her within the castle walls, and to never let her out of my sight.

But then I would truly be just like him.

I can't do this anymore; I can't be around her. I can't be close to her when she won't fight for herself. Being by her side will only throw us both down a path of heartbreak. "Perhaps I have been too...familiar with you." I gesture to our shared room. "I believe it best if we separate ourselves from one another."

She blinks in surprise.

I walk past her, unable to handle seeing her upset anymore.

"I will stay in another room," I say, not turning around. "If you need me, let a servant know and they will fetch me." I thought I could help her, I thought I was doing the right thing, but I can't. I reach the door and continue without turning around. "Please let me know when you would like to go to your forest, and I shall take you."

"Venus," she says quietly.

My hand freezes on the doorknob, but I don't look at her. I pause, frozen, waiting for her to say something, anything.

But she doesn't. So I leave the room and don't look back.

Chapter Thirty-One
Vivian

I shouldn't have said what I said.

The regret settles deep within me, burrowing into my bones as it takes up space. Logically, I know Venus and her father aren't the same. Venus might have inherited some tendencies from him, but they're completely different. Venus might want to lock me up in here, but I know she won't.

She's never outright said she's afraid of becoming him, but based on her reaction, I know she is.

And I took that and threw it in her face.

I'm too ashamed of myself to go to her. Too disgusted with how easily my panic makes me lash out. I can't face her and her anger, her disappointment in me.

How can she even care for someone like me? I'm just a constant reminder of all that's happened.

I find myself wandering the halls, not sure where I'm going until I'm leaving the castle and heading towards where the new souls reside.

The demons guarding the gates let me in without a word. I walk numbly down the path, unsure of where my aunt even lives.

It isn't until I spot the small garden that I see her.

My aunt looks up and spots me, her face lighting up and then clouding once she sees my expression. She quickly floats over to me, her eyebrows furrowed in concern. "Vivian," she addresses me, her voice alarmed. "What is it? Are you alright?"

"I—" No. No, I am not alright. "I wasn't sure where else to go," I admit, shrugging and fighting the urge to bawl in front of her.

She nods, understanding me, even when I don't have the words to express myself. "Come," she instructs, gliding next to me as we go to sit on the bench. We sit in silence, my aunt letting me work through my feelings in my mind.

"I've messed up," I tell her. I tell her everything, sparing no detail of how horribly I behaved and how much I regret it. Her face is open and warm, with no sense of judgment. Once I've bared it all, she asks, "And you have not spoken to the Dark Lady?"

"No." I sigh, sadness and shame leaking from me.

"You should."

"I know, but I can't."

"Why not?"

"Because I'm afraid she won't want me anymore," I admit hoarsely.

My aunt cocks her head in curiosity. "The Dark Lady will never stop wanting you." She says it as if she knows this for a fact.

"How can she after I said something like that?" How can she ever care for someone like me?

She shrugs her delicate shoulders. "You will not know until you speak with her. Tell her all that you told me. Do not hold back because you are afraid."

"Easy for you to say," I grumble despondently.

She gives me a half smile. "You both deserve forgiveness. Make it known how you feel. Do not let your regret grow even more."

Taking a deep breath, I nod. She's right. I'll regret it if I don't lay everything out there, broken parts and all. I look at her, at my features mirrored on her transparent face, and give a watery smile. "I'm sorry I came here under these circumstances."

She chuckles. "I'm happy to see you any time. It gets quite boring here after a while. I enjoy hearing some gossip from you."

I roll my eyes. "I'm glad my life being in shambles is amusing to you."

"I'm only teasing." She shakes her head. "Talk to the Dark Lady, Vivian. She clearly loves you, and you clearly love her. It will work itself out."

I blink at her.

The realization crashes down around me. "I *do* love her," I say, mostly to myself.

Venus is not without her flaws, but who isn't? And I know I'm far from perfect. She's been fighting to help me heal, to ground me when I feel myself floating away. She irks me, drives me crazy, and makes me want to wring her neck sometimes, but that has helped me when I couldn't help myself. She comforts me and takes care of me. She doesn't look at me like I'm some pariah, and even though she pokes fun at my fashion sense, she lets me be myself.

I don't just love Venus—I'm *in* love with her.

A small laugh slips past my lips, earning me a curious look from my aunt, but I wave my hand dismissively.

"Vivian," she says, her face growing serious. "There's something I need to speak with you about."

I open my mouth to ask her what about, but a spear of dark magic streaks from the sky, landing in front of us with an earth-shattering boom.

Venus unfurls her wings as she straightens, her midnight eyes finding me immediately. She rushes over to me, reaching for me without a word.

"What—Venus—"

"There's been a disturbance at the wards. Something has attempted to break through," she informs me as she lifts me into her arms like I weigh nothing, her wings shooting us into the dark sky.

Chapter Thirty-Two
Venus

"Luckily, the wards have not been damaged, but we heard loud booms just beyond it—as if something was crashing into it," one of the witches stationed to survey the wards tells us.

A demon had rushed into the council room, informing us that the wards had been attacked. I had received word Vivian had gone to see Judith, so I wasted no time grabbing her before flying to the location to find a group of frightened witches. The High Priestesses arrived shortly after we did. We all stand in a circle, discussing and observing.

The ward itself is invisible without being trained in magic and knowing where to look. A little shimmer will appear out of the corner of the eye, making someone think they've seen something—but when they look, nothing is there. Wards make non-magical beings turn away without ever knowing why, as their magical properties make them uneasy.

But this ward is different.

Streaks of power electrify it, resembling lightning without clouds. The air is charged, making even me feel uncomfortable approaching it, causing a general sense of doom to sit in my stomach.

It is marvelous.

Vivian is staring at it, wide-eyed, like she can't quite believe what she's seeing. "I made this?" she asks, her voice awed.

"It can be quite difficult to stomach," the young witch replies, which earns a bemused look from Vivian. She clears her throat before dipping her head. "Apologies. It has just been difficult to monitor, given its strength."

"How many times did you hear something collide with the wards?" I ask.

"Not many—maybe less than ten? Whatever it was, I have no doubt it underestimated the power. I would bet it is dead from the magic the wards exude."

The High Priestesses and I exchange a look. It's my father, it has to be—either himself, his pet, or his newest creature. I turn to the young witch and tell her, "You shall be relieved of this responsibility."

She opens her mouth to express her shock, but I hold up a hand. "Not because you have done anything wrong, but I suspect a break from being in such close proximity would be beneficial."

The witch blinks in surprise before her face smooths out with relief. "Thank you, Your Grace—yes, I believe some time away would be ideal." She transforms into her spirit form and floats towards the other witches, who are huddled together, staring at the unbroken wards.

"I doubt he will strike in the same place or in the same way," Aradia muses to us. "Perhaps it was a test to see how powerful the wards are."

"Or to see if I was here," Vivian interjects.

We all turn to her.

"Think about it," she says. "We don't know if he knows I'm here. I'm sure he assumed, but he didn't have confirmation. Now he does; he knows my magic made the original wards. And now that my magic has shown itself here..." She starts fidgeting with her fingers. "When I was stuck with him, he was obsessed with finding out how strong my magic was. Paranoid, even. He would torture me in an attempt to force my magic out, to see its true potential. Him testing the wards has shown him how powerful it is."

Anger radiates off the High Priestesses at Vivian's words. Even my own has come out, though I already know the story.

Vivian continues, seemingly unaware of our reactions to her words and her experience. "He made it seem like he was weakening when he kept me. Maybe it was all a ruse." She spits the last word out, clearly disgusted with the idea. Her hazel eyes connect with mine. "He's clearly getting ballsy. I need to keep training; I need to go back to my forest."

"We could conceal you—maybe it will allow us more time—" Marie says.

"No," Vivian responds confidently. "It won't matter. He'll find me, concealment spell or not."

"The High Priestesses had been working on feeding a concealment into the amulet from your aunt," I interject. "You might be right that it will not stop him, but it could help."

She mulls it over, biting her lip for a moment before she squares her shoulders and says, "Okay. I'll wear it." I nearly breathe a sigh of relief. "We should continue as soon as possible, though," she says before turning to the other witches. "When can it be ready?"

"It needs a few final touches. We stopped once you were taken," Marie says awkwardly, and I can tell Vivian fights the urge to fidget again. My hackles rise at her discomfort. "Give us a day or two."

She nods and looks to me. "Who will guard the wards now?"

"I think it best to station new witches and demons around the perimeter, in case he manages to succeed," I respond.

"Maybe I should stay here, just in case it needs to be repaired—"

"No." The word comes out harsher than intended, but the thought of Vivian being *right here* if Phanes broke through...

Vivian narrows her eyes at me, but Aradia interrupts, "If the wards are broken through, you are the first person he will be searching for. It is best if you are kept in the palace."

"The palace is where he'd expect me to be," Vivian argues.

My shadows buzz around me in irritation.

Isobel chimes in, "It is not only the safest place for you, but the smartest. Besides, the wards were erected just outside the forest—you do not need to be so near the wards to remedy an issue should one arise."

Vivian appears thoughtful before letting out a sigh. "Okay, fine. So, we just go back to the castle?" she asks me.

I can't wipe the irritation off my face. I say to the High Priestesses, "Let us gather the council to strategize how many to station. I'll meet you all there."

They all nod, transform into their spirit forms, and float their way back to the castle.

My aggravation is threatening to overtake me. I lock eyes with Vivian and say with quiet venom, "What was that about, offering to stay by the wards?"

Her mouth pops open and her eyes widen in shock before her face contorts angrily. "He's after *me*, Venus. I'm the reason he attacked Hell in the first place—or did you forget that?"

"You know I haven't," I seethe. "You being in your forest is risk enough. You being right at the wards would lead to more bloodshed than you realize."

"But it might prevent so much more."

"You told me you want to help me rule Hell," I growl. "How is this showing me that you're ready for that? You're reacting with your guilt instead of thinking strategically."

Anger simmers from her; she's nearly shaking. "Like you're the greatest ruler ever. Hey everybody, Venus knows everything about everything and I clearly know noth-ing—"

"I did not—"

"Don't act like I'm some idiot—"

Soon, we're shouting over each other, neither of us hearing the other, both hinged forward, glaring each other down, gesticulating wildly. My wings splay out instinc-tively, and my shadows dart around us, confused about what's happening.

Two predators fighting over an invisible carcass.

"You can't treat me like I'm stupid—"

"What you *are* is an insolent, little brat—"

I'm not sure who stops shouting first; all I know is we eventually both run out of breath. Vivian's cheeks are bright pink, eyes wild. A beat of silence passes between us, unsure of how to proceed.

Finally, Vivian breaks the tension. "That felt good," she pants.

She's right. I feel lighter than I have in weeks. From the way Vivian stands straight, she clearly feels the same.

Still, an awkwardness settles between us from both the spoken and unspoken words that keep us apart.

You are just like him.

I clear my throat. "We should get back to the castle."

Her face dims and she nods before I open my arms for her, flying us back to our other problems.

Chapter Thirty-Three
Vivian

Venus is always on the brunt end of my wrath, choosing to weather it, but I know it drains her. I don't want to lash out at her, but it feels like I can't stop—it's as if I'm watching myself, unable to control the vitriol I spew at her.

Sometimes I think it would be better if she wanted nothing to do with me.

I'm tired of this. I'm tired of struggling to accept that she cares about me, for me.

I have to apologize.

Walking into her temporary room, I find her sitting in front of the fire, a glass of amber liquid in a glass cup that dangles from her hand.

It dawns on me then how tired she looks, how deflated she is. Her shadows are still for once, barely even hovering around her.

She looks over at me, and her onyx eyes have aged thousands of years in the span of a few days.

"I'm sorry," I say, nervously fidgeting with a strand of my hair. "I wasn't thinking clearly when I came before your council, or when we argued at the wards. I shouldn't have said what I said."

Venus lets out a long sigh before she replies, "And I am sorry for the words I threw at you. I do not think you naïve, or broken, or any of the other horrible things I called you."

Tell her, I urge myself. *Tell her how you feel. Tell her that she isn't her father and that you love her.*

I take a deep breath, but the words that come out are not the ones I want. "I meant what I said. I would like to train in my own forest, to see if that helps move things along."

She nods before leaning her head against the back of her chair. Her tattoo hisses at me, baring its fangs. "Then I shall take you. The High Priestesses are nearly done with your amulet."

"Okay," I say awkwardly, "Can we go once it's ready?"

"Sure," she sighs.

I twirl my hair around my finger until it hurts, my fingertip turning red. I'm not sure what else to do now—how to get Venus to look at me the way she did just days ago, how to make things normal between us again.

Tell her.

"Okay," I repeat, trying to inject some confidence into my words, but it falls flat.

Come on, I tell myself. *Don't wimp out now.*

But Venus doesn't look at me, so I turn on my heel and leave.

Chapter Thirty-Four
Venus

My anger has dissipated and all I feel is tired. An exhaustion that sits within me that I can't remove, no matter how I try to alleviate it.

Vivian wants me to be angry at her; she might even want me to hate her. I thought I could handle it, and perhaps I could have before, but now...now I don't have the strength.

I am far from perfect, I know this. I do not know how to make this right with her. I've told her I am not strong enough to defeat him without her soul.

But perhaps...perhaps she must know the theory, the idea that she could become the Goddess of Life, even if it is folly.

Even if all it does is create hope.

But hope is dangerous here.

I struggle being away from her. My shadows keep an eye on her, letting me know she's alright. She spends most of her time in the archives or by the bedroom windows, much as she did when she first came back, her cat sitting beside her. The same cat, apparently, that tried to attack one of my shadows the other day.

The High Priestesses have finished infusing a concealment spell into her amulet. It's time to go to the realm of the living.

My nerves are all jumbled, making it hard to think clearly as I step into Vivian's room.

We lock eyes and just stare at each other—no words passing our lips, but they don't need to. Stepping close to one another, I tap my tattoo three times, letting it slither across us, connecting us.

I've missed you, I say with my eyes.

I've missed you too, her eyes seem to reply as my tattoo brings us closer together.

I transport us to her forest, stepping back immediately once my tattoo is settled in its original place. My shadows cast outwards, scanning the surrounding area, and find nothing amiss. It doesn't ease my nerves about being out in the open, so vulnerable against my father if he wishes to attack, but Vivian was right; I can't keep her locked away in Hell forever, no matter what I might desire.

And Phanes does need to be dealt with. I have never been put in such a position where all outcomes are complete and total shit like this.

Vivian is also observing the area nervously, as if unsure how to proceed. She starts breathing rapidly, panic flashing across her face.

"Vivian?"

She shakes her head, as if unable to answer, her nerves strangling her.

I try again. "Where are you, Vivian?"

Gulping down air, she tightens her hands into fists and grits out, "I'm with you."

"Good," I murmur.

"I'm with you, in my forest, in the other realm, and you are going to keep me safe."

My shadows vibrate in answer, hyper-aware.

After a few moments, her breathing evens out, her body relaxing as she walks to a part of the forest floor still discolored with death and kneels, placing her hands upon the grass. Closing her eyes, she takes some deep breaths, as if readying herself for the onslaught of her magic.

Nothing happens.

A minute goes by, then five, then ten...still nothing—no rumble of her magic, not even a whisper.

My shadows peek around my shoulder restlessly. My body is wound so tightly that I might snap at any moment. I clear my throat. "Perhaps—"

The ground beneath me groans, the soil tumbling over, renewing; the grass beneath my feet turns green and quickly grows; wildflowers peek up and bloom before my eyes, their petals stretching towards the sky. Next to me, a tree stump begins to regenerate, the rings disappearing as it rockets upwards, branches and leaves appearing as it grows.

An incredulous laugh dances from my lips as I watch Vivian bring this wilderness back to life. I look over at her and nearly go to my knees.

She's glowing. A warm light radiates from within; her hair floats upwards on a phantom wind. Her face is peaceful, serene, calm.

I'm struck stupid.

Then her magic peters out, the glow rescinding as she removes her hands from the grass and her eyes open, landing on me.

They're clear—clearer than I've seen them in a long time.

"Extraordinary," I murmur.

She smiles at me, and I swear I see that glowing essence within it. "I knew it would work," she says, mostly to herself.

Neither of us says anything for a few moments, too engrossed with what she's accomplished.

"I'm sorry," Vivian eventually says.

"As am I."

She shakes her head, her blonde hair swaying. "I don't think you're like your father. I just freaked out when you said you'd keep me locked away. I didn't trust you, and I should have. I shouldn't have said what I said."

"You have good reason to not trust me," I relent. "I have done horrible things to you."

"Not since I've been back in Hell," she points out. "You make me feel safe. Cherished, even. You've tried to keep me from losing myself. I know why you kept secrets from me."

"Keeping secrets is second nature to me," I admit. "I've never had anyone I could rely on—not fully."

"I know." Her smile is sad. "But we shouldn't have secrets between us. I need to know what we're up against, even if it'll hurt me."

I still, my nerves fizzling at her words. How can I make that promise to her when I'm still keeping things from her?

Steeling my spine, I decide she's right. No more secrets. "The High Priestesses suspect Phanes can be killed if you were to take his place, not me. That your magic, and by extension, *you* are the true Goddess of Life."

Her smile drops. "I don't get it," she admits, her brows furrowing.

"Think about it. Your magic created the original world before he appeared and stole it, weakening your magic so that it had to go into hiding. He's destroyed all who have possessed your magic—for what purpose other than to stop your magic from becoming strong enough to take back what rightfully belonged to it?"

"But that's my magic. That's not *me*."

"Admittedly, this is uncharted territory for all of us."

"What would be so different this time though? He killed Lilith and destroyed her soul, and we had the same magic."

I force the words out, even as I struggle to speak them. "What *could* be different is you handing your soul over to me. As you know, Lilith had not done so before she was murdered. It's possible that, by offering your soul to me, it would strengthen us both enough to finally rid us of him—but not to strengthen me. It would be to strengthen *you*."

The glow I just witnessed from her has dimmed even further. She looks down at her hands in her lap as she says, "I'll have to think about it."

It feels as if she's reached into my chest and ripped my heart straight out, but I can't put that on her, so I slip a mask of indifference on and reply, "It is your choice what you would like to do." After a beat, I say, "Would you like to continue working with your magic?"

She nods, avoiding eye contact as she stands, quietly walks outside of the lively area she's created to kneel in a patch of death, and begins again.

Chapter Thirty-Five

Vivian

My magic is here, reviving the dead world around me.

I feel a mixture of emotions. Happy I was right; angry that it took so long; upset because my magic and I are still two separate entities. Thinking of when we had a few moments where we supported one another...it felt good. Right.

Swallowing my nerves, I sit on the fresh grass, soaking in the newfound beauty, as I reach inside myself to speak with it.

I have questions for you, I say internally.

It cocks its head, waiting.

I huff out a sigh. *Is any of it true? Are we ready to kill him?*

Nearly.

"Why this time?" I ask aloud. "What will be different than all the other times you showed up and ruined someone's life?"

We need to bond with the Dark Lady first, it replies, ignoring my jab.

Shaking my head, I retort, "But why?"

She has always been the answer. Give her your soul, and you will both be strong enough.

"I ran from her when it was my turn to hand over my soul," I argue. "I felt...like it wasn't right."

You misunderstood then. My past selves all converged to you, showing you their endings.

So I wasn't running because of Venus. I was running because of *him*—of what he had done to the witches before me with the same magic.

"Magic is supposed to get stronger when a witch hands over her soul. We could've easily gotten rid of him then."

My magic swirls angrily. *I have made this mistake before, believing it was time to take back what is owed, but I was wrong. Now, it is different. You are different from all those before you; Venus is different than she has ever been. WE are different. There is finally a chance to destroy him.*

"And how, exactly, am I supposed to do that?"

Give your soul to the Dark Lady. Lure Phanes into the dark and kill him. We will work together.

"Why did you leave me when I needed you? When he did all of those things to me?" I ask, the betrayal sitting heavy in my body.

I am sorry I did not protect you. I was afraid and short-sighted. It shall not happen again.

"I can't go through that again."

You won't. I will not leave you.

"I'm sorry too," I reply, tears pricking my eyes. "I'm sorry for shoving you away and blaming you for how my life became. It wasn't your fault or Venus's fault. It was his—it has always been his." And I would no longer let him have control. "No more," I tell it. "No more leaving me to fend for myself. If you're too scared to fight, you'll never win. And the only way to win is if we work together."

It flares inside me, casting out into the earth beyond, confirming the answer.

My head swims from the bomb my magic has dropped on me. I puzzled through it all as I went inch by inch, section by section, bringing death back to life. It was my magic that created this world, not me...so what will happen to me once I kill Phanes—*if* I can kill him? There's no guarantee I'll be successful.

Even if he's destroyed, will my magic simply overtake me? What point would I have for my magic anymore? I can't help but feel like a vessel, a simple meat suit for it to harbor inside until it's finally ready to act. Just like the witches before me, simply holding onto the magic until it was potentially strong enough.

But maybe...maybe it doesn't matter.

I'm tired of trying to outrun my fate, even if my fate is to die so my magic can be free again.

Surprisingly, I feel like I'm taking this news very well, considering how I've reacted to every other bit of information that's been dropped in my lap. Maybe that's because it feels...right. I can't put my finger on it, but it's almost as if my body and my magic know this is what we've been moving towards this whole time.

My magic doesn't interrupt my thoughts, too focused on the task at hand. Eventually, it returns to me, exhausted. I take a few gasping breaths and realize I'm exhausted too, both physically and mentally.

"I'm done!" I shout to Venus, who has kept her distance, but I have no doubt is anxiously monitoring both me and the world around us for any threats.

She steps through the newly grown foliage and holds out her hand, which I take eagerly, ready to curl up in a ball and sleep for a week. I rise, but my knees buckle, causing me to slump back to the ground.

"Sorry," I pant. "I didn't realize how much it took out of me."

With a grunt as her only response, she collects me into her arms. Her tattoo quickly slithers across us, gathering us together, until we're back in our—my room. Venus quickly, but gently, places me on the bed and heads to the door without a word.

I want to stop her, to ask her to stay, to tell her how much I need her, but exhaustion weighs me down, stopping my mouth from forming the words.

My eyes are closed before she exits the room.

Chapter Thirty-Six
Vivian

The next few days pass in a blur. I'm either training physically or rebuilding my forest. At the end of each day, I'm exhausted, and sleep deeply until I drag myself through it all over again.

My magic and I have started talking to one another, which I can tell unnerves everyone, especially when I'm caught whispering to myself. It isn't all the time—for the most part, it leaves me to command it how I see fit without any input. But at night, we whisper to one another, discussing our plans, our fears, our dreams. It's like having someone else living in my body.

I feel like I should be concerned by it, but honestly, I'm not; it feels like the final puzzle piece I was missing has finally been found. Trusting my magic again may seem naïve, given how it's clearly acted out of its own self-interest most of the time, but I find myself *wanting* to trust it.

I tell my magic about my worries about being able to kill Phanes, and it replies that I need to give Venus my soul.

The only thing I don't ask is if I'll cease to exist if Phanes dies.

Venus assists with my training, but we aren't spending much quality time together. She's quiet except for when she's instructing me on how to position my feet or how to best attack. Whenever I try to talk to her, she simply makes up an excuse and leaves me alone. I can tell she isn't completely over what I said to her in front of her council.

My magic's words bounce around in my head: *Give your soul to the Dark Lady. Lure Phanes into the dark and kill him. We will work together.*

For the past ten years, my life has revolved around keeping my soul for myself...but now that I know the truth, what's really stopping me from giving Venus my soul?

Butterflies flutter in my stomach as I think it over, eating in the dining room alongside Steve. Venus hasn't joined me for any meals.

"I should just do it, then, shouldn't I?" I muse to Steve, who is too busy with his sausage links to really listen. "Since it's a bigger threat to keep my soul rather than give it to her, I shouldn't be stupid and short-sighted." I sigh before spearing a piece of cantaloupe with my fork, lifting it to my mouth, and chewing slowly. "And," I continue, my words muffled around my food, "if giving my soul to Venus is the best way to, like, level up my magic, then I need to not be a baby and just do it. Besides…" I pause, trying to say the words. "I love her."

I look over at Steve, who didn't hear a word I just said. Swallowing the food in my mouth, I clear my throat, and he turns his head to lock eyes with me. "You're a terrible listener," I complain.

He meows in response.

Sighing, I push back from the table, a newfound determination coursing through me. I'm giving my soul to Venus, dammit.

I make quick work of the walk from the dining room to the room Venus has been staying in. I'm not even sure if she's here, but I don't bother to knock before I push the door open. Stepping in and doing a visual sweep of the space, I spot Venus sitting on the edge of her bed, wings and shadows both out, head dropped down, shoulders curved inwards.

A fallen angel.

It stops me dead in my tracks.

"Venus?"

She doesn't look up. Instead, her shoulders curl more and her shadows dart around her, trying to shield her from me.

Approaching hesitantly, I hold a hand out for her shadows to know I'm not a threat and to let me through. A few circle my wrist and travel up my arm before parting.

"Venus, what is it?" I ask, alarmed and confused.

Then she shudders and looks up at me.

Tears pool in her onyx eyes.

"What happened? Why are you crying?" A million possible scenarios flicker through my mind, unsure of what would cause her to cry. I cup her face and search her expression. "What happened?" I repeat more urgently.

"I'm so tired, Vivian."

Her words ring through me, an understanding of what she means feeling so familiar, it's as if I said the words myself.

"I am too," I reply hoarsely.

A tear glides down her golden cheek, and I lean forward to kiss it away.

"I wish it was just us—no Phanes, no magic, just...us," she admits softly.

"I know." My heart aches because that's what I want too. It's *all* I want. I suck in a breath before I press my lips to hers. I want to show her that I understand—not just what she's saying, but that I understand *her*. I understand her fear, her anger, her sadness. I have and feel it all myself.

My entire world explodes behind my eyes, my body lighting up in a way I've forgotten but am desperate to hold onto. Her lips are soft and warm against mine, and I melt into the kiss.

She kisses me back greedily, hungry to share in this grief of accepting our potential fates while mourning a life we want. My fingers slip into her silky hair, tugging at the strands to tilt her head back, positioning her the way I want. Her arms wind around my waist, pulling me flush against her. Her tongue lightly skirts along my bottom lip, asking for entrance. With a little whimper from me, I open, letting her tongue explore and dance with my own.

She groans into my mouth and I swallow the sound, the need to swallow every noise that comes from her nearly overwhelming me.

I missed this. I missed her. I never thought I could have this again.

Too soon, she pulls back. I open my eyes and see all my arousal mirrored in Venus's gaze. "Oh how I have longed to do that," she admits gruffly.

A laugh bubbles out of me, and I lean in and kiss her again. She quickly reciprocates, her hand moving to hold the nape of my neck, keeping me in place.

"This isn't what I planned to do when I walked in," I admit as I break the kiss, my lips lightly skimming hers.

"And what was it you were planning?" she asks, her voice low, her breath warming my skin.

"I was coming here to give you my soul."

Venus rears back, dropping her hand, cutting off all contact as she eyes me with alarm.

"What?" I ask, laughing slightly at how concerned she looks. "I'm sure it's a shock, but—"

"Why are you giving it to me?"

Her question makes me pause in confusion. "My magic told me I should, and I don't see a reason why I shouldn't." I furrow my brows. "Does it matter?"

She's staring at me, an unreadable expression on her face. "Yes, it matters."

I can't help the incredulous chuckle that slips past my lips. "Uh, since when?"

Her dark eyes are guarded; her shadows slither around protectively. "It just does."

I blink. "Are you being serious right now? You've desperately hunted my soul for a decade, tried tricking me out of it, and *now* you decide you don't like the reason I'm giving it to you?"

"Yes." Her tone is firm.

I'm at a loss for words. It feels like my mind is unable to process what she's telling me. "So...you don't want my soul?"

"I don't."

Chapter Thirty-Seven
Venus

It feels like everything is happening too quickly. Vivian is running full steam ahead after speaking with her magic. Now that she has this newfound purpose, she's relentless; she's either training with me or near me, or she's mumbling to her magic. She briefly told me what she and her magic discussed a few days ago when they finally reconnected, and it left my stomach feeling sour.

What will happen to Vivian once her magic takes over? Will she continue living or will she die?

Meanwhile, Phanes is breathing down our necks, just waiting for the perfect time to attack with his new god and whatever other creatures he's concocted.

It's making my head spin; I'm losing my grip on the reins I've held tightly my entire existence.

Now, Vivian is telling me she wants to give me her soul because her magic decided that's what she should do.

I want her to give me her soul because *she* wants to, because *she* has chosen to. Because she has chosen *me*.

She's staring at me with a look of pure bewilderment. "You're unbelievable."

I don't say anything for fear of my unchecked emotions getting the better of me. I try to tamp them down, to shove them into a tiny box in the back of my mind.

She continues, "Venus, what the fuck? Don't you want to defeat your father? You told me I could get my revenge," she growls, her face shifting from incredulous to irritated. "And when we're finally getting somewhere, you don't want to do the *one thing* you've been hounding me for?"

Swallowing the emotions working to lodge in my throat, I tell her, "Your reasoning isn't good enough."

Her mouth gapes. "Is that why you've been avoiding me? Because you decided you didn't want my soul? I thought it was because you hadn't forgiven me for saying you were like your father."

I flinch before I can control my reaction. Of course, Vivian caught it, her eyes widening as she observes me. "I truly didn't mean it," she says softly.

"I know."

Tentatively, she reaches her hands up to brush her fingertips across my cheeks. "I wouldn't give you my soul if I thought you were like him, Venus."

For some reason, it makes my breath catch to hear her say this. I fight the urge to hide, to throw something back at her that will hurt her the way she hurt me.

I don't want to hurt her.

So I suck it up and say, "I want you to give me your soul because you want to—not because it will defeat Phanes or help your magic or any of that. I want your soul because that is what *you* want." Vivian lightly caresses my skin again. I shut my eyes and blurt out the rest. "I want you to give me your soul because you choose to. I'm trying to allow you space to make your own choices."

"My life has never been about my own choices, Venus."

I squeeze my eyes shut harder at how horrible that makes me feel. "I want you to give me your soul because you love me."

There it is.

I open my eyes to find Vivian staring at me, still as a statue. Her scent doesn't show any fear or anger—it's just neutral.

I rush to get the rest out. "You don't have to love me as much as I love you, but I want it to be done out of love. I don't think I can take another thing from you."

"You love me?" Her voice is so small.

I nod, unable to speak anymore.

Her eyes turn glassy with tears, making me panic. For all that is unholy, what have I done?

"I'm sorry," I murmur, taking Vivian's hands from my face and holding them in my own. "I didn't mean to upset you, I—"

"You're such an idiot, Venus."

My brows narrow. "Excuse me?"

She shakes her head, a tear slipping free. "Of course, I love you. I think I've loved you for a while now."

Before I can detangle her words and her emotional response, she slams her lips onto mine. The taste of salt reaches my tongue as her tears cascade down her cheeks. Her mouth moves against mine with a sense of urgency, with ferocity, that I can't help but lose myself to. Her tongue darts out to caress my bottom lip, asking for entrance. Groaning into her mouth, my tongue dances with hers to a melody only we have heard. This is not a kiss of claiming, but of love, of understanding, of knitting ourselves back together.

Her hands leave mine and tangle in my hair, pulling lightly at the scalp, causing a delicious burn. I reach out and grip her waist, pulling her against me so there's no space between us.

She pulls back slightly, breathing ragged, as she asks, "So when do you take it?"

What?

Oh, her soul.

I lean forward and gently nip her bottom lip. "Whenever you'd like," I say once I release her.

Her eyes are hooded as she peers down at me. "I want us to do something first."

Chapter Thirty-Eight
Vivian

I'm not going to let my trauma stop me from having what I want. And Venus is what I want.

Feeling pleasure felt tainted after Phanes forced me in his castle. It felt like my body's response was no longer mine—but if I'm going to potentially yield myself for my magic, then I want what little time I have left to be spent enjoying it.

"I need you to take me," I tell Venus.

"Take you where?" she asks, not understanding.

My cheeks heat, but I stand firm. "I need you to *take* me."

It takes her a moment to understand what I'm saying, or maybe my scent has made my words make sense, because her midnight eyes widen. "Take you how?"

I clear my throat, not letting myself chicken out. "Take me however you want to. Chase me. Fight to keep me down. Restrain me. Use me."

"I don't want to frighten you." Her voice sounds strained.

I shake my head. "You could never frighten me. I want his hands off me and I want my mind to replace his with yours. I want *us* to take back my pleasure—together. I need to feel out of control, and you'll make me feel safe when I let go. Does that make sense?"

Her eyes soften. "Yes. More than you know."

"I need this," I whisper, my breath shuddering through me.

"What if it becomes too much?"

"We can use a safeword," I offer. "Something simple, like 'red' when we want it to stop."

"Do you swear to use it?" she asks quietly.

I hesitate. I know I should, but the thought of having any control whatsoever doesn't comfort me, only because I know Venus knows me and knows what I'll need.

But I nod.

Venus transforms before my very eyes. Her wings flare out menacingly, her shadows now darting around her, a few slipping under the door, I assume to tell everyone to clear the fuck out. A slow, evil grin spreads across her mouth as she reaches out, too quickly for me to react, and grabs me by the throat. She gently places her thumb under my chin, tilting my face up at an uncomfortable angle.

"Then you better run."

Once her hand releases my neck, I don't think twice before I spin around and haul ass out of the room. I burst into the hallway, nearly slamming into the opposite wall with the inertia.

I push myself to keep moving, to not look behind me.

I can feel her shadows slither along the floor but not getting too close. Toying with me.

Hooking a right, I scramble down the next hallway, and then the next, and one after that. I'm not sure where I'm going, but it doesn't matter. My breath saws in and out of me, my legs are on fire, but I don't stop.

Just when I think I've outrun her, a shadow wraps around my ankle and knocks me to the ground. The breath in my lungs whooshes out as I hit the floor. I don't have time to react before another shadow wraps around my body, then another, then another, until they're stretching me spread-eagle in the middle of the castle hall.

Tugging at them, I test their restraint, but they aren't letting go of me. Not until Venus wants me released.

More shadows come to loosen my clothes, leaving my skin bared to the draft flowing through the hallway. I shiver, my back against the cold floor, silently hoping no one finds themselves needing to walk in this direction.

Then I hear her. Those ass-kicking boots.

She strolls towards me, unhurried. Her wings rustle as she stops in front of me.

Looking down her nose at me, she shakes her head in faux disappointment. "You couldn't even make it that far," she scolds. "Were you even trying?"

Irritation flares inside me and I squirm against the hold.

She chuckles, the sound of it skittering across my bones. "Of course you weren't really trying. You're just a little slut who wants it so badly, aren't you?"

Unholy shit. Hearing such filth from Venus's lips makes me pant with need.

Venus lowers herself to her knees between my spread legs and lightly skates her fingers along my inner thighs. My pussy clenches around nothing, desperate to be filled. When her fingers finally part me, she croons, "Already wet. See, I knew you weren't trying to flee."

She grips my thighs tightly, her fingers pressing hard into my skin as she flattens herself on the ground, her mouth just hovering over me. "Say please," she commands.

"Please," I whisper hoarsely.

"Again. Beg me for it."

"Please, Venus, please, pl—"

Her tongue parts me slowly, lapping at my show of arousal. I try to gyrate my hips, but her shadows keep me in place. I'm completely at her mercy.

"Venus," I whine. "I need more."

She doesn't listen; her tongue caresses me slowly, dragging my pleasure out of me.

Giving my control over to her, to the only being I will ever trust completely, is what I wanted.

Her tongue flits over my clit and I can't stop the whimpers that escape me. She drags her tongue from my ass up to my clit and back again, soaking me. Her strong hands grip my thighs, holding me open, bared to her.

The feel of his hands flashes through my mind. Panic starts to creep up my spine. Gasping, I fight to free myself from the shadows holding me down.

Images of him touching me, his greedy eyes devouring every inch of my exposed body.

"No, no—" All the pleasure of Venus's touch leaves me and I'm left with dread, of the feel of his wandering hands—

"Where are you, Vivian?" Venus asks me.

I look down and see her staring up at me from between my legs. It's not him, I remind myself. "Where are you?" she asks again.

"I'm with you," I gasp out.

"Good," she praises as she lightly strokes the inside of my thighs. "Keep going."

Gritting my teeth against the wave of panic, I continue, "I'm in a hallway, on the floor."

She lowers her mouth to me, her eyes still locked on mine.

"And?" she says against me, causing a shiver to curl up my spine.

"And you're using me, just like I asked you to."

She hums, her tongue moving in slow, languid circles against my core. Pleasure starts to roll through me again, dragging a gasp from my lips.

"And?" she prods again, keeping me firmly rooted in my body.

"I'm in Hell. I'm home."

Chuckling, she slips the tip of her finger into my center and I immediately clamp down on her. I close my eyes at the sensation of her, of the gentle caressing her shadows are doing, even as they hold me tight.

"Eyes on me, Vivian."

I snap my eyes open. The sight of her makes me moan. Her finger slides in and out easily, creating a rhythm that builds and builds until I think I'll never survive it.

"Tell me again where you are," she demands.

"I'm with you," I sputter out, watching her devour me, taking my pleasure to new heights. "I'm home. I'm with you and I'm home."

She adds another finger and fucks me in earnest as I keep repeating my words.

I'm with you. I'm home.

Venus moans as she laps at me, her midnight eyes hooded with pleasure. Seeing her enjoy this almost as much as I do makes arousal spread through me like wildfire.

"Are you going to give me what I want, Vivian?"

I gasp, feeling release gather in my body, but I can't make it that easy for her. With a wicked grin, I pant out, "Of course not."

She growls and lightly sucks my clit into her mouth. I buck my hips as stars dance in my vision.

Swirling her tongue over my clit again and again, fingers pumping into me, shadows keeping me spread, I break. I cry out, my back arching, pulling against the shadows that give me no leeway. Pleasure continues to roll through me, leaving me breathless, unable to stop. Tears stream down my face as she works me through it, never giving me reprieve.

When I've crested and come down, my body is limp—I can barely hold my head up to look at her. The tears don't stop, but they're silent now. They aren't tears of sadness—they're tears of release. Of relief.

Of feeling safe for the first time in a very long time.

Venus pulls herself out of me and prowls up my body, her shadows still keeping me pinned to the cold floor.

She latches her mouth onto mine, letting me taste myself on her lips. I groan into her mouth, our tongues dancing with each other's. When she finally breaks the kiss, she holds herself above me, a devious smile on her beautifully talented lips.

"Oh, Vivian, you can't possibly be this tired after just one. We're just getting started."

Ever since Venus took me, I feel like something inside of me has healed. There's no longer a festering wound growing larger every moment, but now, the wound is beginning to knit itself back together.

Venus and I have been going at it like bunnies ever since. Letting her take control of me still feels safer than gentle, loving sex. When she decided to switch it up this morning, caressing my skin softly as she descended my body, panic overtook me and I blurted out my safeword. Venus stopped immediately, gathering me up in her arms as I sobbed into her chest.

I feel closer to her than ever.

What's concerning is that she hasn't taken my soul.

I brought it up over breakfast this morning, asking her when we would complete the ceremony, but she rebuffed me, claiming there's too much to do before she can take it.

She's stalling, my magic hisses to me as I make my way down the hallway, heading towards the High Priestesses' workroom.

"But why?" I whisper. "All she's wanted is my soul."

I know. Perhaps she is afraid of what having your soul might mean.

"Which is?"

It will set everything into motion. Once your soul is hers, it will be time to find the pretender.

"We were already planning to kill Phanes," I point out.

The Dark Lady is scared. For you.

I hum, considering my magic's words as I reach the High Priestesses' workroom.

There's one other person I need to make amends with.

I stand outside the door, readying myself to knock, when the door slowly swings open on its own.

Guess my presence was already known.

Stepping into the room, I find Marie tidying her shelves of pickled dead things. She doesn't turn to me, clearly ignoring me.

I clear my throat and say, "I was hoping to speak with you."

"So speak," she responds curtly.

Swallowing my nerves, I step further into the room. Marie keeps her back to me as I say, "I am truly sorry for tricking you into providing me with information. I shouldn't have done that."

Marie's shoulders stiffen and she replies, "You lied. You made me think the Dark Lady was treating you unfairly."

"I know," I say, shame burrowing into my stomach. "I shouldn't have done that, either."

She looks over her shoulder and, if looks could kill, I would be struck dead. "You let me believe we were similar."

I grimace. "I'm sorry."

She turns back around and continues dusting her jars. I take that as a dismissal, slumping my shoulders and shuffling towards the door, when her airy voice travels to my ears. "My last lover, while I was alive, is the reason for my death."

I halt, unease spreading throughout my body. Turning back around, I whisper, "What happened?"

"He told everyone I was a witch," she replies as she continues dusting. "Granted, I *was* a witch, and he was not, but I was young and in love. We were mere children, you see, so lovesick that we were to get married after a few short months of knowing one another."

She turns to face me, her icy eyes boring into mine. "My mother warned me to hide my magic from him—this was at the height of witch hunts in the area, resulting in the deaths of both witches and non-witches alike, but I didn't listen. The night before our wedding, I showed him." She holds her hand out towards me, palm up, and fire erupts from her fingertips. Closing her hand, the flames go out. She drops her arm and continues. "I showed him my fire and he was horrified. I knew it was foolish, but I was foolish in love. I believed he would love me, regardless of my magic—maybe even love me more because of it. But he didn't. He panicked when he saw my fire and ran, telling the townsfolk, and they gathered with pitchforks and torches. I tried to run, to escape, but they sent hounds after me. I was dragged back, had rocks tied to my ankles, and was thrown into the river. What could my budding fire magic do against that?"

My stomach churns. "Did anyone try to save you? Your mother? The Dark Lady?"

She laughs, but it's hollow. "My mother had warned me and saw this as a fitting outcome. As for the Dark Lady..." She trails off. "She does not concern herself with the realm of the living—this new fascination only began with you.

Once I arrived here, she offered me a place on her esteemed council, recognizing something in me." She looks down at her hands for a moment, then back at me. "I will not begrudge her for not rescuing me from my own idiocy. She has given me a role I could not have imagined for myself and is always fair."

"I'm sorry if I got you in trouble with her," I reply.

She shakes her head. "She did not punish me for your stunt; she knew you ultimately acted alone."

I let out a relieved breath at that.

Some of her hair slips free of its knot at the base of her neck as she leans her head back, looking up at the ceiling. "I am still angry with you," she admits.

"I get it," I say. "You don't have to accept my apology. I just wanted you to know."

She looks at me, and the ice in her gaze has somewhat melted. "But I am happy that you apologized."

One corner of my mouth tilts. "Good."

She cocks her head, seeming to consider something for a moment, but keeps silent. She doesn't say anything as she turns around, going back to her task of dusting.

Noted.

I clear my throat awkwardly and say, "See ya," and leave the room—nearly walking face-first into Luke. His large hands grip both my forearms as he stops me from careering into him and immediately lets go once I've steadied myself. He dips his head in greeting.

I raise my brows. "What are you doing here?"

"I have business to attend to with the High Priestesses," he replies.

"Oh. Well, only Marie is in there," I tell him.

"That's fine," he responds a bit awkwardly.

I purse my lips as I scrutinize him. Luke is a formidable being, that can't be denied; his red skin is the shade of spilled blood, his horns could rip my stomach open, and his pitless eyes make it hard to know where he's looking. "So you, one of the most powerful archdemons in the realm, is going to sit and wait for the other Priestesses to arrive? Don't you have more important things to do?"

He grunts in response.

I hum dramatically. "I thought you weren't into witches?" I tease, recalling one of our first conversations.

"Careful, Lady Vivian. You might be under the protection of the Dark Lady, but I have no qualms with tossing you right out the window."

I snort. "You wouldn't have the balls," I say with a saccharine smile. "I warmed her up for you, don't worry." Flipping my hair over my shoulder, I turn and walk down the hall, Luke's half-ass snarl trailing behind me.

Chapter Thirty-Nine
Venus

All I want to do is touch her.

The need overrides my mind and makes me feel like a feral animal, needing to grab her, hold her close, and destroy anyone who dares to look at her for more than a moment.

I once told her patience isn't my strong suit, but my fear of frightening her, of pushing her too hard before she's ready, is what keeps me from acting on my base impulses.

My impulses will need to wait.

Vivian and I sit at my desk, discussing what her magic told her.

"My magic said to lure him out," she shares, her brows bunched in thought. "I'm not quite sure how, though."

"It didn't tell you how to?"

She shakes her head. "Not exactly. Just to lure him out into the dark. My magic says handing over my soul will set everything in motion. I'm assuming we'll have to come face-to-face with him after you get my soul."

I hate that idea. The last thing I want is to have Vivian and Phanes face each other on the battlefield.

"Any other nuggets of wisdom?" I sneer.

Vivian tsks. "Don't be like that."

"I don't like this. I don't like how we're dropping everything to do whatever your magic says."

She holds out her hands. "What else can we do? It's not like we have a lot of options."

"Of course, we do," I counter. "We go back to existing the way we did before—him in his realm, us in ours. We leave each other alone, and you stay safely in Hell."

"Venus." Her tone is almost...pitiful. "We can't do that. We have to end this."

I know we do. Leaving my father to create even more gods and corrupting the world again cannot continue. It makes me want to vomit. I want to strangle my father until the light leaves his eyes. But most of all, I want Vivian, safe and guarded.

Loosing a breath, I murmur, "I don't like listening to your magic. It's always acted out of self-interest."

"I know," she sighs. "You just have to suck it up." She straightens in her chair. "We should plan for an attack. How did you do it last time?"

"Last time, we lost," I remind her. Images of the final battle threaten to drag me back into the recesses of my mind.

"Well, we'll need soldiers—I'm assuming demon ones. Doesn't the forest have beasts?"

Her question pulls me from my memories. "It does," I answer slowly.

"Can they fight? If we're up against Phanes and this new god, maybe they can help us?"

I shake my head. "They despise me."

She blinks. "Really? Why?"

"Because of a decision made long ago," I sigh. She opens her mouth to press me, but I shake my head again. I definitely don't want to rehash that right now.

She shrugs. "Okay, well, let's just focus on the demons then."

As Vivian continues brainstorming, her words flowing a mile a minute, I fall into my own worries.

How can I survive going through this again? Fighting Phanes and losing Lilith nearly destroyed me; doing it all over again, but with the potential of losing Vivian, makes it seem impossible.

I've been putting off taking Vivian's soul for this exact reason. Much as I want it, crave it, need to have it...it's not worth the Hell it is going to unleash.

Vivian continues animatedly, gesticulating with her hands, and I consider how to pump the brakes on this. I want her to be prepared, but not prepared enough that she runs headfirst into danger. Keeping up with her training should do it; maybe teaching her how to use her magic in battle would be beneficial. Maybe that will keep her busy enough so that she won't inquire about me taking her soul—at least for a while.

"Venus, are you even listening to me?"

I snap back to myself at the sound of my name. Vivian is staring me down, her arms crossed, her face showing her annoyance. I give her a feline grin. "Of course I was, my love."

"Then what was the last thing I said?"

She's got me there. I roll my eyes. "Okay, fine, I wasn't listening."

She huffs in annoyance. "That's exactly what the captain of the yacht I was partying on a few summers ago did wrong; he didn't listen to me when I told him those guys had smuggled drugs onboard..."

Chapter Forty
Vivian

Venus and I stand in the clearing of the monolith, facing each other. A gentle breeze lifts the silky strands of her hair, and her face is calm but determined.

"You have been working hard to restore the forest." Her voice booms through the open field. "But if you are to kill a god, you must be prepared in more ways than one."

I shift my weight from one foot to the other nervously. "How?"

She rolls her shoulders back. "The only witch I met with your magic was Lilith, so I only know how the magic manifested in her. She could create towering mountains or deep fissures in the earth. I believe you can do the same. Maybe even more."

My magic flips in me, ready to fight. A feeling of blood-thirstiness rolls through me, an intense desire to take back what I lost.

Venus cocks her head to the side. "Your magic wants this."

I'm not sure how she can tell that, but she's right.

Venus continues, "You're thinking about it too much. Just picture what you want your magic to do. Try to manipulate the earth around us to disarm me."

I snort dismissively as my eyes zero in on her. "I don't want to hurt you." At least not right this moment.

A smirk graces her full lips, irking me already. "No? Come now, Vivian, I know you have a fury in you that could destroy the entire world."

Anger flares in me, searing hot, catching me off guard and blinding me from my hesitation and nerves. My eyes narrow and I picture it—

A root from a tree to my left spears through the air, racing towards Venus. She snaps her arm out, and the root snakes around it. Venus flexes and grips the root in her hand, holding it steady as it tries to drag her into the forest. Her eyes never leave mine.

The root continues to struggle, but Venus isn't even breaking a sweat, her feet planted firmly, an arrogant smile on her face. "Is that it?" she goads.

I bare my teeth and picture a flood of roots wrapping around her, keeping her immobile. As soon as I think it, they burst from the ground and shoot towards her from all different directions.

Only to be swatted away with the flick of her free wrist.

They keep coming, one after the other, trying to grab her, but it's no use—she simply bats them away like pesky flies. She tugs on the root still firmly wrapped around her wrist, causing the entire tree to groan as if she's ripping it apart.

"Don't hurt them," I snarl, losing myself to my anger, to my magic's desire for vengeance.

Venus promptly releases the root, but her easy grin makes me see red. "I truly expected more," she chides. "Perhaps your magic isn't as strong—"

Venus insulting my magic riles me up, and she knows it. A scream passes my lips as I feel myself gather my magic within me and burrow it into the earth, picturing the ground rising to capture her. My magic gleefully races from me, shifting and shaping the flat surface into a hill of rock, reaching for Venus.

She rolls to the side to get out of the way, but I follow her relentlessly, chasing after her as she continues to dodge. Small hills break through the grass with thunderous booms. Sweat beads form on my forehead as I channel my magic to go harder, faster, to show no mercy. Venus runs towards me and flaps her wings, looking for escape.

That won't do. My hand raises towards her, and the rocky earth rises to greet her.

It slams into her from all angles, surprising her, giving her no time to react. It constricts around her like a snake, molding to her body, even as she struggles to break free.

The more I channel my magic, the easier it becomes to use. A mere thought from me, and it does my bidding.

With my hand still raised, I close my fist slowly and the grasp on Venus tightens and guides her over to me until we are at eye level.

It would be easy to crush her.

Her golden skin is flushed from exertion, her midnight eyes wild as she continues struggling.

I let out a triumphant chuckle. She should know her struggles are pointless.

I feel invincible, like there is nothing that can stop me. In a blink, I could crush her with almost no effort at all.

Flashes of Phanes hurting me dart past—his eyes clouding as he ripped me apart from the inside out, ignoring my pleas for him to stop, for the pain to stop.

A snarl rips from my throat as I zero in on the threat I have in my grasp.

Destroy it, I think. Destroy everything he created.

"You've made your point, Vivian," Venus gasps, and I blink, the anger leaving me immediately. I release my fist and drop my arm, the earth depositing Venus on the ground carelessly as it returns to its natural state.

"Shit," I breathe as I rush to Venus, who is sprawled face-first on the grass, coughs wracking her chest as she pushes herself onto her back. "Venus, I'm so sorry—"

A breathless laugh passes her lips and she pants. "That was truly magnificent."

I blink at her. Did I squeeze her too tightly and accidentally scramble her brain?

Kneeling beside her, I watch her take deep breaths, trying to regulate after what I did. "I could've killed you," I groan, shocked and horrified at how I simply lost control, too focused on destroying a perceived threat to think clearly.

She huffs out a laugh. "Good. That means you won't hesitate to rip him limb from limb."

I shake my head incredulously. "You're not right in the head," I tell her.

Her eyes shine as she gives me a serpentine grin, causing my blood to heat. Maybe I'm not right in the head either.

"How did it feel to use your magic this way?" she inquires, her breathing evening out.

I chew on my bottom lip as I consider it. "It felt...good," I admit, "like almost as natural as breathing. But if I think about it, it was also terrifying—I lost myself in my anger, and simply...reacted. I didn't even see *you* anymore. All I saw was a threat that I needed to eliminate."

Venus's eyes hold no judgment. "Your anger will push you to make decisions you might not make otherwise—if you are to meet Phanes on the battlefield, you cannot afford to hesitate. Let your anger guide you during those moments. Let it protect you."

Her words nearly take my breath away. Isn't that what I wanted? To channel my anger into something useful?

My magic is settled within me, no signs of stepping forward for the time being, but I know it agrees with me.

Venus sits up, her face nearly touching mine as she leans forward. "We will keep practicing," she vows. "Until we're ready. Have you gotten your magic out of your system for today?"

I nod. "I'm ready. I think I need a bath."

She sniffs dramatically and nods.

I roll my eyes. "Well, I guess I won't be inviting you into my bath then," I joke.

She stills.

I grow serious as I say, "It's the last thing I'd like to rewrite."

Venus doesn't say anything in response—she simply leans forward and presses a kiss to my forehead, her snake tattoo slithering across our skin, transporting us back home.

I'm beyond nervous.

I know I need to do this—for her and myself. To replace my horrible memory of him with moments of her.

But it doesn't calm my nerves.

Once her tattoo has left my skin, I step away from her, needing a bit of space to think. I fight the urge to gulp down air and throw up all over the floor. I breathe in for four, out for four. In for four, out for four. Again and again, until I feel the panic subside, reducing itself into manageable anxiety. Letting my body feel how it wants to feel and letting it pass without judgment.

Venus doesn't approach, but she and her shadows assess me nervously. One shadow comes and swirls around my wrist in a show of comfort.

"I'm okay," I tell them. "Just overwhelmed, I guess."

"We don't have to do this," she urges.

"No, I know." I shake my head. "I want to, I do. My body is just reacting."

Hesitantly, Venus steps closer until our chests are pressed together. She smooths my hair back as her shadows caress my arms and my legs, comforting me. Her eyes hold mine, nothing but understanding swirling in them; no judgment, no pressure to move things along.

It infuses me with confidence. "I'm ready."

She nods and steps back, gesturing to the bathing room. "After you."

I stride into the other room, Venus on my heels. I refuse to let a bathtub break me down. I am not these things that have happened to me—I can conquer my own fears.

Without turning around, I step up to the tub and begin removing my clothes, shucking them onto the floor. Venus's magic turns the water on, and I dip my fingers in the pooling tub, testing the water temperature.

With one last deep breath, I step in and lower myself, letting the water swallow my feet, my legs, my pelvis, my stomach, my chest, as I sink. Pressing my back against the tub, I raise my eyes to Venus, fighting to not let my horrible memories drag me under.

Venus removes her own clothing and spirits her wings and shadows away.

It's just her and me. As it always has been, and how it always should be.

Without saying a word, she steps into the large tub and prowls into the water, pressing her back against the opposite side of the porcelain. The water ebbs and flows as we disturb it, but eventually, it settles against our bare skin.

I can feel my anxiety slithering its way up my body, my muscles locking, fear of being touched against my will coming to the forefront of my mind.

"I'm with you," I tell her, even though she didn't ask like she usually does.

She nods approvingly. "That's right. You're with me. And we shall never be apart again."

I grunt affirmatively, noting each part of my body and working to relax it, starting at my feet, my legs, my stomach and chest, reaching my arms and up my neck.

I work to turn my attention to Venus. The ends of her onyx hair disappear under the water, covering her breasts. Her legs are bent, with her kneecaps breeching the water, as if she's trying to avoid touching me.

I can do this. I want to do this.

Letting myself relax in the water, my eyes skate over the beautiful being across from me. "I'm okay," I tell her.

Her sharp features don't soften, making it clear she doesn't believe me. My eyes travel from her intense stare, down her nose, to her full lips. The column of her throat as she swallows. Her clavicle that juts out slightly, connecting to her powerful arms.

She's mesmerizing. A siren calling out to me.

I blurt out, "You are so beautiful." She clears her throat, seeming to feel uncomfortable with my words. "It's true,"

I say. "Sometimes, I'm struck with how beautiful you are, how addictive it is to simply look at you."

She rises slightly and places her elbows against the lip of the tub behind her. My eyes can't help but dip to her breasts as they leave the water, her smooth skin and pert nipples just asking for me to caress them.

Licking my lips, I say to her, "Don't move. Don't touch me at all, unless I say you can."

She freezes, her eyes wide in anticipation.

Arousal begins to heat my skin. I'm wound tight enough to snap. Shifting, I glide myself over her body until I'm straddling her.

"I have missed your touch," she says to me. All I do is nod—it requires no words. I have missed her touch, her closeness, and the noises she makes.

I won't let this be taken from me. Not when it comes to Venus.

I press myself against her, our chests lightly caressing each other, eliciting a gasp from her.

I smile, lifting my hands and slowly moving them down her neck, across her collarbones, down her muscular arms. I peel away, enough to work my hands down her gorgeous chest, lightly running my fingertips across her nipples. She shivers under my touch.

It's kindling for the fire building inside of me.

I continue to run my thumbs over her nipples, feeling them pebble under my touch. Her hips tilt forward, seeking me out. Chuckling, I move to cup her breasts, feeling their heavy weight in my palms. "I love these," I murmur, transfixed by the goosebumps rising over her skin as I touch her.

"Vivian," she groans. Her hips shift again. "I need—" Her words cut off as I release her breasts and trail my fingers down her stomach, dipping under the water to her center. We both suck in a breath as my fingers explore her. She stretches her arms out to grip the bathtub, her knuckles turning white.

"I can tell how wet you are, even in the water," I comment, swirling my finger through her arousal before moving up to her clit. She gasps and her hips jerk. I place my other hand against her stomach to still her.

We lock eyes and electricity sparks between us. Her eyes are hooded, her mouth slightly open as she whimpers.

I circle her clit, working her up, until I move my finger down and push it inside of her. She moans as my finger enters her and slowly thrusts in and out. She wants to gyrate her hips, I can tell—but my other hand keeps her pinned in place.

"So perfect," I murmur, curling my finger in her. She throws her head back in ecstasy. I press the heel of my palm to her clit, hitting her in the best spots at the same time. "I know you want to touch me."

"Yes," she pants to the ceiling. It makes my breasts ache, seeing her spiral out of control all while not letting herself go out of fear she'll frighten me. "Please, Vivian. Please let me touch you."

My fingers move faster, in and out, working her to her climax. I swear she's gonna crack this tub with how hard she's gripping it.

"Vivian, *please*, I *need* to touch you. I need it more than I've needed anything—" Her pleas turn garbled as I work her higher and higher, the water sloshing around us.

I've never seen anything as marvelous as her.

"Come on my hand, Venus," I instruct, needing her release almost as much as she does. She clenches down on me immediately, her cries filling the bathroom. She locks my finger inside of her, and I let out a little whimper of my own.

It is single-handedly the sexiest thing I've ever seen.

She finally comes back down and goes limp, and I slowly remove myself from her.

"Beautiful," I breathe, simply awestruck by it, by her. Without thinking, I bring my mouth to hers, my desire roiling through me. She yields to me immediately, her mouth opening to let me in. Her tongue darts out to play with mine. We're a clash of tongues and teeth as we fight to merge into one, to be closer than physically possible.

"Touch me," I plead against her lips.

She doesn't need to be told twice. Her arms snake around my waist and she hugs me to her chest, our wet skin sliding together as we grab at each other like horny teenagers. I gasp into her mouth as one hand trails down my stomach while the other snakes down my back, both traveling to different destinations. Her fingers touch my clit and my ass at the same time, swirling around and around, teasing, taunting.

I've done ass play, like, twice in my life and it never interested me much. Until now.

"Venus," I gasp, rocking my hips back and forth, urging her to just do it, to put herself in me—

The sensation of her fingers entering both holes at the same time makes my body light up. A low moan escapes my lips, and Venus latches her mouth back onto me, swallowing the sound. I feel full, unable to think about anything besides the feeling of her inside me. My ass struggles to accommodate her but relaxes once she's past the initial opening.

"How does it feel?" she asks against my lips, her fingers pushing all the way in.

"It feels—ah—so...good, so full—" I pant, way past being coherent. Pleasure has taken over me and I grab at her, trying to find purchase before I tumble over the cliff of desire.

Slowly, so torturously slowly, she thrusts in and out of me, alternating so I'm always full.

"You're mine," she growls against my lips, moving her own lower to latch onto my neck. I cry out as her teeth sink into my skin, and I mewl as she releases me and licks to soothe the hurt.

"Yes," I agree breathily, ready to agree to anything, to say anything—

"Say it."

"I'm yours," I pant, beyond needy.

"No one will ever touch you again. No one will dare look at you. You are mine for eternity."

I let go, yielding control to her as she pumps her fingers into me, faster and faster, the pressure building—

Her name spills from my lips as I clamp down on her, my entire body contracting with the power of my orgasm. My mind goes blank. All I can do is feel how amazing this is, how right it is—

"Mine," Venus groans before capturing my mouth in a searing kiss, locking us together as I nearly leave my body.

Once I come down from the high, my body slumps against hers, completely exhausted. Her fingers slowly slide out of me, and I hiss at the soreness from behind.

Venus pulls back and inspects me anxiously. "Did I hurt you?"

I let out a tired chuckle and shake my head. "Next time, better lube," I say sleepily, my head resting on her shoulder, my eyes drooping closed.

Her arms wrap around me, and I feel myself being lifted. Instinctively, I wrap my legs around her waist as I hear the water slosh around from the disruption. Venus pads into the bedroom, not worrying about drying off, and climbs into the bed, still with me attached to her. I finally let go once my head hits the pillow, but Venus simply positions herself next to me, her warmth seeping into me as we press together.

I let out a long sigh, my body still high and relaxed from the realm-shattering orgasm, as I feel her press her chest against my own, her chin resting on the top of my head. I breathe in the scent of her wet skin, letting it soothe me to sleep.

Chapter Forty-One

Vivian

I check my roots in the mirror and frown. "Venus!" I shout, hoping she'll hear me from the bathroom.

She's through the door in seconds. "What is it?" she asks, looking concerned.

"I think I need to get my hair done," I announce.

She steps behind me, looking at me in the mirror, and tilts her head. "And why is that?"

I gape at her. "Do you not see my roots?"

She rolls her eyes. "I don't mind them."

"Oh, so you *do* notice them." I roll my eyes. "I don't care if you mind them. *I* do." I pivot to face her.

She looks down at my outfit and can't help but give a look of approval at my denim overalls with pink crop top underneath. I've been back to wearing my own clothes for a bit now, but Venus always seems happy to see what my ensemble is for the day.

Wearing my clothes again feels both familiar and for-eign. I find myself feeling randomly uncomfortable, suddenly too aware of myself.

Now, I try not to squirm in my skin. "Can you take me up to the living realm? Maybe back to town, just outside my former coven? There was a really cute salon there, and I'm still wearing my protective amulet. Just for a few hours," I plead. I know the risk of being in the realm of the living, but Phanes hasn't shown himself since he tried breaking through our wards.

Now that my magic and I have been working together, and I finally feel at peace with letting my fate play out the way it's supposed to, my anxiety has lessened dramatically. I know facing Phanes is inevitable, and I'm tired of wasting what little time I have being afraid.

She pretends to consider it, but I know she's just happy to see glimmers of the old me again. So she shrugs and takes my hand, and we're off.

Four hours later, I'm nearly prancing down the sidewalk next to Venus. I got the greatest stylist in the world who made me the perfect shade of blonde. I nearly cried.

Venus immediately picked up on my mood and wanted to capitalize on it, suggesting we stop and get our nails done while we were at it. It was the most shocking thing that has ever come out of her mouth.

Watching Venus get a manicure was the funniest thing I have ever seen. The poor nail technician couldn't do anything without Venus demanding to know what she was doing to her and why she was doing it. I made sure Venus tipped extra.

Now, with my bright red nails and my gorgeous locks, I strut confidently for the first time in a long time.

Maybe a bit too confident, as I nearly walk straight into a woman because I'm too busy looking at my manicure.

Venus, with her quick reflexes, grabs me and deposits me on the other side of her, putting herself between us.

"Oh, sorry about that!" I say, smiling. Until the woman locks eyes with mine.

"Vivian?" she asks.

I blink. "Yes. I'm sorry, do I know you?" I ask politely.

Venus nearly growls next to me.

The woman's eyes widen as she approaches me, her hands outstretched as if to touch me. "It's Kirsten. Remember? We grew up together."

I suck in a startled breath.

Kirsten was a witchling the same age as me. We were always forced together and spent most of our days learning next to one another. She was horrible to me, giving me nasty looks if I answered a question right or outright laughing if I answered it incorrectly. She mercilessly ridiculed me for spending time in the woods, sneering that I was more of a wild animal than a witch.

"Sorry, doesn't ring a bell," I say, my tone dripping with sweetness. I start to turn from her, but she grips my arm to stop me.

Venus does actually growl this time.

"I'm sorry," Kirsten says, dropping my arm but not cowering from Venus the way I expect. "It's just that I'm shocked to see you. You look"—her green eyes rove over me—"really great."

"Leaving the coven proved to be the best thing for me." I throw her a sarcastic smile. "I didn't have to deal with everyone else's judgments anymore."

She swallows nervously. "I'm not shocked to hear that," she admits.

"If you'll excuse us, we have much better things to do with our time," I say, flipping my hair over my shoulder.

"It's just—" She takes a step towards me, like she might reach for me again, but shoots a glance in Venus's direction and thinks better of it. "I just wanted to say I'm sorry." My shock at her words makes me pause. "I'm sorry for the way I treated you when we were younger. You know, I always was jealous of you."

I bark out an incredulous laugh. "Jealous of me? What could you have possibly been jealous of?"

"You had someone who loved you," she replies sadly. "It was clear to everyone that your aunt loved you unconditionally." She looks down at her shoes. "I never had anyone to love me like that."

I take a deep breath, my thoughts churning. Looking at her, I know she's telling the truth—while I had my aunt try to shield me from my mother, Kirsten clearly didn't have anyone.

"My aunt was wonderful," I reply.

She nods, her eyes rising to mine. "I'm sorry about her passing. I hope you and her will be reunited in Hell."

"How is the coven, after..." After Venus sent my mother's ass down to Hell's dungeons.

She laughs bitterly. "Same story, different day."

"What do you mean?" I ask, furrowing my brows.

She waves her hand dismissively. "Your mother is gone, but the other elders remain. They cannot let go of how things were, so they don't. The new matron is the same as your mother." She shrugs.

Knots form in my stomach.

"I was hoping you would come back and take over as matron," she admits sheepishly, "to show witchlings that they don't have to follow in their foremothers' footsteps. To change things for all of us."

"And why can't you do that yourself?" I snap, irritated at the assumption that it's my responsibility to fix this problem.

"You were always different. I just thought..." She shakes her head, her glossy brunette hair shifting with the movement. "Never mind." She looks back at me and attempts a smile. "It was lovely to see you looking so well, Vivian, even after all this time." Then she bows her head to Venus. "Your Grace." Kirsten gives us her back, walking down the quiet sidewalk.

"Insolent," Venus mutters.

I watch Kirsten until she disappears down the street, a lump forming in my throat. When I ran after my failed ceremony, I never considered how my actions might impact the others. My fellow witchlings were always nasty to me and were never really my friends. I hadn't stopped to think why—that they might not hate me for being different but resent me for it. For having someone who loved me. For having even the tiniest bit of space to think for myself, to *be* myself.

"You once told me I should lead my former coven," I say to Venus.

She wraps an arm around my shoulders and pulls me into her side, leading us in the opposite direction as the witch. "I remember."

"I don't know the first thing about being a leader."

"You readily agreed to assist me with Hell," she reminds me.

I shake my head. "Yes, but that's different. I meant, like, working behind the scenes, not being the new ruler entirely."

"You ran from me, making a choice that none have done before, and while most would consider what you did to be incredibly reckless and idiotic," she shoots me a faux irritated look, making me grin, "some might see it as an act of courage. A sign that the status quo needs to be changed."

I chew over her words as we continue down the sidewalk, passing cute storefronts. When I stop walking, Venus pauses and turns to me. I get up on my tiptoes and press a kiss to her cheek.

"What was that for?" she asks as I pull away.

"Just...for seeing me," I say, emotions threatening to bring me to tears. "For fighting for me to come back to myself. For not giving up on me."

Her onyx eyes soften as she nods. What she feels, what I feel, is almost beyond words at this point.

"Can you take me to my forest? I'd like to heal some more."

Her smile is so bright, it nearly brings me to my knees. "I would enjoy nothing more."

Scanning the empty sidewalk for unsuspecting people, she summons her wings.

"Okay, just fly carefully. I don't want to ruin my new—" My words are swallowed by my scream and Venus's answering laugh when she grabs me and shoots us into the sky.

Chapter Forty-Two
Venus

The days pass with no news of Phanes. No attempts to break through our wards, no sign of him at the forest Vivian is rebuilding, and no attack from this new god he might have created.

It makes both Vivian and myself uneasy.

He wouldn't simply give up, I considered one afternoon. *Especially if he feels he has lost. He will do anything to make sure he doesn't lose again.*

This only makes us want to work harder, to be as prepared as possible to finally end it, to end him. Vivian and I now go to the forest every day, strengthening her magic and reviving the woods bit by bit. Each time, it seems to take less energy to summon her magic and heal a wider area of forestry.

The wards Vivian erected still seem to hold. I visit them every day, checking in with the demons and witches stationed around the perimeter. They always seem to be on edge—from the magic of the wards, from my daily visits, or from being stuck with one another when they would rather not be. I tend to break up more fights than I care to.

I guess this is part of my role now.

Dipping through the bedroom window, I can't wait to close my eyes, just for a moment. Vivian is seated on the bed, a book in her lap, with her cat lounging next to her. She takes my breath away. Her blonde hair is tied back in a braid, and her skin is glowing in the candlelight. I want to devour her beautiful lips, and her hazel eyes capture mine just as her sweet scent playfully drifts over to me. She licks her lips as her gaze travels up and down my body at a glacial pace, seeming to drink me in.

Steve leaps from the bed, seemingly annoyed and wanting to be as far away as possible.

I snort. "What is his problem now?"

Vivian grins at me. "I think he can pick up on the sexual tension."

"I can too."

"You can scent it. There's a difference."

"I'm not sure why we're arguing about semantics when you're clearly in need," I point out.

"And what about you?" she argues. "Aren't you in need?"

My eyes widen at her question, causing a sinister smile to spread across her mouth.

"I want to try something different," she tells me, flipping her braid over her shoulder. "I miss taking charge, and I know you miss it too."

Desire ravages me, too quickly for me to control. "What I want is what you want."

She snorts. "You're worried about upsetting me."

"You made it clear what kind of sexual interactions work best for you, and I am more than happy to provide them."

Gliding off the bed, Vivian approaches me slowly, and I go still—even my shadows pause in anticipation. "You taking me the way you have is helping. It helps replace bad memories with good ones. But..." Her eyes skate down my body and up again. "I do miss seeing you at *my* mercy."

I shoot her a lazy grin, trying to hide my desperation. "If that is what you wish."

"You're being so respectful," she croons. "More respectful than I'm going to be with you."

With that, she steps back, making her way back to the bed. "I can read you like a book, Venus. I know you miss it. So I took the liberty of arranging a few things."

She's right. I do miss it. I've been too afraid of upsetting her to try anything different than what we've been doing. Besides, I do enjoy dominating her.

I try to hide my confusion as she stands at the foot of the bed. "And what, exactly, have you arranged?"

She looks over at me and bats her eyelashes. This witch knows what she's doing to me. "In the bathroom cabinet, there's a gift for you. Fish it out and bring it to me."

I don't hesitate—I nearly run to the bathing chamber, darting to the cabinet. I yank it open to find a large pink, sparkly cock with a matching harness set in the drawer.

She had to pick the most obnoxiously colored toy, didn't she?

Scooping them out, I take them into the room.

"Good dog," Vivian chirps before gasping and clutching her heart dramatically. "Is the Dark Lady scandalized?"

I roll my eyes. "Are you asking me to put it on?"

"No." She grins. "It's for me to wear."

I make my way over to her as she begins to strip off her clothes. My eyes dance over her body as she exposes it to me, unable to stop my mouth from watering.

Once she's undressed, she stands confidently before me and holds out her hands. "Give it here."

I thrust them into her awaiting hands.

"I'm going to fuck you with this," she tells me patiently. I nod, my shadows buzzing around her. "You're going to ride it like the good little whore I know you are. Isn't that right?"

Heat pools in my stomach at her filthy words, her dominance. I nod again, desperate for her, to have her take me however she wishes.

She wastes no time getting herself into the harness, fixing her newest appendage into place. Once situated, she climbs onto the bed, placing her back against the headboard, and crooks her finger at me as she spreads her legs. "Sit on it, Venus."

My clothes instantly vanish, and I climb up to straddle her, my entrance pressed against the tip of the toy. I can't hide my excitement, my desperation.

Vivian grips the base and slides it back and forth against me easily, collecting my arousal. She tsks playfully. "I love how desperate you are. Go on, but slowly. Only the tip."

A whine snakes out of my throat as I bear down, the tip stretching me wide open. Stars burst in my vision as I feel the cock enter me, spearing me. I need more, I need it all. "More," I pant, placing my palms on her shoulders. "More, Vivian."

"Not yet," she commands. "Just ride the tip."

I obey, lightly lifting my hips and lowering myself down. I clench around it, pleasure building rapidly between my thighs. Little moans fill the air as I fuck myself, but it's not enough—not yet.

Without warning, Vivian grips my hips and slams me down on the cock. I cry out as I'm stretched to my limit too quickly. My nails dig into her shoulders as I try to shuffle off, a bit of pain mixing with pleasure, but she holds firm. "Good girl, Venus. I knew you could take it."

The praise warms my skin. Whimpering, I tilt my hips back and forth, trying to get used to the girth.

"That's it," Vivian coaxes, her sultry voice sending shocks of arousal sparking through my body. "Just like that. Get used to the size of my cock in you."

I groan, my hips swiveling faster, the pain dissipating the faster I move. A devious grin lights up her face as she watches me. "So greedy. Go ahead and fuck yourself. Soak me." Our eyes lock as she reaches up and grips my face—hard. "But you will only come when I say so." Her eyes brook no argument.

I nod furiously, worried I'm going to come right then and there.

She releases me and slaps her hands on my ass. "Go on."

I waste no time—I begin bouncing myself up and down, desire spiraling deeper and deeper with each thrust. Vivian moves one hand to my clit, placing a feather-light touch, and I clench down on her, needing release. My vision turns hazy as I dive further into pleasure.

"Only when I say," she reminds me.

I want to beg her to let me come, to not stop me, to never stop—

"Stop," she commands.

A small whimper breaks through my lips. "Vivian, please," I beg—I can't believe I'm begging. Her finger still caresses my clit, causing my hips to jerk.

She hums. "Only good girls get to come. Are you being good?"

I keep begging, willing to say or do anything to keep going.

She sighs as if exasperated, but her eyes are alight with arousal. "Alright, keep going."

Letting go of her shoulders, I lean back, resting my hands on her knees as I fuck myself hard. My hair is plastered to the back of my neck, a layer of sweat now coating my skin.

Vivian looks ethereal under me. Her eyes are glassy as they flit from my face to where I ride the toy as if she needs to see both. Her breasts move as I do, demanding to be held in my hands.

"You really love it, huh? You're soaking everything, even the bed. Maybe you've lubed me up enough to fuck your ass. What do you think of that?"

My movements stutter. Is she being serious?

She outright laughs at my bewildered expression. "Maybe next time." She slaps the side of my breast, causing me to yelp. "I didn't tell you to stop."

I do stop—or rather, Vivian forces me to. Three times. Three times, I nearly reach my climax before Vivian simply tells me to halt. I babble my pleas, telling her I'll do whatever she wants, to please, please, please let me come.

I even try distracting her by running my fingertips over her nipples, causing her to arch into me. Kissing her neck and murmuring sweet nothings into her ear, hoping she won't notice I'm trying to get myself off.

But she does. And makes sure I pay for it.

By the fourth time my orgasm starts to creep up on me, she pushes me onto my back, with her between my legs. She swivels her hips as she moves in me, splitting me in half. I'm lost in my pleasure, unable to do anything but take it, to let it wash over me.

"Vivian," I groan. "I can't take it anymore."

She pistons in and out, setting a punishing rhythm, her finger expertly stroking my clit as she smiles down at me. "Come all over me," she instructs, finally showing me some mercy.

Release slams into me, my entire world shattering apart and being remade. I throw my head back as I ride the wave of pleasure, wondering if the world around me is actually shaking or if it is just me.

A bead of sweat glides down the exposed column of my throat, and Vivian leans forward to lick it off. I wrap my arms around her, pressing us together as we both work through my climax.

Once I return to myself, Vivian eases the toy out of me. Hazel eyes connect with mine, and I see the need shining in them. We aren't done yet.

Once her face reaches mine, I capture her mouth. Our lips fit together like puzzle pieces as we fit ourselves into one another. My hands wander over her back, traveling lower until I help her shimmy out of the harness. I need to taste her *now*.

Her mouth releases mine with a startled squeak as I grip her ass and push. I'm lifting her up, up, up until she's pressed right up against my mouth.

I take one long, languid taste of her, and we both groan. I will never tire of this, will never get enough. I don't require any other sustenance but her.

"Venus," she gasps just as I press a finger into her channel, and she implodes, catching me off-guard with how quickly she's reached her peak. Clenching down on me, she gyrates her hips faster, chasing her high. I pulse in and out of her, giving her a taste of her own medicine.

Once her hips slow and her moans quiet into little gasps, I remove myself from her, guiding her down my body so we're pressed together.

A content sigh slips from my lips as we hold each other, as if we are the only two left in this universe.

Chapter Forty-Three
Vivian

The threat of Phanes still looms over us, even with his inaction. I keep throwing myself into connecting with my magic, strengthening us, but I know I will always be limited—that Venus will always be limited without my soul, powering up our respective magics from the connection.

Venus still hasn't taken my soul.

It's starting to piss me off.

"I'm ready," I announce as I throw open the door.

Venus is sitting at her desk, pouring over some book that I'm sure is super boring but probably helpful.

She looks up from me, her brows furrowed. "Ready for what?"

I swallow my nerves and approach her desk. "You're taking my soul today, Venus. No more waiting."

Surprise lights her face as she pushes back from the desk and stands before me. Her midnight eyes show every emotion she's feeling in real time. Shock, longing, and a bit of suspicion.

"Vivian, I—"

"I don't want to hear excuses. We need to do this."

"I'm afraid," she admits.

I reach forward and take her hand in mine. "Of what?" I ask, even though I already know.

"I'm afraid of what will happen after I take it."

She has to get over it, my magic grumbles.

I squeeze her fingers. "We can't fight fate, Venus," I murmur. "I know you want to, but we can't."

"Your magic is keeping things from you," she growls.

I sigh. "I'll be honest, I haven't asked it what will happen to me."

Venus rears back in shock. "Why not?"

"Because...because it doesn't matter. What happens to me doesn't matter."

"How dare you speak like that." Venus's shadows vibrate with agitation. "You might be lost forever, and you don't care?"

"Part of me does, I think. But if I stop to think about dying, will I go through with it? Probably not. So, no, it doesn't matter."

Venus's face shifts in anger. "I'm not letting anything happen to you, regardless of what tales your magic spins," she spits with venom.

"Don't blame my magic," I scoff. "Blame your father."

Her anger dissipates, unveiling her fear beneath. "I can't live without you," she admits.

It makes my heart ache. I let go of her hand and reach to cup her face. "I want to enjoy the time we have together with no worries about what's next. I want to be here with you."

Leaning forward, she presses her forehead to mine and shuts her eyes. I close my own as our breathing intermingles, just feeling the presence of one another. Her wings shift around us, keeping us close.

Venus looses a breath. "Marry me, Vivian."

I blink my eyes open and pull back to scrutinize her face.

Nothing but determination in her onyx eyes. "We don't really follow the laws of the living in Hell, but I want us tied together in every possible way."

"You want to marry me?" I squeak, my heart feeling ready to burst.

Her head tilts. "Is that not what you desire?"

A bewildered laugh escapes my lips. I've never considered marriage for myself; I always thought it was something that was out of reach for me.

Because of Venus. Now, the one who made me feel marriage was out of the equation is the one who wants to marry me.

"I want to marry you, too" I say softly. "I love you."

Her smile is radiant. "I am simply yours. I am your lover, your defender, your confidante. I am the one who will not demand your soul but will take it gleefully if you offer it to me. I am your equal. And now, I would like to be your wife. I will spend eternity making you realize how much I love you."

I nearly remind her that we might not have eternity, but I don't want to ruin the moment. "I want to give my soul to you. Let's do it now, before I come to my senses," I joke.

She throws her head back and laughs. "Very well, my courageous, little witch. I will finally have your soul."

Venus takes us to the monolith outside my former coven, both of us giddy, despite the uncomfortable feeling of teleporting. We're both grinning ear-to-ear, looking like two lovesick puppies.

Until we hear screams in the distance.

We look to the source and see Kirsten sprinting towards us. She's in pajamas that are covered in mud and has little nicks on her face and arms.

"Vivian!" she shrieks as she sees us. She skids to a halt. "Your Grace," she gasps out. "I came to call upon you. I—we—something has attacked the coven."

Venus's shadows immediately rush along the forest floor toward the coven site, racing against time. My magic leaps out of me, digging into the earth, spreading through the dirt to understand what is happening.

It reaches the coven site and turns sour.

Phanes has finally come back for me and has left destruction in his path.

Starting with the coven.

Chapter Forty-Four
Venus

When Phanes attacked the covens looking for Vivian, he made sure to do it stealthily: slip under their wards, leave the exterior of the homes intact, and render the witches prone so none would know they were next.

This time, he destroyed as much as he could to send a message.

He wants us to know what is to come if we do not yield.

The homes have been completely leveled, smoke billowing from the rubble. Screams and cries fill the air, injured witches at every turn.

It's complete chaos.

The ground rumbles with the sound of his serpent retreating. I soar towards the beast, rage propelling me forward, my wings beating hard. The giant snake slithers over a hill, and I don't hesitate, sending a blast of power spearing towards it. The monster turns to look at me, and my magic lunges directly for its large eyes. It rears as my magic makes contact, letting out an ear-piercing shriek, blood spurting out before it slams its eyes shut. It writhes in pain, distracted by its sudden lack of vision.

I rally my magic again, ready to strike—when it hits and careens off a protective ward that wasn't there a moment ago.

My stomach drops. Phanes must be here.

The sound of the beast's screaming is muffled by the new protective ward. I pivot, searching for him, now panicking—what if he gets to Vivian? She's wearing her protective amulet, but all he would have to do is go back to the coven site...

"You've blinded my pet."

I turn in the air at the sound of his booming voice. He stands on the hill, out of the way of his pet writhing around, whipping its tail back and forth. Seeing him strikes a mixture of fear and pure wrath in me.

The last time we faced each other like this was when he took Lilith from me, and history might just repeat itself.

"Your pet," I snarl, "has destroyed entire covens." My vision gets hazy around the edges, my heart pounding with fury.

"Tell me, my errant daughter, where is my Vivian? I've missed her dearly."

My shadows vibrate in agitation at the sound of her name on his lips.

"I have missed my little flower," he goads. "She was so delicate, ripe for the picking. The sounds she would make…"

I shut out his words, the knowledge of what he did to her, of what she had to endure. I send a blast of pure night magic towards him, aiming to kill, to destroy—

He counters with his own streak of lightning. Our magic collides, sending the earth below us trembling from the sheer power.

My magic presses into my skin, ready to try again, to land the killing blow, but then I remember Vivian is not ready to step into Phanes's role. Not yet.

I keep myself aloft in the air and look down at my father.

I can't doom Vivian. She has to be the one to do it, to finally right the wrong Phanes did eons ago.

Perhaps I am my father's daughter, but I will be better than him.

"When we see each other next," I say looking down my nose at him, "it will be on the battlefield." A cruel smile graces my lips. "Your little flower will be your undoing."

His face contorts with rage, his bloodshot eyes narrowing. "If you are not careful, she will end up just like your mother. Dead without a name. Is that what you want?"

My mother's soft, angelic face flits across my mind. I bare my teeth at him. "You have no right to mention her."

He lets out a sadistic caw. "I had her depict the truth, but she got too bold, too interested. So I had to end her. Just how I will end Vivian; just how I will end you."

I knew it. I knew he had killed her. My magic is bubbling in me, desperate to rip him apart.

He gives me a smirk, knowing he hit his mark. His veins seem to pulse under his skin, looking like ink beneath the flesh. I blink, trying to understand what I just witnessed, but he and his serpent disappear, presumably back to the safety of his palace.

Or to steal Vivian away from me again.

Without even having to command them, my shadows race towards the coven site, as desperate to keep her safe as I am. With a mighty push of my wings, I follow, ready to face what is at my back.

Chapter Forty-Five
Vivian

Half the coven is dead and it's all my fault.

Phanes came here to send me a message, to lure me out. He picked my former coven to hurt me, to show me what would happen if I continue to disobey.

Hate is too weak a word to describe what I feel towards him.

Kirsten and I bandage one of the elders with scraps from her dress; her leg is split open and blood quickly soaks the cloth.

None of the witches in the coven are naturally inclined healers, Kirsten told me. All they know is what might be in their grimoires.

Still, a few fellow witches are working what healing magic they can over those more injured than them, dumping potions onto gaping wounds and creating tourniquets with whatever fabric they can find.

A witchling's cries reach my ears and I instinctively look over to find a child, no older than five, covered in debris, slowly stumbling towards us.

"Can you handle this?" I ask Kirsten, who simply nods, and I rise and rush over to the child.

She looks up at me with huge grey eyes, unsure of who I am. I kneel and say lightly, "Hello there. I'm Vivian. I'm a witch, just like you." I work hard to make my face appear warm. "What's your name?"

"Eliza," she says quietly, her tears sticking to her eyelashes, but at least they've stopped flowing.

"Now that's a pretty name," I tell her. "Would you like me to clean you up? I bet you'd feel so much better."

She nods, her eyes unblinking, and I hold out my arms for her. She hesitates for a moment before walking into them. My heart calms a bit at not seeing any dire injuries.

As I pick her up, a thick wind beats through the commune. Everyone begins to shriek as darkness descends over us, swirling around, dodging through the destruction, circling me. Venus's shadows, here to make sure I'm safe.

Eliza begins to tremble in my arms and buries her face in my neck.

"It's alright," I soothe. "They belong to the Dark Lady. They won't hurt you."

As her shadows settle, I hear Venus's wings before I see her. Relief nearly brings me to my knees. Once I see her, searching for any injuries, I can't help the few tears that slide down my cheeks. She appears unharmed.

The Dark Lady lands gracefully in front of me and gathers my face in her hands, inspecting me the way I just did her, with a wild look in her eye. "You're alright."

Not a question, but I nod. "I'm alright."

She lets out a breath before releasing me and surveying the damage.

"Half the coven is dead," I inform her. "Most everyone else is injured. They can't stay here."

"I agree," she murmurs before stalking into the middle of what's left. Everyone stops what they're doing and stares at her with a mixture of awe and fear. Addressing the coven, she says, "It is not safe to stay in this realm any longer—at least, not until the threat has been dealt with." She looks over her shoulder at me for a beat before continuing, "You all shall have a choice: stay in the realm of the living or take temporary refuge in Hell."

Murmurs rise up from everyone, shocked that the Dark Lady herself would be giving them a choice and not a command.

Pride swirls in me.

"What will happen to us if we stay, my lady?" an elder named Mabel asks.

"We shall provide concealment spells for you," Venus answers, "to hopefully protect against you being detected as a witch, but I must say, I feel coming to Hell is the safest option."

Nervous murmurs continue again until Kirsten steps forward. Blood coats her trembling hands, but her face reveals nothing except determination. "I will go to Hell with you, so long as I can be taught how to protect myself."

"We can provide you the protection you need—"

"No." A muscle in Kirsten's jaw flickers. "I want to be taught how to do so." She looks around at the destroyed homes. "Some others may want that too."

Venus raises an eyebrow in surprise and runs her eyes up and down the witch—to my surprise, Kirsten does not wilt under the gaze.

"I'm sure we can accommodate your request," Venus finally answers.

Little Eliza peeks up, raises her hand, and says, "I want to go too."

One by one, the surviving witches all agree to go to Hell.

Chapter Forty-Six
Vivian

Venus transporting what's left of the coven took a few trips, and she was nearly asleep on her feet once it was done.

The next few hours pass in a flurry of activity. Spirit healers usher the coven to the infirmary, working to heal any wounds they can. I'm not a doctor or a healer, but I try to be as helpful as possible, fetching water, cleaning up soiled bandages when someone's bleeding wouldn't stop, and holding a witchling's hand as her arm is stitched up.

If anyone from the coven recognizes me, they don't speak on it. I don't even receive any weird looks. I think we're all in shock over what happened.

In all the commotion, I lose track of Venus—she isn't anywhere to be seen in all the madness. Once the healers seem to have gotten to everyone and the infirmary feels more settled, I wander off to see where she went.

On my way through the castle, I find Kirsten speaking with Marie, leaning towards each other, whispering.

Kirsten's hairline has dried blood crusted to it, and she's covered in dirt, but her eyes are clear. Standing pressed against her leg is Eliza, looking much better than she did a few hours ago.

Smiling at the little girl, I say to her, "Did one of the nice ghost ladies get you cleaned up?" She nods at me, her grey eyes somber, her little fist clutching Kirsten's pant leg. I raise my eyes to the two witches. "You should have the healers check you over."

"I'll live," Kirsten says grimly.

I let out a breath. I'm not going to battle her about her own health.

"What *was* that?" Kirsten asks me. "I've never seen any-thing like it. It was like a massive python."

I throw a glance at Eliza and say, "Perhaps we adults should discuss this. Privately."

Marie looks down and smiles at the child. "Come, little one. I'm sure there are some sweets Lady Vivian has hidden in the kitchen."

"I haven't *hidden* them," I grumble a bit defensively under my breath as Marie takes the girl's hand. They make their way down the hall, leaving Kirsten and me alone.

I take a deep breath to steady myself, to not let my nerves get the better of me. "That thing that attacked is...a pet of sorts." She furrows her brows and opens her mouth to interrupt, but I continue, filling her in on my magic, Phanes taking over and creating the gods, including Venus, and Venus rallying witches to destroy them. I gloss over the details of Phanes holding me hostage, both because I don't want to rehash that here, and also because it doesn't change the predicament we're in—or what he's done to the coven.

"So, he was looking for you," she says flatly.

The urge to defend myself kicks in, but I nod. "I'm sorry. I've been trying to make myself ready to kill him, but it's taking much more than we anticipated."

"And he can steal our magic?"

I blink at her question. "No, he can't do that. Why would you ask that?"

"I saw it," she breathes. "I saw him pull the magic from my mother's body. It was like he was taking her entire life force." She shudders. "It made the veins...pulse and slither, and then he..." Her eyes are haunted by what she had to witness.

Alarm bells are ringing in my head. "Are you sure?"

She nods. "I know what I saw. It left her looking like an empty husk." Her voice lowers to a whisper.

Memories of the covens he attacked filter through my mind—the feeling of the life being sucked out of the witches before they died.

Kirsten scrutinizes me for a moment before letting out a breath. "All this time, I can't believe we do not learn the true history of our alliance with the Dark Lady. Why? Why keep that from us?"

I shrug, trying not to let the questions running through my head show on my face. "I honestly don't know. Maybe to keep us happy and blissfully ignorant?"

"So if your magic is the true creator of this world," she muses, "that means you and the Dark Lady are equals."

"In a sense, yeah, I guess so."

She lets out a tired laugh. "It's ironic—the one witch who was adamant she did not want to give her soul to the Devil is now irrevocably tied to her."

We size each other up for a moment, unsure of how to proceed. Do we want to be enemies or do we want to be allies?

"If what you say is true, it sounds like there would be no need for future generations of witches to sign their souls over to the Dark Lady. When you defeat him, will you still require witches to give their souls to her?" When—not if.

I roll my shoulders back and say confidently, "I believe we should get to choose."

Something like appreciation and gratitude shine in her forest green eyes. "Then I guess I need to prepare myself for what is to come."

Chapter Forty-Seven

Venus

By the time I drag myself to the council room's doors, I know everyone else is already in their seats, anxious to discuss the events that just unfolded. I send my shadows out to find Vivian, but surprisingly, she's somehow already on my heels. Blood is smeared on her clothes, on her hands, in her hair. My heart drops and I quickly gather her into my arms to scent her.

Not her blood. The relief I feel nearly makes me weep.

"I'm okay," she tells me, her words muffled against my chest.

Pulling back, I let myself see that she's uninjured. She gives me a small smile as she steps out of my grasp. "There's something we need to discuss."

"That is the understatement of the millennia."

She shakes her head. "It's more than what we think. Kirsten said she saw Phanes literally suck her mother's magic out of her body."

Shock makes my mind go blank, and I realize the witch is standing a few steps behind Vivian. "Our meetings are closed to those not on the council," I snarl, too exhausted to control myself.

"Venus, please," Vivian pleads, her hazel eyes wide with concern—and fear. "She saw Phanes—saw him take magic from her mother."

"That's impossible," I argue.

"We can't rule this out," Vivian whispers urgently.

Fine.

Narrowing my eyes at the other witch, I growl, "We will call you when we are ready."

Kirsten merely nods.

I push open the council door, gripping Vivian's hand and steering her to the head of the table where my seat resides. I guide her into it while I stand behind, my hands on the raised back. Everyone's face alights with surprise but wisely decide against commenting.

"Phanes attacked Vivian's former coven—sent his serpent to destroy their homes and murder half of them," I announce. The High Priestesses look ill at the news. "The remaining witches and witchlings have been transported here for their safety."

"How likely is it that he will attack other covens?" Isobel asks, her amber eyes wide as saucers.

"It is unclear," I admit.

"He attacked them because of me," Vivian adds, her guilt reaching my nostrils.

"There is more we apparently need to know," I inform them. My shadows slither across the floor, opening the door for Kirsten to enter.

She confidently strides in, her head held high as her eyes sweep across the room before landing on me. She nods to me, looking me in the eye without flinching.

I raise my eyebrows at her, at the fire that seems to spark within this young witch, as I reply, "You believe you witnessed Phanes attack your mother."

"I don't simply believe it," she contradicts smoothly. "I *did* witness it. I witnessed him stealing her magic."

The council scrutinizes her.

"And how would you know of such a thing?" I fight the urge to snap at her interruption.

The witch doesn't back down. "It felt like my magic was reacting to it, like...like my magic was trying to hide." She swallows. "I had felt wrong all day, like something bad was going to happen, even though it was just a normal day. I expressed this to my mother, but she dismissed me, telling me she felt nothing out of the ordinary. I went to my room, but I couldn't sleep; I kept tossing and turning, unable to get comfortable. After a few hours, I felt a disturbance."

"A disturbance?" I press.

She nods. "I couldn't hear anything different, but I just *knew*. It felt like...evil was near." Fear rolls off her in waves, tainting the air. "I went to my mother's room down the hall. The door was open a crack, and I peeked in, and that's when I saw him."

The room is charged with anxiety at her words. "Go on," Vivian encourages.

Kirsten licks her lips. "He stood over her bed, and I'm not sure how, but she was rendered speechless—her mouth was open in a scream, but no noise came out. He had a hand hovering above her chest, and I *felt* the magic leave her." Her words end on a stilted intake of breath, her eyes pained. "When he was done, she was nothing but an empty shell."

"And he didn't sense you just beyond the door?" I ask, skeptical.

She shakes her head. "No—or at least he didn't seem to. He simply disappeared into thin air. A few minutes later, I heard the first home being destroyed."

"That's why he's gotten stronger," Vivian breathes. "He didn't make a new god. He's been stealing magic from witches."

"He must have destroyed the homes to get rid of the evidence," I muse, "so we wouldn't know what he'd done."

The room is eerily silent, everyone trying to grapple with this realization. I think back to what Vivian's magic had informed us when we were investigating the covens' disappearances. The feeling that the witches were immobilized and their life force drained from them.

We had assumed it was their souls being destroyed, as their souls never made it to Hell. They should have made their way to me after their death—it's the reason they even sign their souls over to me to begin with. I had wondered if he somehow managed to work around it, by trapping their soul before it reached me. But...he was stealing their magic instead.

"I think I'm going to be sick," Marie announces, her pale skin now nearly matching the hue of Grigor's.

"What do we do?" Aradia asks, her eyes pleading for answers.

"He must be stopped before he can hurt any others," Isobel adds.

"If he's getting stronger, I'm not sure how we can," I admit.

"It's my fault," Vivian whispers.

"No," I snap without thinking.

"It is," she argues, twisting to look up at me. "He figured out what coven I used to belong to and attacked them to get to me."

"Perhaps he felt your magic working in your forest," Isobel offers.

I shoot her a look that conveys she's not helping matters.

Vivian turns to the council and declares, "We must warn all covens and give them the same choice the Dark Lady gave mine. Come to Hell or stay on their lands, but urge them to come here."

"But if Phanes can steal their magic, why would staying behind be beneficial to them?" Aradia looks panicked now. "Haven't we lost enough witches to him?"

"We can conceal the covens who want to stay—place the spell into an object that the coven can keep with them. The ward Vivian created is impenetrable. Perhaps, if she assists with creating concealments, it will truly keep the covens safe," Azrael argues, rubbing his horns contemplatively.

"I'm sitting right here," Vivian grumbles under her breath, to which Azrael dips his head sheepishly.

"Apologies, my lady."

She waves her hand dismissively. "No problem, man—er, demon."

Isobel interjects, "Azrael is right. We will need your help, Lady Vivian."

Vivian nods. "I can do that."

Grigor clears his throat. "Forgive me, my lady, but where could we possibly house these witches? How would we feed them? You are the only living person to reside here—it is not meant to be a place for the living."

I bite back my growl, letting Vivian stand on her own two feet for this discussion, but ready to remind my council if they overstep. She straightens her spine as she addresses him. "Hell's city is massive, full of homes that spirits reside in. Spirits don't need the homes. We'll ask them to share with the living witches. Besides, it's not like there's a lot of witches out there. For food, maybe we ask the witches to pack up what they can and bring it with."

Luke nods. "That sounds reasonable."

"You have still not given the Dark Lady your soul," Aradia points out to Vivian. "That may be the final piece to this, to strengthen you both."

I bite back a growl. "I think we have more pressing matters to attend to right now."

I expect Vivian to fight me on this, but she nods in agreement. "We need to get the witches to safety first so he can't swoop in and steal more magic. Once they're safe and he's not able to reach them, then I can hand over my soul."

Chapter Forty-Eight

Vivian

Days later, everyone is still rattled by Phanes's bold display. The council is meeting every day, for hours at a time, trying to pick up the pieces. Venus sent word to every coven, explaining the dire situation and offering them the choice to either take refuge in Hell or have the High Priestesses and myself create a concealment spell within an object to keep on their lands.

Many were understandably frightened, unsure of who Phanes even is—but some had heard of the mysterious deaths that had occurred not too long ago. Venus told them everything, aside from my magic's and my piece in it all. Most of the covens decided to come here while a few felt comfortable with a concealment spell. Venus tried to reason with them, to tell them how dangerous it would be, but they had wanted to stay. I have a sneaking suspicion they considered Venus's words as a test to see which covens were unafraid and confident in their magical abilities, as if to win her favor.

Venus had seemed inclined to force them to come here but had relented, so now the High Priestesses and I are working on these concealments. My magic works to embed itself into various stones quickly and efficiently. Creating these concealments is a completely different experience than when I created Hell's wards—it doesn't hurt or require much energy. My magic simply settles into the stones, which Venus transports to the covens that want to stay behind.

Everyone is frazzled and dealing with it in different ways. Venus's patience has burnt out and she's struggling to let go of any ounce of control she thought she had. Meanwhile, I feel a constant urge to draw Phanes out myself so that no one else gets hurt. I know I have no choice—our inevitable meeting looms closer and closer.

And I'm tired of running away.

My magic agrees with me, constantly growling that his time has reached an end. We seem to be fueling one another's rage.

I'm speedwalking down the halls on my way to the High Priestesses' workroom when I spot Kirsten. She and I regularly run past each other on our way to different parts of the castle. We give one another a nod of approval and mutual understanding before we head off in different directions—her to the infirmary, and me to either meet with one of the High Priestesses or with Venus.

"Oh, I believe your lover is this way," she calls when she sees me.

I halt. "She's in the infirmary?"

She nods. "She stops by to check on everyone—doesn't stay for long though. Probably not to distract."

Trying to hide my surprise, I trail behind Kirsten, both of us silent as we walk down the halls. Guilt sits in my stomach as we get closer. I haven't been to the infirmary to check on anyone—not since the day they first arrived.

Should I? It's bad enough that I feel responsible for what happened, for the death and the complete destruction of their homes. But also, this was a group of people that bullied me, belittled me my entire childhood, saw how my mother treated me and did nothing.

I have to let this go, I think to myself. *Their opinions don't affect my life anymore. I have to let this go.*

The infirmary is less chaotic than I anticipated. Healer witches flit back and forth in their physical forms, softly speaking to the witches that occupy the beds which are evenly spaced out with curtains to offer some privacy. All look clean and relatively calm. Some are even asleep.

In the corner, I see Venus and Isobel, their heads bent together as they speak quietly to one another. Shockingly, no one seems to pay them any mind—I wonder if Venus is using her magic to shield them from everyone else's view.

I walk up silently, not wanting to disturb anyone. Venus's head snaps up, probably scenting me, and her eyes soften when she smiles at me. It nearly steals the breath from my lungs.

I turn to Isobel as I approach. "Helping out?" I ask softly.

She nods and Venus interjects, "Isobel's affinity for water manipulation is crucial for healing. She's been assisting us since the coven arrived."

Us is interesting. I give Venus a curious look as I ask Isobel, "Can I speak with the Dark Lady privately?"

Isobel nods her goodbye, not needing to be told twice, and I grab Venus's hand, taking us out into the hall.

"I wasn't aware you were coming down here," I note as I stop and turn to face her. I go to take my hand back, but she holds fast, intertwining our fingers together.

"I'm their ruler. I should be assessing the damage and see what they need from me. You taught me that." I blink in surprise. "You taught me that I need to be a better ruler," she reminds me. "And ruling includes things such as this."

My magic leaps with pride in me. "That's very...leader-like of you." She snorts. "I haven't been down here at all," I admit, my shame making my skin feel oily. "I wasn't sure if I could face them, you know?"

"I assumed that was the case." Her eyes hold no judgment. "I do not want you blaming yourself—for what Phanes did, or for not checking on your former coven."

"But I'm the reason he did it. It was to send me a message."

"You know that Phanes, and Phanes alone, is responsible for what he does. And that we are working on getting rid of him so that something like this never happens again."

I nod, but my unease doesn't go away. "We have more things to talk about."

"Like what?" she asks.

Like how we probably don't have much time left. Like how I want to spend every waking moment I have with you—before it's too late.

"Later," I tell her.

Her eyebrows narrow at my evasiveness but gets what I'm saying: this isn't something to discuss in the hallway, when there are injured witches just on the other side of the wall. I pull my hand from hers, which she allows, and with a parting smile, I head back to our room, contemplating how I'm going to get through this.

Chapter Forty-Nine
Vivian

The council sits around the table, each looking worse for wear. No one has gotten much sleep the past few days, too busy reeling from the coven attack and working to protect everyone.

Azrael looks like he's about to fall asleep at the table when one of Venus's shadows pokes him, making him jump in his chair.

"We should consider luring Phanes out," I explain for what feels like the millionth time.

"My lady, forgive me, but are you ready?" Marie's eyes hold concern.

"I will be, once the Dark Lady has my soul." I can't help but fling the words at Venus, who sits across the table.

The coven attack has stopped Venus from wanting to take my soul. Every time I bring it up, she pumps the brakes, arguing that we're still dealing with too much to consider it, and that we aren't ready to set things in motion.

My magic and I are starting to get restless.

"I'll lure him to my forest, and we'll finally take care of him."

"No." Venus's magic rumbles through the room.

"Aren't you tired of having the same argument, over and over?" I ask, exasperated.

"I am. I wish you would drop it."

"And I wish you would just take my soul, like you're supposed to."

Luke clears his throat, reminding us that we're wasting our time. "The witches who are here seem to be acclimating fine to their new surroundings, although it has become crowded. We should consider how long we're going to exist like this."

The room looks at Venus, who has an unreadable expression on her face. She leans back in her seat and tells us, "Prepare the witches to be here for the foreseeable future."

I want to throw something.

Venus dismisses the council as I grow increasingly annoyed. Shoving back from the table, I stalk out, Venus on my heels.

"Vivian—" Her voice reaches my ears, but she's interrupted by a group of witches standing outside the council room.

"Is there something you all need?" Venus inquires as we all stop to greet one another.

Kirsten takes a deep breath. "These witches and I," she says, gesturing to the group behind her, "have been talking and we've decided that we want to help. We want to fight."

It stuns both Venus and me into silence.

"We want to help," she repeats. "If Phanes is killing witches, we want to avenge them. They're our sisters in magic, and they deserve to be honored. Let us go."

"I—we," I say, gesturing to Venus, "can't ask that of you all. It's too dangerous."

"I want to be useful," Kirsten says to us, then gestures to the witches behind her. "We all do."

"Phanes will kill you. You're willing to hand over your life for this?" I ask.

The intensity in Kirsten's green eyes surprises me. "I want the threat to us, to the world, eliminated. If I must lay down my life to succeed in that, then I will." She gently grips my wrist, her fingers cool to the touch. Venus moves as if to rip Kirsten's arm from her body, but I stop her with a look. Kirsten takes a deep breath and closes her eyes. I feel a tingling sensation where she's touching me, as if my arm has fallen asleep and is just waking up. I look down at the inside of my wrist and see my veins *moving*. I'm about to freak out, but light-headedness starts to take over. My eyes droop and I feel my body sagging. Then, as quickly as it came on, it recedes, making me feel energetic, like I could run a marathon or even fly—

"Enough," Venus barks.

Kirsten releases me and I immediately feel like myself again.

I look from her to my wrist, then back to her. "What *was* that?"

"I can manipulate blood," she admits, blush tinting her cheeks. "I'm not particularly strong yet, but I've been working with Isobel"—Kirsten and the High Priestess share a quick glance— "to hone it. I don't need to touch someone to manipulate their blood anymore, although it does make it easier."

Unholy shit. That's incredibly useful.

And also disgusting.

Kirsten continues. "The High Priestesses have spent the little time we've had together helping all of us understand our magic—how to wield it, to sharpen it. To become something to fear."

My breath catches. How badly did I need that, *want* that for myself? How can I deny that to these witches, when that was what I needed?

Venus, surprisingly, says nothing—as if to let me handle this, to see what I think and what I'll decide.

I look Kirsten in the eye and see nothing but determination. I can't strip someone else of this decision, but...I don't want this to happen.

I could say no, tell them to simply wait it out down here like any reasonable person would do, but that would go against this new world we're fighting for—a world where we are not stripped of our choices.

"Alright," I murmur, my insides twisting. "If you all wish to fight alongside us, then that is what you all will do."

Relief spreads across Kirsten's face.

"The archdemons will have to incorporate you into their ranks," Venus adds.

"I will tell them myself," Isobel offers.

The witches share feral grins among themselves as Isobel shuffles them down the corridor.

"Explain to me," Venus starts as we continue down the hallway, "why the only witches that have ever defied me all happen to be from the same coven?"

I roll my eyes. "Kirsten isn't defying you."

"She has openly questioned my authority in front of other witches. You wouldn't consider that challenging me?"

Shrugging, I reply dryly, "Defying you is second nature to me, so it's hard for me to tell what is and isn't."

"It must be something in the water supply," she grumbles.

Cutting a glance at her, I say, "I'm worried about sending the witches to help us with this."

"As am I." Her tone is somber. "But as you have taught me, choice is important. We will provide them with all the necessary information and magical protection that we can, and they can make an educated decision on how to proceed."

"I'm shocked you're cool with that," I admit.

She shrugs. "Seeing the repercussions of you being stripped of autonomy, especially after doing that to you myself, has made me rethink matters."

I can't help the pride that glows in me. "Is that your version of an apology for stalking me for so long?" I joke.

Venus rolls her eyes at me.

"What if he manages to capture them and take their magic?" I ask, keeping us on track. "It'll make him stronger—too strong."

"I know," Venus murmurs, her brows pinching together. "Perhaps we use them as a last line of defense, only to be utilized if the situation looks dire."

"How will we determine that?"

"If we are already dead."

I start. "Let me get this straight…if he kills us, then you'll send the witches after him? It'll be too late."

She nods. "If you die, I will have no reason to continue. He can have this world, and I will die with you."

"Venus—" Anxiety starts to cloud my vision.

"I will not argue about this." Her tone is definitive. "You are allowed choices. Am I not allowed the same?"

A lump forms in my throat. I don't want anyone to die for me, especially not Venus.

"But you will not die," she states, still not letting go of her denial.

I shake my head. "I need some time to myself. I'll see you at dinner."

She sees right through me but doesn't push. Without another word, I beeline for our room where I slam the door shut and press my back against it, trying to regulate my breathing. No one else was supposed to die for me. I can't send the witches out there.

Then don't, my magic pipes up.

"I can't stop them," I groan.

Of course, you can. The pretender only wants you.

I blink. "Are you telling me to go on my own?"

Lure him out. Go to your forest and send him a signal. He'll slither out to retrieve you, like the pathetic, little worm he is.

Shaking my head, I whimper, "I can't do it."

This may be our only chance.

"Venus still needs my soul."

Drag her to the monolith to complete the ceremony.

"Have you met Venus? I can't drag her anywhere," I argue.

"Vivian?"

My muffled name travels to my ears, startling me. Venus is on the other side of the door. She knew something was up.

I push myself off the wood and spin around when she opens it and walks in. Her brows are narrowed, and her eyes track around the room before landing on me. "Were you speaking to someone?"

"My magic," I explain, still trying to calm my breathing. "It's nothing."

She nods before walking to the bed and lying back, her feet still on the floor. Silently, I go over and get her out of her boots. She sits up to help, but I simply push her back down and quickly shuck them off. Climbing onto the bed, I press myself into her side, my head on her chest.

We listen to each other's even breathing for a while, simply beyond words. Words can't comfort us now anyway, but the closeness is what calms us, centers us.

Her hand reaches up to lightly stroke my hair, her fingers brushing through the tangled locks.

"Venus?"

She hums, her chest rumbling under my ear.

"I just want to say...I'm happy we got the time together that we did. I wish I hadn't wasted so much of it, but I'm glad we got a little bit of time together."

Her fingers still in my hair. "What makes you say this?"

I swallow the lump in my throat. "I just wanted you to know, that's all. And I wanted you to know that I love you."

Her other hand grips my hip in warning. "You are not going to die, Vivian."

"We're not arguing about this again."

"There is nothing to argue because you will not die."

"Venus," I sigh, my weariness seeping from me.

She pushes forward. "I don't believe the universe is so cruel that it would separate us. We are meant to be, as sure as the stars glittering in the living realm's sky, as sure as the earth under our feet."

Unease twists itself inside me, not quite believing her words but wanting to more than anything.

"I can't have you die," she whispers, her voice cracking. "If you die, I will follow you in death. We shall never be apart again."

She says it as a promise.

I don't want to hear this anymore—to have this same conversation again. So I shut my mouth, trying to undo the knots forming in my stomach.

Even now, Venus can't accept what's right in front of us.

Raising my head from her chest, I look up at her. Her onyx eyes are unblinking, drilling holes into the ceiling, as her serpent tattoo coils across her skin anxiously. Dark, silky strands of her hair are fanned across the pillow.

If this is the only time we have with one another, I don't want to spend it bickering. I trail my fingers over her stomach, grazing the fabric of her tunic.

Venus lifts her head to lock eyes with me, one eyebrow raised, but says nothing. I glide my fingers up to her chest and her throat, relishing the feeling of her skin.

"No more talking," I purr, earning me a low rumble from Venus. "I have a better idea of how we should spend our time."

Venus's nostrils flare, scenting me. Her eyes sharpen with need. The look alone makes my body feel like it's been doused in gasoline and Venus has the match. I'm burning up from the inside, a raging fire enveloping me.

She senses my readiness and quickly straddles me, her onyx hair providing a curtain over us. She pushes my legs apart with her knees and settles into the space she's created.

Her nimble fingers dip beneath the waistband of my jeans and lightly brush against my center.

"Already wet," she snickers.

I bite back a moan, not wanting to give her the satisfaction, but when she parts me and places the tip of her finger in, I can't hold back—I gasp and feel myself clench down, wanting more, needing more.

She knows it. Her eyes flare with arousal and triumph as she removes her finger from me, leans back, and rips my pants from me, the denim breaking away under her strong hands.

"Venus!" I groan. "Stop ruining my clothes!"

She lets out a cackle before gripping my legs and pushing me open, baring me to her. "You know I don't like anything getting between me and your perfect little cunt."

She dives in and her tongue glides over me. I cry out and grip the sheets underneath me as waves of pleasure begin to roll through me. Her shadows start tearing at my shirt, and I hiss at them, but it ends in a whimper as they swirl over my exposed nipples, teasing me as Venus fucks me.

Release is already building in me, but Venus pulls back. I buck my hips as she sits up, demanding more, but she simply gives me a sadistic smile before she reaches into the nightstand, pulling out a small vibrator.

"You aren't the only one with toys, Vivian."

Fuck me.

Venus's clothes vanish, presenting herself in all her naked glory before turning the toy on and pressing it to my clit.

The vibrations take my pleasure to new heights in the blink of an eye. I throw my head back and grip the sheets, rocking my hips against the toy.

"Look at me, Vivian."

My toes curl at her voice, her demand, and I lift my head just as she presses herself against the vibrator too.

A low moan escapes her, making my eyes nearly roll back in my head.

"Oh," I pant, feeling needy, feral, unstoppable—

"Let's see who will break first," she breathes, her eyes glazed with desire.

I give her a small laugh. Challenge accepted. "You like teasing me," I croon. "But I know you like it even more when I tease you."

Her eyes narrow as she circles her hips, keeping us both pressed into the vibrator.

I grit my teeth against the wave of arousal that crashes through me. "What do you want more, Venus? Me to tell you what a greedy whore you are, or what a good girl you are?" She bares her teeth at me, which just urges me on. "Or maybe both? A good, little slut?"

Venus bites down on her bottom lip, but it doesn't stop the groan from coming out. I've hit my mark.

I'm winning this, I think, feeling triumphant as pleasure continues to build in me. "My good, little—"

Venus snaps forward, her hand circling my throat, as she growls, "Quiet, Vivian." She applies light pressure to the side of my neck, not cutting off my air supply, but showing me she easily can.

Fuck. My body feels like it's on fire, my release building in me. I open my mouth as a last-ditch effort to win, but a shadow slithers in, gagging me.

A feral grin spreads across Venus's face as her hips continue to grind against the toy. "Not so mighty when you're gagged, are you?"

Another shadow lightly presses in my center, filling me, overwhelming me.

The vibrations, her hand, her shadows, and the mischievous glint in her eye, all throw me over the edge. My back arches and I scream around the shadow gag, pleasure threatening to destroy me. It's too much—I'm free falling, unable to stop myself, to slow it down—

Venus tumbles over the edge with me, her hips rocking back and forth, chasing her own high.

I feel a rush of wet warmth between my legs, and tears leak from my eyes from the overwhelming pressure being released inside me.

Venus pulls back from me and asks incredulously, "Did you just squirt?"

I let out a whimper in response.

"For all that is unholy," she mutters before removing the toy and replacing it with her tongue. I scream again, the feeling too much, too overstimulating, but I don't want her to stop.

Eventually, she settles and pulls back, her shadows removing themselves from me. She gathers me into her arms as we lay next to one another, soaking in the orgasm afterglow.

Except...

"The sheets are all wet," I grumble tiredly.

"I love it," she mumbles.

I let out a huff of annoyance, though it quickly dissipates as I settle against her muscular frame.

We stay like this for a few hours, talking about everything and nothing until Venus falls asleep. I stare up at the ceiling, waiting until her breathing becomes deep and it's clear she won't wake easily.

It's time, my magic tells me.

Slowly, I detangle myself from her and sneak into the bathroom to retrieve some new clothes. "Ugh, were you listening to that?"

I've figured out how to retreat so I don't have to be subjected to it.

I shove my legs into a pair of athletic leggings before throwing on a black razorback top. Grabbing my bright pink sneakers, I quietly make my way to the bookshelf. Finding the book I need, I ease it from the shelf and open it to reveal the summoning stone to my former coven's lands. I traveled through the stone once before; I'm confident I can do it again.

Setting the book down on the desk, I slide my shoes on and remove the amulet from around my neck, placing it inside the false book, and then picking up the summoning stone.

The witches agreeing to fight against Phanes was the final straw. I can't let them, or anyone, go to their death because of me. Because that's really what this is: a struggle for power between him and me. No one else needs to die—especially not for me.

I look at my slumbering goddess one last time, taking her in, trying not to let the guilt and devastation of what I'm about to do stop me. Closing my eyes, I grip the stone and will myself through it, picturing where I am to go.

As I'm pulled through the stone, I can't help but feel a deep sadness that Venus doesn't have my soul.

Chapter Fifty
Vivian

I land with a thud on the ground of my forest, dry heaving from the feeling of being ripped apart by the space-time continuum.

Does traveling this way ever get easier? I doubt it.

I rise on shaky legs and get myself as far away from the monolith as I can in the clearing, leaving the summoning stone to take itself back to Hell.

The forest is quiet with anticipation, as if it knows something is about to happen and it's holding its breath.

I spool my magic from me like a ball of yarn, but instead of burrowing into the earth, I cast it out into the sky beyond. Glowing, bright magic rockets into the night, illuminating the world beyond with its undiluted power.

A beacon. A signal.

I can't let Phanes destroy anything or anyone else because of me. If he wants me, then that is what he will get. Even if it will destroy me instead.

I wait impatiently, tapping my foot against the grass.

I'm about to send another blast when I feel it—his foreboding presence, a sickening electricity moving through the world.

Phanes swaggers out of the trees, his white hair loose and flowing behind him as he eyes me like I'm an object he has desired for quite some time. Memories of him holding me down, of him touching me without my consent, flood my senses.

I despise him. I hate everything he is, everything he's done—to me, to Venus, to my magic, and all the witches that carried it before. My magic and I let our hatred and disgust of him fill me until I feel I'm about to burst.

He looks around the clearing before his greedy eyes land back on me. "You came alone, didn't you, my little flower?" He stalks toward me, a hideous grin on his face.

I swallow my terror at being so close to him again. "I did."

His grin widens into a smile. "I look forward to having you once again."

Another step, another, then another. I can't stop my panicked steps backwards to keep distance between us.

"You came to realize no one else needed to die for you," he sneers, cocking his head as he scrutinizes me. Another step closer.

"I did," I answer meekly. "I don't want anyone else to die."

Another step.

He sighs as if he's speaking to a child. "Unfortunately, my little flower, it is too late for truces."

I retreat with each one of his steps toward me, closer to the monolith. This was a mistake, I can't do this—

"My daughter managed to blind my creature," he growls, his face quickly contorting with anger, an unhinged look entering his eyes. He's close enough that I can see how bloodshot they are—can see the stolen magic slither through his darkened veins. It looks like he's been infused with oil. "I wonder if blinding you would be punishment enough."

He could grab me now, he's so close. He could reach out and grab me and take me away.

If I can get back to the monolith...just a few steps away, I just need—

"But it is no matter. I have made more," he continues nonchalantly.

Fear strikes my heart at his words.

I hear them before I see them, hissing and writhing through the grass. Slowly, they slither out through the trees, their hisses reverberating around the wilderness. The unnaturally large serpents come from all sides, surrounding the area. I refuse to put my back to Phanes, but I can feel them behind me, waiting for their chance to tear into me.

The ones I do see look...wrong. Some are much smaller, half the length of the others with deformed eyes or mouths. It looks like his stolen power makes him unable to recreate the vision of his original pet.

Just then, the original slinks up behind him, its eyes now replaced by two angry oozing gashes. Ready to do its bidding for its master.

I'm nearly at the monolith, just inches away—

Phanes lunges for me, and my magic leaps, digging into the ground, creating a deep fissure in the earth, circling me and the monolith, separating me from the immediate danger. He stumbles back, shock rearranging his face before he growls, "Did you really think your pathetic magic would stop me?"

I don't answer. Instead, I spin around and face the monolith, slamming my hand onto the cool stone and funneling my magic into it. A spear of light erupts from the obelisk, a blinding, white light emanating through the forest. I slam my eyes shut as hisses and snarls from the light reach my ears.

After a moment, the light recedes, throwing us into darkness.

That is the true signal.

A spear of dark magic flies through the night sky as if the moon itself sent its unearthly power down from the skies. Venus dives from above, her wings tucked in as her magic slams into the fissure I created, causing the earth beneath us to separate even further. It feels like an earthquake as the ground shakes uncontrollably and the trees groan in protest. I place my back against the monolith, letting it steady me.

Then it stops, and an eerie silence falls over us all.

Until Hell's forest beasts begin climbing through the crack in the earth.

They crawl on spindly legs, their claws digging into the earth as they pull themselves into the realm of the living. With maws dripping saliva, hungry for blood, they snarl at the serpents awaiting them, rushing to crush their enemies.

Venus swoops low, blasting her magic again, but this time, at her father. He dodges her and sends his own careening toward her. They're now locked in a battle of magic as chaos ensues all around.

Venus and I had discussed this a few days ago, and while she seemed hesitant to let me go on my own, she knew the beasts wouldn't respond to her. *They despise me,* she'd told me. When I pressed her about it, she sighed and said, *because of a decision made long ago.*

So I entered the forest on my own.

I scan my surroundings diligently as I disappear into the forest, the darkness swallowing me whole. The only time I had been in here, I was so consumed by my self-loathing that I hadn't noticed what was around me.

The trees here are the size of five normal trees combined, their trunks massive and their tops disappearing into the dark sky above. The wood on each tree is surprisingly uniform, a deep brown that's nearly black. I wouldn't be able to see anything, except there are a few small orbs of light, clustered close together, blinking on and off. I squint, trying to see what they are—maybe some sort of firefly?

A snarl rips through the air and skitters across my bones. I spin, trying to find the source, but it seems to come from every direction. Is it one beast or multiple?

Perhaps it doesn't matter. One beast is enough to rip me to shreds.

Then my stomach nearly falls out my ass.

A giant beast steps out of the darkness. Its four legs end in claws the length of my forearm, its leather skin is littered with dark spikes, and thick horns grow out the top of its head. And the orbs—they're the eyes of this forest beast. Four eyes that hold a pure, blue flame within. It blinks, and its mouth pulls back to show off its sharp canines that could impale me with one bite.

In this instance, my body is unable to choose between fight or flight and decides to freeze, unsure if this monster will eat me or if it prefers to play with its food first.

Its claws dig into the soft earth as it stops directly in front of me. It has no nose, only two slits set between its four eyes and its large maw.

"What a curious, little witch, wandering into my forest." The monster's voice is like granite, making my body quake in fear. "I have seen you once before. So small, so sad you were." It tilts its head to the side, as if scrutinizing me. "I sense less sadness from you now." Its nose slits open and close a few times, scenting me. "I know what you are. I know what it is you seek."

I'm tired of my emotions being scented by the beings in this realm.

"Perfect," I say with as much confidence as I can muster, even though I feel like I'm about to piss myself with fear. "Then this can be a short meeting."

It chuckles, making the hairs on the back of my neck stand on edge. "Careful, little witch. I have no loyalties to you, and neither do my brethren."

"You want something," I guess.

Its eyes blink and it hisses, "Yes."

"What is it?"

"Tell me, little witch, do you know what I am?"

I'm about to say 'a monster,' but think better of it and just shake my head.

"I am what those demons originate from—my brethren are their ancestors."

"They've never mentioned that," I say, then quickly snap my mouth shut.

It growls, "They have become bothered with the ways of society. They have lost their way."

I don't want to unpack this monster's issues with modern demons right now.

"My kind want the demons to return to us—to return to their primal state."

I shake my head. "I can't promise that."

It brings its head down so our eyes are level, its mouth widening as it huffs out air, which sends my hair flying backward. "The demons belong to us."

"They have their own lives, their own agency—"

"It was foolish of them to stray from us," it snarls.

"This isn't up to me," I manage to say, my voice hoarse.

"Then we do not have a deal."

"If you don't help me, all will be destroyed. Even you," I grit out.

"Child of the earth," it croons, saliva dripping from its maw. "That is what we require in exchange for our service to you."

Suddenly, orbs in groups of four begin to pop up in the darkness: green, red, orange, yellow...

All these monsters, staring out at me.

Fuck. Fuck fuck fuck—

It turns away from me, about to disappear into the darkness again, but I blurt out, "Wait!" I take a deep breath as it peeks back at me. "I can offer a meeting with the archdemons. They can decide whether or not to join you. But that is it."

Turning back around, it chuckles, making me feel sick. What have I just done?

"It is a deal," it replies.

"It's a deal," I repeat, and with those words, our fates have been decided.

With mighty roars, the beasts run headfirst towards the serpents and begin clawing, snapping their sharp canines around them, crushing them. Both roars of triumph and shrieks of pain fill the sky as witches and demons pour through the realm. Demons with insatiable bloodlust howl as they join their estranged brethren, gleeful to rip something apart. The witches willing to fight swoop low on their brooms, sending blasts of power raining down on Phanes's creatures. I see Kirsten flying on a broom, her magic spearing down to immobilize a serpent, controlling the blood within, while Luke approaches and slices cleanly through its neck with a razor-sharp sword.

I don't have time to be pissed off that the witches are already here. As the fight rages on, I pull Venus's dagger from my back pocket—the same dagger I used to slice my hand open in this very spot over ten years ago. I press the tip into my palm, quickly drawing blood, and place it upon the monolith.

The world around me fades away as images slam into me just like before—death and decay and rotten flesh—

My body is no longer my own as my magic's past lives show themselves to me. All destroyed—not by Venus like I had once believed, but by Phanes. I fight the urge to look away, to not see the death and destruction and devastation he has caused. I must bear witness to this, to what has been done. Each witch, unique to her own kind, destroyed. One by one, he came and ripped their souls from their bodies, like a weed to be pulled.

Yet, like a flower growing through cement, the magic remained persistent, biding its time, determined to find the one who would end his reign and take it back. To set the balance right once again.

And that one is me.

I feel it then. My soul, small and fluttering like a butterfly made of pure light, gliding through me and into the stone. It flares once, as if to say, *we're home*, before it is absorbed by the stone and goes out.

Once it departs, the structure lets me go, and I fall backward, landing on the grass.

Sounds around me come back—monsters and demons and witches fighting against Phanes's newest creations.

Pulling myself together, I pick myself up and weave around dead demons and snakes, around witches slamming their magic into serpents, around trees that have been knocked over and ripped from the ground, and hide behind a tree trunk that is now discarded on the earth, with burn marks charring it.

I need a minute, just a minute—

Scanning the battlefield, I see that Phanes and Venus are still locked in battle, but Venus does not obliterate him like she could, now that she has my soul—because she's waiting for me.

"Here goes nothing," I mutter before getting on my knees and slamming my hands into the ground, digging until they're embedded in the soil. I send my magic deep into the earth, illuminating it from beneath, bending it to my will, to my desire. I grit my teeth against the pressure, the feeling of the life being sucked out of me, as my body starts to glow. My eyes close as I concentrate, as I tell the earth what I want.

After a few moments, I feel something gently wrap around my wrist. Opening my eyes, I look down and see a tree root softly caressing my skin, as if to say, *I remember you.*

Sobs wrack my chest as I watch entire trees—the same trees I used to climb and nap in as a child, that I loved so dearly and worked tirelessly to bring back to life—raise themselves out of the earth and transform their trunks, creating two legs and feet made out of bark and begin stepping into battle, shaking the earth around them with each step. One by one, the trees lift out of the soil, extending their branches like limbs to wrap around the serpents, crushing them, ripping them in half as they move.

Witches and demons are picked up by the trees and gently placed on high branches as the forest sweeps through, clearing the earth of Phanes's creatures. Hell's beasts run alongside them, desperate to keep killing.

I remove my hands from the dirt and stand, mesmerized by the place I loved so much transforming with my magic.

There is only one thing left to do.

I search for them, struggling to know where they are as the trees continue to move. Eventually, I spot them, still fighting against one another. A tree passing by wraps branches around me, lifting me up, and carries me so I can finally take back what is mine.

Chapter Fifty-One

Venus

I blast my magic again and again, trying to wear him down, to weaken him to the point where Vivian can make the kill.

I hated waiting for Vivian's signal to attack. Leaving her vulnerable for even a moment made me panicked, even though it was all part of our plan. Vivian has taught me to trust her—even if her ideas are risky and nearly give me a heart attack.

We finalized it last night. Vivian lowered the wards earlier this evening, allowing our army to cross over. Phanes would be too focused on stealing Vivian, thinking she came alone, to be prepared for our attack.

He brought his own monsters with his plans to infiltrate Hell, but we were ready.

My father and I battle on the ground, for my wings being exposed provide more places where he could hurt me. I'm breathing heavily, sweat pouring down every part of my body, but my magic doesn't peter out. In fact, I feel stronger than ever. Unfortunately, Phanes doesn't relent. He has dark, black blood dripping from his nose, from his eyes, out the side of his mouth.

The magic he's stolen and corrupted seems like it wants to destroy him as much as he wants to destroy us.

A flash of blonde hair enters the corner of my vision, and I nearly let out a sob of relief.

My emotions must be on my face because a bloody smile slithers across my father's face. "I look forward to welcoming Vivian back into my home. I'll make sure to fuck her over your corpse."

A blinding fury threatens to distract me, but I know that's what he wants. So instead, I grin right back. "And when Vivian kills you and turns you to dust, I shall make sure no one ever remembers your name."

I send my shadows out now, weaving through the air, surrounding him, grabbing him too quickly for him to react. He fights against them, his power striking at them.

They don't work to hold him—they mean simply to distract him.

Vivian is slowly deposited on the ground behind him by one of her trees, my dagger gripped in her hand. "And I look forward to taking back what you stole," she says as her magic shoots out of her, hitting him in the back and sending him flying into the trees.

Vivian and I lock eyes, and I nearly weep at seeing her. She *glows*. Her eyes are a bit wild, magic radiating out of her skin, a warm, gentle light pouring from her.

I nod to her, trying to convey everything I need to. *I love you, I'm in awe of you, you can kill him and take all that you deserve.*

She nods back and mouths, *I know*, before sprinting after Phanes.

With a little incredulous laugh, I race after her.

Chapter Fifty-Two
Vivian

I rush into the trees, trying to find where he landed. The earth looks disturbed a few yards away, with dark blood soaking the grass, but no other signs of him. I pivot, searching for him, trying to hear him—

A bolt of magic cracks the tree right behind me, splitting it in two. I duck out of the way, covering my head from any falling branches. I look up and see Phanes gliding towards me. Adrenaline courses through me at the sight of him. I'm finally ready.

And he has no idea.

I give him a feral grin as I stand, my skin glowing with magic. "It's time for you to finally meet your end."

He spits blood onto the ground. "You are nothing but a cunt to be used," he snarls.

I roll my eyes. "That's really what you want your final words to be?"

He keeps stepping closer, his magic twining around his fingers. A bolt of lightning crackles between us as it spears for me. Just before it makes contact, the earth rises, shielding me from the attack.

I channel magic into the ground, the earth forming multiple shields of rock that flow like waves over the surface, attempting to trap him. He dodges them, crackles of power shooting from his hands, causing the rocks to splinter and send debris flying in every direction, but I keep creating them, shifting them, throwing them again and again.

I push harder, gritting my teeth as my magic roils through me, demanding more blood—

His magic surpasses my shields of rock and slams into me, knocking me off kilter. It feels like I'm being electrocuted. I'm gasping for air as I fall backward into the grass. My eyes scramble to see through the tears of pain, but I can't see Phanes anywhere.

I try to channel my magic, to alter the world around me so he can't reach me, but it feels like my magic has short-circuited.

My head is yanked backward, the pain searing through my scalp as I cry out and try to grab the hands pulling my hair. My hand releases the dagger, and it lands with a soft thud next to me.

"You thought you could defeat *me*?" Phanes cackles. He stands behind me, his blood dripping onto my face as he leans down. He's close enough now that I can see how bloodshot his eyes are, how much the stolen magic has corrupted him. I fight the urge to vomit at my proximity to this monster again.

Pain ripples through me, my brain feeling ready to explode. He's in my mind, I realize in panic. Memories, young and old, fly past my eyes as he infiltrates it, perusing through my life like it's a book.

Growing up alone, never feeling welcome by the coven.

Running from Venus.

Hiding my magic for so long.

My aunt's death.

Every moment I was stuck in his castle.

You shall die, just like the others, he says to me.

It feels like I already have.

Over and over, the worst moments of my life play on a loop. I'm not sure if I'm screaming or crying or simply lying in silence as he violates me in this final way before he kills me.

Until a moment with Venus flits past that catches my attention. It was the moment she came to my mother's home to apologize. A moment where we came together, where I forgave her. Despite his attack, I focus on the memory. Lean into how it felt to hear those words from her.

I start forcing my mind to replay my favorite moments with her. Seeing Hell's city, her telling me she loved me, showing her my lake, her telling me to rebuild my forest. Over and over, these memories push him out, dampening his influence in my mind.

You are not more powerful than me, he snarls.

I think about the moments with my magic. The ones where we've united, where we've worked together, talked to one another, kept one another company. Even if it plans to shed my skin, I willingly lay down my life for it.

It's enough to throw him from me completely. I become aware of myself again as he releases my hair and stumbles back. I whirl on him, breathing heavily, blood flowing from my nose and down my lips.

His breathing shudders out of him, his mouth drawn in a snarl as I stand on shaky legs and point. "My magic and I are tired of you telling us what we are."

Phanes tries to steady himself as he pants, "Give up now, Vivian, and I'll spare you and your little lover."

"My *little lover* is your daughter." My anger presses against my skin, the need to destroy him is so intense I can taste it. I reach for the dagger I dropped, the need to stab him strong in my veins.

"She is no matter. She will never be strong enough to kill me." He raises his hand and shoots a bolt of magic into the sky.

Right where Venus is flying overhead.

To distract him enough so I could surge my magic forward, tree roots lashing out, grabbing him from every angle. Twisting and twining around his body, they overwhelm him—he attacks one and three more appear in its place. They constrict around him like snakes, ready to devour their meal.

As he struggles against the restraints, I slowly approach, a cocky, wild grin on my face. "You are nothing," I tell him, my voice not wholly my own. "Your corruption ends here."

And I sink the dagger into his throat.

Black blood spurts out, his eyes wide with shock as he gargles, desperate for air. His mouth is open in a silent shriek.

The hatred I feel for him is visceral. It propels me forward and I pull the dagger from his throat, only to drive it into him again.

Again.

Again.

Again.

A guttural scream belonging to a rabid animal claws its way up my throat, shaking the world around us. Fury radiates from me as I make a mess of him. The one who hurt me, who tried to take everything from me, who tried to break me.

But I am unbreakable.

Whispers of his power try to break through, his veins pulsing now, blackening, but I don't give his body a chance to repair itself.

Maybe I take a bit longer than necessary, just to make sure he feels as much pain as possible as I slowly sever his head from his body. My entire arm is coated in his tainted blood and my face is sprayed with dark droplets.

It's a small price to pay for vengeance.

I snap the final cords, and his head tumbles off his body onto the grass. As soon as it lands, my magic releases his corpse, dumping it like it's a piece of garbage.

Suddenly, a rush of power unlike anything I've ever felt before surges through me. It feels like every atom inside me is being fueled with this power, like it's too big for my mortal body to manage. I scream, feeling like I'm being ripped apart from the inside out—

Until everything goes black.

Chapter Fifty-Three
Vivian

My bones are splintering apart, bit by bit. My DNA is being altered, shifting and twisting me into something else completely. Something *other*.

Then I hear it. The earth, crying out to me, reaching for me, needing my help.

I feel power—raw, unflinching power—tunnel through me and out into the world around me, letting it know I'm here. The world bursts behind my eyelids.

I am the earth itself. I am everything.

I'm going to right every wrong, destroy every bit of evil that has polluted and corrupted my creation. All it would take is a breath, a thought, and everything will bow to me. I'm desperate for my revenge.

I will wipe the slate clean.

Vivian.

Like a shooting star across the sky, a familiar name reaches my ears, breaking through my bloodthirstiness. A name I might have known before, in another life.

Vivian, come home.

Is this voice speaking to me? I try to find where the name is coming from, to find who is speaking, but my eyes won't open.

Vivian, come home to me.

A gasp escapes my lips, even as I'm not sure why, not sure who they are or who they're speaking to. The raw magic within me seems to pause, too, in anticipation of the voice.

I know who it is.

Venus—my home is calling to me.

My anchor to the physical world, where we belong with one another. I'm just not sure how to return to her.

It is time, the magic within me says.

Time for what? I try to ask, but I can't form words.

It is time for you to take over.

I don't understand, I want to say, as the magic within me seems to shift, taking its voice with it. I don't understand. Where's Venus? The world around me tilts. I try to find my body, try to find where her voice is coming from, but I can't.

Come home.

I focus on the voice, letting it hold me as I try to stop myself from being lost.

Chapter Fifty-Four
Venus

My father is dead.

I never thought I would see the day.

He shot the last bit of stolen magic he had at me, but it was a mere whisper of power. His magic was no match for mine, now that Vivian's soul has been given to me. I knocked it away like a mosquito buzzing in my ear.

As Vivian sank the dagger into his throat, I swooped down behind her, letting her claim his death. His head fell to the ground, his eyes staring at me as his head rolled.

A copy of my eyes, dead.

My tormentor, my enemy, has finally been destroyed.

Vivian curls in on herself, screaming to the skies.

I run to Vivian's hunched body as her screams pierce the air, sounding like the cries of some otherworldly being finally released from the cage it was trapped inside. Her entire body lights up, as bright as a star, and a surge of power so great reverberates through the ground, sending me flying backward.

The air is ripped from my lungs as I land on my back a few yards away from her. Her screams die out and she slowly turns to face me.

A gasp escapes my lips as I take her in.

Vivian's body is made entirely of light. Her hair flows around her as if she's underwater. Her curves are on full display, like the magic simply ripped her clothes to shreds.

The entire forest quiets—the trees stop moving and wait with bated breath.

She is claiming her rightful title as the Goddess of Life.

This newborn star looks down at Phanes's body for a moment before she blinks, and the earth surrounds him, infiltrating him. His body decomposes before my very eyes, his skin and muscles melting away until all that is left are his bones. The earth then swallows what remains.

As if he was never there.

Then her gaze turns to me.

She glides over to me, her feet barely disturbing the grass beneath them. I rise but do not approach, unsure of what to do.

I hold myself perfectly still, squinting at the brightness she exudes as she places her hands on my shoulders. Her touch is warm. Her glowing eyes seem to take me in, scrutinizing me. Maybe she recognizes me as Venus, her lover, or as Phanes's child who also needs to be destroyed.

"Vivian," I try, unsure if she can hear me or process what I'm saying.

Panic begins to worm its way through me. Is this still Vivian or is it just her magic that remains? Is this all that is left of her?

I try again. "Vivian, come home." Tears have started pooling in my eyes as my worst fear begins to shape before me. She can't be gone. I'd get on my knees and beg for it—or for this new goddess to simply end everything if Vivian is no more. I won't survive without her.

Her head tilts, as if seeming to register my voice.

"Vivian, come home to me." My voice breaks, thick with desperation. I want to hold her, want to force her to come back—

"Venus," she says in a voice that is her own and yet not, a voice that belongs to the earth and the witches that came before.

"Yes," I breathe, the relief of hearing my name on her lips flowing through me.

Her eyes close, and the glow slowly recedes, revealing Vivian's creamy skin underneath. Her hair floats back down, and a halo of pure light flashes around her brow before it dissipates and Vivian collapses into my arms.

Chapter Fifty-Five

Vivian

I wake up on soft, silk sheets, grinning like a fool as I stretch my limbs out on the bed. There's nothing better than a comfy bed.

Okay, there are a few things better than a comfy bed, but it's definitely high on the list.

My foot bumps something warm and fuzzy. I peel my eyes open and look down to see Steve staring daggers at me with his ears back in airplane mode.

"You're the one sleeping by my feet," I grumble at him, which earns me an annoyed noise of his own—but he's not too annoyed to actually get up from the bed.

Snorting, I roll over and see Venus sitting in the chair beside the bed, a book in hand, watching the exchange through lowered brows.

"Don't tell me you're taking his side." I gape.

Her eyes flit to me and then down to her open book. "I'm not getting involved."

"Mmhmm."

It's been a week since I killed Phanes and ascended into a goddess. I don't remember much of what happened after his head fell from his body and my own felt like it was going to explode—but I do remember one thing.

The goddess sitting by me.

The tether holding me to the physical world, pulling me back to myself so that we could be together again.

When I woke days later, I told Venus this, and she immediately burst into tears. She had gripped my face and kissed every part of it, murmuring how terrified she was when I didn't wake up and that she couldn't lose me, that she would gladly follow me into the next life if that was where I was going. She soaked my face with her tears, pressing kisses into my neck, across my collarbone, until she made it down further south... and then she showed me how much she loved and missed me in another way.

As much as we wanted to stay in bed and fuck each other's brains out, we now each have our own realms to manage.

My fear of being cast aside once my magic was strong enough was, luckily, unnecessary. My magic and I have finally united, now operating as one being. I no longer hear its voice in my mind or feel its influence trying to steer me. Before, my magic would act with its own intentions, its own wants—but now, my magic *is* me. If I want my magic to do something, I do it myself.

Part of me almost misses it. When we finally started getting along, it felt...comforting to have it with me. But I don't need it as a companion anymore. Not when I have Venus.

I stare at her unabashedly, my eyes traveling up and down her body. One side of her hair is back in braids and the other shimmers freely in the candlelight. Her skin is near-glowing, apparently an after-effect of handing over my soul.

In fact, we both seem to glow now. Not constantly, but whenever we feel intense emotions, our bodies radiate from within.

Venus seems to sense my gaze because she looks up from her book and locks eyes with me. She offers me a soft smile, her eyes warming as she takes me in. I sit up, beaming at her as I ask, "What's on the agenda for today?"

"We're meeting with the new matron of your former coven."

"Mm, that's right. Well," I sigh, swinging my legs over the opposite side of the bed and prancing to the bathroom, "I best get dressed then."

I can feel Venus's eyes track me as I waltz across the floor. Throwing her a look over my shoulder, I croon, "Are you staring at my ass?"

Sure enough, Venus's dark eyes are laser-focused on my behind, looking like she'd rather eat me than go about our day. Flipping my hair, I say sweetly, "Take a picture, it'll last longer."

Venus's laugh follows me as I saunter out.

Kirsten enters the council room, her head held high and her back straight, but I can sense her nerves.

I sit at the head of the council table, with Venus standing behind me, her strong hands gripping the back of the chair as we both assess the witch before us.

I give her a slight smile and gesture to the chair at the other end of the table—the one that was always empty until I came along. Unless Venus decides she needs me to sit in her chair, which she does quite often, looming over me as we conduct meetings.

Kirsten quickly pulls the chair out and sits, her hands politely folded in her lap as she makes direct eye contact with me, then with Venus, then back at me. "Dark Lady, and...what should we be calling you, again?"

"She's the Goddess of Life, and should be referred to as such," Venus instructs.

I fight the urge to roll my eyes. "For this meeting, Vivian is perfectly fine." Before Venus can contradict me, I continue, "You were brave to assist us during the battle, even though it was not required or expected of you—especially after your coven had been attacked."

She raises her brows, picking up on my word choice. *Your* coven, not *our* coven. It has never been mine. I used to resent that, but it feels good to finally let that hurt go.

"I wanted to do it," she answers. "I wanted to defend those who couldn't defend themselves."

One of Venus's shadows slithers down to perch on my shoulder, assessing the witch before us. Venus takes up the thread of the conversation. "Now that your coven is without a matron, a new one will need to be established."

"Is there someone you have in mind?" Kirsten inquires carefully.

"We do," I tell her. "We would like you to take over as matron, if you would like that."

She blinks in surprise—either at me saying we've picked her or for the simple fact that we're offering it to her instead of demanding she take it, I'm not sure. She swallows before she responds, "I would happily serve as a matron to my coven, but..." She bites her lip nervously before she continues. "I grew up in that coven, too, Vivian—all the beliefs, all the hatred they instilled in me...I don't know if I can overcome those things." Her eyes hold guilt as she looks at me. Guilt for how she treated me, how she behaved when we were mere witchlings.

A small smile blooms across my lips as I reply, "Perhaps it is time for us to forgive ourselves and try to be better—for each other, but also ourselves. I forgave you the moment you helped after the coven attack."

An olive branch.

She seems to realize it, too, because her forest green eyes widen a bit. "And what of future witches' souls? Will witches still be required to hand them over to the Dark Lady?"

"We've discussed it," Venus interjects, "and we see no reason to demand such a thing. If witches would like to, they are welcome to, but there is simply no need for it now."

A small smile. "Then I accept."

"Good," Venus replies, "because there's a lot of work to be done. Work with the High Priestesses to see what can be done about your coven's lands. I know you're already acquainted."

A blush creeps up Kirsten's neck at that, and she sputters, "I will. Thank you," before she pushes her chair back and scurries out of the room.

I look up at Venus and ask, "What was that about?"

Venus just chuckles at the secret she seems to have, her shadows nuzzling against my cheek.

"I thought we said no more secrets," I remind her, my eyebrows raising.

"It isn't my fault you aren't as observant as I am," she quips, earning a light smack on the arm.

"I deserve to know all the Hell gossip, Venus."

The playful look in her eye cools as she sucks in a breath. "There *is* something I've been keeping a secret from you…"

There is one last thing to do, to finally allow all of my wounds to heal.

Four demons flank me, with Luke leading the way as we descend the stone stairwell into the depths of Hell's dungeons. The air is thick and hot, reminding me of humid summer days. My skin immediately feels damp, my clothes clinging to my skin. There is little light down here—just lit torches embedded into the stone walls. Every few minutes, we pass iron doors, one on the left and one on the right. Each is the door to a single cell.

No windows to look out through. Not that there's anything to see.

I knew I needed to decide what should be done about Jessica eventually. Venus seemed happy to let her rot down here, but I needed to speak to her—to close the door for myself.

When Venus told me the truth, I nearly ran to Judith to demand she tell me it wasn't real, that I didn't endure abuse from my aunt instead of my mother. The thought of my real mother letting that happen made me see red.

Venus tried to calm me, told me not to react out of anger and say something I might regret.

Ripping Jessica a new one, however, is not something I'll regret.

Luke doesn't speak as we make our way down the stairs. He's still angry at me after I promised the beasts in Hell's wilderness that the archdemons would meet with them. When Venus and I told the council what they demanded, the other three archdemons had roared their anger, claiming I had no right to do that—which was silenced by a simple look from Venus.

She was acting on official orders, Venus informed them. *There's no argument to be had.*

Luke had remained quiet through the discussion though, staring me down the entire time, the aggravation rolling off him in waves. At the end of the meeting, he had stormed out without a word.

We haven't talked since.

Eventually, he stops next to a set of doors and unlocks one with a skeleton key. I'm about to scoff at a place full of magic using a simple key to keep the most dangerous souls locked away, but I think better of it as the door creaks open and Luke steps back without a word. I glance at all the demons around me, but no one says anything or gives me a reassuring look—nor do they swear to me they won't lock me in here themselves.

Apparently, my promise to the original demons has made the rounds.

I face the open door, the darkness within, and send a bit of magic to the surface, letting my skin illuminate in the dim space. I take a deep breath and step into the cell.

The space is a small rectangle with the same stone walls and floor as the stairwell. No light source, no window. No bed or signs of comfort. Just a small, dark box.

The witch is seated on the floor against the far wall, her thin arms pressing her bent legs into her chest. She looks up at me and hisses, the light I'm emanating making her squint in discomfort.

I've always shined a bit too bright for the woman who claimed to be my mother.

"Hello," I say politely, even as my stomach feels like it's full of cement. I tamp down my magic so I'm not blinding her, but so that we can still see one another. I want her to see me—I *need* her to see me. To see how I flourished without her, in spite of her.

Her eyes widen at my voice, realizing it's me who has finally bothered to visit. "Oh, my daughter," she weeps, her face contorting strangely, as if she's trying to make herself cry but no tears are created—as if she's never cried before. "I am so happy to see you, my beautiful child."

"Save it," I snap, not interested in the theatrics. "I'm not busting you out of here."

She drops the act immediately, her face now changing into a scowl. "Then what are you doing down here?"

I tilt my head. "I came down here to see."

"To see what?" Her tone is bitter.

"To see how it would make me feel to see you down here, in this state."

"And to laugh at my misfortune?"

"Maybe. Probably."

"You will have to live with the consequences of this," she hisses.

Shrugging, I reply, "I wanted to see if I'd feel guilty too. Venus told me—"

"You dare speak her name, you traitorous bitch," she seethes.

I hold up my left hand, my wedding ring—a heart-shaped pink sapphire with a dainty gold band—glittering against my glowing skin. "She's my wife, so I can call her whatever I please."

She balks at me, at a loss for words.

My smile is cruel as I assess her. "You were—are—a horrible mother, a horrible person. You abused me, belittled me, and made sure I never felt an ounce of love from you. I know you aren't even my mother. You forced Judith to hand over her only child so you could earn the Dark Lady's favor.

"But you know what?" The question is rhetorical, which she seems to pick up on, as she doesn't respond. "I survived it. I survived you. I have even done what you would be proud of me for. Not only am I the Dark Lady's wife, but she also has my soul. I'm her equal. I did not do it for you or even in spite of you. These are not your accomplishments. They are *mine*."

Her eyes flare with anger, but I don't stop. "The coven has a new matron who wants future generations of witches to challenge the status quo that you so gleefully forced onto us, and you will be nothing but a forgotten witch—no one will ever utter your name again."

Panic replaces her anger at my words. I know I've hit my mark. "What *are* you?" she asks, as if seeing me for the first time.

My mouth quirks upwards. "I'm the newest goddess around here." Letting my magic spool out of me, I rattle the tiny cell, making the entire space shake. Jessica cowers, covering her head as dust drifts from the ceiling.

I let out a little sigh and flip my hair over my shoulder nonchalantly. "That's all. Hope you have a nice existence down here!" I chirp.

Turning on my heel, I stride out of the cell, leaving her screaming at my back until the door closes, locking her in there for eternity.

Sometimes, revenge must be enacted against the one who harmed you. Other times, the best revenge is forgiving and moving forward—but never forgetting.

My enemies no longer have control over me.

Chapter Fifty-Six

Venus

"There's a throne room here?"

"It's a castle, Vivian," I reply.

"I know!" she says a bit defensively. "I've just never seen it, is all."

"There's much of this castle you haven't seen. I will admit, I tend to neglect the areas where I am not needed."

Hand in mine, I guide her to the throne room doors at the end of the hall.

"Woah," she breathes, taking in the ornate doors with serpents depicted throughout, winding and curling themselves around the handles.

"We might have to redecorate after all we've endured," I say, only half-joking, but Vivian shakes her head.

"Your beautiful snakes don't even compare to his fucked-up ones."

We lock eyes and grin at each other as if time has stood still.

Vivian, my stubborn, brave, remarkable goddess, is still here with me, through trials and tribulations I never thought we could get through. But we did, and now it feels like our lives can finally begin.

Without looking away from her, my shadows pull the doors open to reveal the throne room. Vivian breaks eye contact first and gasps at what she finds inside.

The room juts out from the rest of the castle, making it feel as if we are stepping out into the perpetually dark sky, which can be seen through the glass ceiling.

The space is bursting with color—paintings cover the entirety of the walls, illuminated by a large, black chandelier and floating candles dancing in the air. A deep red strip of carpet leads from the door to the dais. And on the dais sits my throne.

It truly is a work of art. Black stone chiseled to provide a seat, with serpents depicted winding around the circular back of the chair.

Vivian lets go of my hand to approach the paintings, her fingers lightly brushing against the depiction of a winged beast roaring to the sky.

"My mother painted these," I say. "She was always a beautiful artist. When I finally left home and resided down here, I asked her to paint whatever came to mind—nothing was off limits."

"They're beautiful," Vivian says, a sad smile on her face as she turns to me.

I swallow the lump that forms in my throat. "I wanted you to see where we will rule together."

"Shouldn't I get my own castle?" She twirls a strand of hair around her finger. "I'd love a pink one."

"I'll have one made for you," I promise, "but only if it's in Hell."

She grins. "Deal."

I secretly hope she's joking, but I know I'd make it for her. I cannot deny her anything.

"We're also here because I have something for you."

"But it's *not* my pink castle?"

I playfully roll my eyes and open my arms for her, which she gladly steps into. I snap my fingers, and my shadows bring forth the surprise, seeming to struggle with the weight. They place it next to my throne and zip away, revealing what was underneath.

A throne for Vivian.

The structure is a deep oak covered in flowers of all shades, vines twisting around the legs, the arms, and the circular back—and on the circular back are yellow, orange, and red flowers blending together to depict the sun.

She gasps as she looks from the throne to me, to the throne, then back to me again. "That's for me?"

"I can't imagine it would be for me," I jest. "As you well know, I'm not a fan of color." I give a mock shudder, which earns me a playful scowl. I jerk my chin to the dais. "Go and see for yourself."

Vivian looks at the throne, biting her lip. "It seems strange."

"What does?"

"That I even need a throne."

"You don't *need* one," I argue. "I just thought you might enjoy sitting side-by-side. But, if you prefer, we can cover it with a sheet and pretend it doesn't exist."

"No!" she nearly shouts at me in alarm. "It's the most beautiful thing I've ever seen. I would never wish to hide it."

I raise my eyebrows at her, waiting. She straightens her spine and confidently strides across the carpet up to her throne, lightly brushing her hand over the flowers before she gasps and whirls to me. "They're real flowers?"

I shrug. "Of course. What good would your magic be if you couldn't keep your own throne decorated?" I ask dryly.

She narrows her eyes at me in faux suspicion. "Someone is awfully playful this evening."

I can't help the answering smile that graces my lips. She's right—I haven't felt this relaxed or so at peace. Seeing the magnificent creature before me, alive, happy, and finally confident in her power has soothed me, buffing all my jagged edges.

Vivian shoots me a soft, serene smile before turning back to her royal seat. She touches more of the flowers, as if connecting with them, getting a sense of who they are before she turns slowly and seats herself.

The same halo I saw in the forest appears, glowing like a fallen star upon her brow. She places her hands on the armrests, and the throne answers—the flowers stretch towards her, their petals becoming more vibrant under her influence.

The Goddess of Life, finally restored to her rightful place. It takes my breath away.

She's smiling ear-to-ear at me, and it's brighter than her glowing crown. "Are you going to leave me here, all by my lonesome?"

I huff out a laugh before I summon my wings and make my way to my own throne, my shadows dancing around, inspecting the flowers and the vines until they cluster together to create my matching crown of darkness.

Sitting upon my throne, I look over at her and give her a wink, which causes her to giggle. I hold out my hand for her, my dark banded wedding ring—Vivian was appalled I didn't want a matching pink one—glistening in the reflection of her halo. We snuck off a few nights ago, asking Aradia to wed us in the way living mortals do. I doubt this marriage would be recognized by their standards, but we're goddesses, so we can do as we please.

Vivian slips her hand into mine and squeezes.

Together, we sit in our empty throne room that won't be empty for long.

And together, we shall live and rule as equals, as lovers, and as eternal beings. Forever.

Or until Vivian's beloved cat demands her attention, sauntering into the room and testing out the acoustics by meowing loudly.

Vivian gasps, rips her hand from mine, and holds her arms out to him.

"Steve!" she squeals, causing the cat to jog down the carpet, his primordial pouch swishing back and forth. Without a care for royal decorum, the cat jumps up the steps and into Vivian's awaiting arms. She pulls him close and presses her face into his fur, causing him to purr wildly.

"I can't believe I come second to a cat—by my own wife," I grumble, trying to conceal my smile.

"Get used to it." Her playful words are muffled by the cat's fur. Steve settles into her lap as Vivian gives me a sultry grin. "So, can we fuck on these thrones?"

Epilogue
Venus

Six Months Later

"Vivian, I can't take it anymore."

"Yes, you can, Venus. Just one more."

I groan, my body completely wrung out of pleasure, covered in sweat, straining to get away from Vivian's tongue that dances between my legs.

We have a game, she and I, where one of us tries to wake the other up with sex, depending on who wakes up first. It makes me excited to fall asleep every night, wondering which of us will surprise the other.

This morning, I woke up to Vivian's tongue skimming over my core, and I knew that she already won this round. Now she's pushing my body past its limits. I've lost count of how many times I've come.

Vivian's tongue swirls around my oversensitive clit, causing my body to tighten from both pain and pleasure.

She wants me to beg her, wants me to be a mess of release and sweat and tears.

I already give her everything. I might as well give her this too.

"Vivian, please, I can't take any more," I whimper, my back arching as she moves her tongue down to lick at my opening.

Her answering laugh is sadistic. "You can take it. Unless..." She trails off, popping her head up to lock eyes with me as her finger starts circling my clit. "Is my wife tapping out?"

My wife. Hearing that on her lips makes me fall over the edge, release spiraling through me, my entire body shaking from the impact. Stars dance behind my eyes as Vivian bites down on the inside of my thigh, her finger stroking me. My garbled pleas merely earn me a feline smile—she's not stopping until she's decided we're finished.

Finally, my orgasm leaves me feeling boneless on the bed, the sheets underneath me soaked. Vivian pulls herself from my center and crawls up my body, her face devious.

"You cheated," I growl half-heartedly.

She gives me a look of feigned innocence as she presses her body on top of mine, our skin sticking together. "I have no idea what you're talking about," she lies sweetly.

"You know I love it when you call me that," I argue.

"Call you what? My wife?"

A moan slips past my lips before I can stop it, arousal pooling in my stomach again. For all that is unholy, this goddess will lead me to my death.

She kisses me, my own taste bursting on my tongue as our lips collide. I shift us so we're lying on our sides, lightly stroking each other's bodies.

Vivian has come leaps and bounds from when she first came home. Her magic no longer speaks to her, which is a relief for all of us. It was a bit unnerving, having her mumble to her magic throughout the day.

Now and again, her nightmares will wake her, making her disoriented, tears streaming down her cheeks as she struggles to pull herself out. I simply gather her into my arms and remind her where she is—that she's in Hell, at home, with me and her little gremlin cat. She settles quickly and falls asleep again, clinging to me like she can't let go.

The world around us has changed drastically since Phanes's death. The realm of the living is thriving under Vivian's care, the earth flourishing in ways that baffle the mortal scientists. She easily creates new human souls, even though her magic was not accustomed to this. When I theorized her tapering off on creating humans, as they were Phanes's creation, she seemed shocked I would even propose that. So, she learned how to do it, and she now breezes through it with minimal magical effort.

Things have changed for Hell too. Witches are no longer required to hand their souls over to me; it felt unnecessary to continue with the tradition upon his death. Some witches still choose to do so, but only after they have been taught the history—the real history of Phanes, of Lilith, and of Vivian's magic.

"What should we do today?" I ask, my nose lightly caressing Vivian's throat.

She hums, arching into me to provide me better access. "I thought we were meeting with the archdemons today."

I place light kisses on her neck and up to her jaw. "We are, but maybe we reschedule and stay in bed."

Her chuckle rumbles against me. "I don't think that's a good idea. They're still pretty angry with us."

"With *you*," I correct.

"We're a package deal, so it's impossible for them to be mad at just me."

"So, all those who hate me, also hate you?"

"Let's not get carried away."

She's right about the archdemons. Since Vivian rallied the forest beasts to aid us, promising them time with the archdemons, tension has been thick. The meeting has not been set, as neither Vivian nor the beasts specified a time frame, but it will need to happen eventually.

Luke is taking it particularly hard. He barely says two words to either of us unless it is business-related. This doesn't bother me, as Luke works for me and I do not need his approval to do anything, but I can tell it bothers Vivian. She enjoys Luke and saw him as a potential friend. Losing that potential has been difficult for her, even if she won't express it outright.

If that wasn't enough drama, Vivian still hasn't spoken to Judith, her real mother. I've decided not to push it—she'll see her when she's ready.

A disgruntled meow echoes off the walls, alerting us to Steve's presence.

Vivian gasps and jumps off the bed, cooing for the little beast that saunters across the room into her awaiting arms. She scoops him up and buries her face into his black fur.

"Not on the bed," I grumble. I'm tired of waking up with cat hair in my mouth.

"Don't be such a baby," she scolds before climbing up, Steve's smug expression making me narrow my eyes. We have a bit of a truce, he and I, but we like to keep our distance. Vivian, however, regularly forces us together.

She presses her back against the headboard and Steve climbs from her arms, curling up next to her instead. I crawl over, laying my head in her lap, closing my eyes as her fingers comb through my hair.

The city below rumbles with noise, citizens going about their business. The living witches went back to their homes, although a few decide to come down to visit from time to time, connecting with loved ones who have departed. Vivian and I decided that crossing between realms should be easier, but on a case-by-case basis. We don't want to overwhelm the living with the dead or vice versa.

For the first time in my existence, tranquility overcomes me. Like the universe has finally balanced itself after being tilted for so long.

And I have no one to thank but the goddess that chooses time and again to love me. To bring me into her heart, despite all that has happened to her. I look up at her and see her smiling gently down at me, as if she's thinking the same of me.

I give her an answering grin, soothed that, now, we will never be apart.

THE END

Thank you so much for reading When Death Blooms!

If you want some bonus content of Vivian and Venus, sign up for my newsletter.

Acknowledgements

I can't believe this book is finished.

The version you just read is leaps and bounds from the original version I created. Be it writer's block, imposter syndrome, or just general anxiety, I struggled to write this story. It felt like I had a huge clock looming above me, telling me to hurry up, but to also make sure it was *perfect*. My biggest fear was letting down Vivian and Venus. After a few kicks in the ass from my beta readers and editor, I realized I was doing everyone (especially V+V) a disservice by forcing it.

Thank you to my beta readers, Kelsey and Gennifer, for telling me when the story was "slow" or just flat-out "boring".

Thank you to my editor, Kristen, for helping me open my eyes to the better story, and for putting up with my em-dash obsession—even though I will never let them go.

And again, a thank you to Gennifer for proofreading.

Thank you to Erika, my PA, who reached out one day and wrestled the reins I was gripping way too tightly out of my hands so I could focus on this book.

Thank you to my cats, Cookie and Jade, for sitting on my lap and blocking me from writing when I needed a break or meowing at me when I needed some feedback.

And, of course, a thank you to you, dear reader. This book wouldn't even exist without you.

About the Author

G.E. Masters is a writer of sapphic romance. Ever since she was a child, G was fascinated by imaginary worlds and created complex characters in her head.

Now, she's writing those stores to share. She lives in Chicago with her two cats.

The Deal with the Devil Duet is her debut.

You can email her at gemasterswrites@gmail.com, or follow her on Instagram or Tiktok.

www.ingramcontent.com/pod-product-compliance
Lightning Source LLC
Chambersburg PA
CBHW031111160726
47991CB00004B/1332